Back Roads Literary Review
Short Stories – Autumn 2025
Volume 3 – Issue 2

Michael Van Natta, Editor-in-Chief
Cover art by Joann Schissel

ISBN: 979-8-9916653-5-3 (Paperback). Any references to historical events, real people, or real places are used fictitiously. Some of the places depicted are fictitious embellishments of actual places but beyond that, names, characters, and places are products of the author's imagination.

Copies of this book may be found at the Back Roads Literary Review website: www.BackRoadsLiteraryReview.com

First printing edition 2025. Printed in USA.

Back Roads Literary Review
1699 Highway 14
Knoxville, IA 50138
www.BackRoadsLiteraryReview.com

TABLE OF CONTENTS

FOREWORD

Michael Van Natta
Editor in Chief

In every edition of Back Roads Literary Review, after having steeped and luxuriated myself on the diverse and fascinating imaginations of our authors, I find it interesting that certain themes coalesce, different every time, as if the collective minds of writers are somehow "tuned-in" to the moment, linked in some larger sphere of consciousness, as they labor at their solitary writing desks. The very concept of consciousness as a spiritual entity, existing somehow both inside and outside of us, somehow gives credence to the notions contained in these scary stories herein.

In this unsettling and elegiac collection, the familiar dissolves into the odd, the strange and the unfamiliar. The living find themselves wandering over and through tenuous landscapes where absence carries as much weight as presence. You will find elements of these in the work of Joy Wright in *A Campfire Miracle* as well as *The Horror of Wichdun*, by Romana Tamm, Stephen L. Braytons's *Culvertown Cavern*, and the timely and pertinent poem (the first poem we've published) *Forbin's Nightmare*, penned by Stewart Lethbridge.

Missing persons haunt not only police reports and old photographs, but also the memories of those left behind, memories that shift and crumble like cliffs eroding into the sea. The settings–creepy hotels, old homes with locked wings, decaying mansions with shuttered ballrooms, sprawling estates where forests and silence have grown thick, and uncanny geological formations that seem to lean toward us–are as much characters as the people who stumble through them. Shudder while reading *Haunting in the Hollow*, by Teresa Tallman. Wince, as I did while reading Michael Chatham's *Trophy*. Worry a bit over things that go bump in the night in *The Ghost in Room 17*, by R. H. Riffenburgh, and things that actually do bump you on the head in *Deadfall*.

Insects, better left unseen, find their eight-legged way into everything, including the pages herein. Witness: *Wriggle Inside*, by Ember Purrian, and *Creep*, by C.B. Butler.

Ghosts, of course, move here too, though it is never certain if they are real or imagined, or whether they are born from guilt, longing, or the slow trick of a mind losing its grasp on what once was solid. Observe the transformation of our main character in *The Girl in the Painting*, written by Ember Purrian, In *Dust Bowl*, L.A. Curry paints a landscape of remorse and recompense. Deb Miller's *A Second Chance* reanimates notions of the mystery of the deep south, and *The End*, by Bailey Primus, in a weird way, takes characters full circle.

Dementia and addled minds thread through these tales, showing how memory, the loss of own's mind and identity can become an isolated haunted house–one with doors that refuse to open, and others that open onto rooms not recognizable. The past becomes both a torment and refuge, flickering in and out like a loose lightbulb, demanding to be acknowledged even as it slips away. I hope you enjoy *The Corner of My Eye*, by Rose Wilson, Pamela K. Kinney's *Death of the Apostrophe*, and *The Key*, by Larry Brown as much as I do. In *Ghosts of the Silver Mine*, Joann Schissel toys with alchemy between a tormented miner and indigenous spirits.

And yet, amid the spectral unease, there are moments of quiet recompense. Some characters find closure in ways they never expected; others discover that kindness, persistence, or even sheer endurance brings its own strange reward. These stories insist the only way to overcome is by passing directly through the darkness–through the haunting, the forgetting, and the fear–and emerging, changed, into a place where grief and grace coexist. Witness *The Game*, by David Matthis and *Fallen Flowers* by J.L Wheaton. Also in this vein, *The Noise* by Geraldine Birch. This is not a collection about evasion, but about confrontation: the courage to walk wherever life travels, facing unexplained mysteries in distinctly human ways, and still find, however faint, the possibility of light.

The Girl in the Painting

Ember Purrian

I love antiques: dusty wood, porcelain figurines, cupboards worn smooth by time. They remind me of afternoons at my grandmother's feet, cookies in hand, a new blankie in her knitting.

I took the day off for a garage auction. Few people came, so winning was a breeze. My bank account protests, but I still smile.

I haul home treasures: a delicate tea set, figurines, a broken clock, five dusty leather-bound books, a dark oak cupboard… and one painting.

That beautiful painting.

I hang it in the center of my living room. Its frame glimmers with faded gold leaf. A maroon house sits on a prairie, misted mountains behind, smoke curling from the chimney. I stare, dreaming of curling up inside.

A soft brush on my legs–Tigress, hungry and curious, inspects the cupboard beneath the painting, clearly approving.

After a day of carefully arranging my newly acquired antiques and reading one of the leather bound books, sleep takes me.

I wake to a faint swish. It's 2:37am. A cool breeze seeps through the small crevice of my window. Tigress jumps off as I stand up and close it.

Before long, drift back to sleep.

The Saturday morning sun spills through the salmon-coloured curtains. I stretch and shuffle to the kitchen, letting the kettle hiss while searching for Tigress. Coffee in hand, I sink into the couch and savor the first, warm sip.

When I glance up, Tigress lies there, curled up right beneath the painting on the cupboard.

My gaze snags on the painting. Sunlight glows across the house. At the window, a girl–blurry, faint, with blue eyes, curly blonde hair. Was she always there? I chuckle. Probably missed this small detail. My grandmother said the smallest things hide until they choose to be seen.

The day drifts by–dusting books, lazing among antiques. Tigress sprawls on her newly claimed cupboard. The girl lingers–calm, watchful, almost alive.

Night came, and I lay curled up in my bed. Tigress still hasn't joined me. Is she still on that cupboard? I fall asleep, cosy and warm in my crimson and cream duvet. The smell of old leather books lulling me to dreamland.

I wake from a faint whisper again. I think nothing much of it.

Then, a breath against my ear.

"Help."

My skin prickles. Is it Tigress? The wind? I slip on my slippers, straining to listen. It draws me toward the living room, where the hush hangs heavy and the air runs cold. Tigress lies curled on the cupboard, asleep. My gaze drifts to the painting.

The girl.

She isn't at the left window anymore. She leans from the right one now, elbows resting on the sill, chin propped on her hand, gazing skyward.

"Help me." The words are clearer this time, scraping along my nerves.

I stare too long. Too hard. And I swear her painted eyes flick toward mine.

I jolt awake. Morning sunlight spills through the curtains. My heart hammers, breath short. Was it just another dream?

I rush to the living room. Tigress sits neatly on the cupboard. I stroke her gently as my eyes perk up towards the painting.

She's gone.

My head spins. Did I … imagine her? Did I imagine yesterday?

Sunday drifts by, yet I keep returning to the living room. Tigress perches on the cupboard, tail flicking. The girl—one moment at the window, the next gone—baffles me. I tell myself I'm tired, yet I can't look away. Something about the house, the girl, quietly tugs, until I feel I might drift into the painting.

I barely manage to read before sleep drags me under. But just as I begin to doze, a whisper cuts through the dark, louder and clearer than ever.

"Help me!"

The voice gives me chills. I slip into my slippers, stumbling toward the painting. My heart flutters, stomach twisting. The house's door yawns open, a dark void. There she stands–painted, yes, but undeniably alive.

Tigress lies curled beneath it, one sharp eye tracking my every movement.

My chest tightens. My pulse hammers in my throat. *This is just a dream.*

Her gaze latches onto mine. Something inside me twists–dread, wonder, an almost irresistible pull. The void behind her seems to breathe. Then she whispers again:

"Come."

My feet move forward of their own accord. My breaths catch, my hands tremble. Inch by inch, I lean closer, drawn toward her presence, until she fills my entire vision.

I jolt awake. Sweat beads my skin, my breath ragged, my heart still hammering as if it hasn't stopped from the nightmare. Another dream, I tell myself. Just another dream.

Sunlight spills gently through the curtains, painting the room in a warm, golden glow. The fabric sways faintly in the morning breeze, their soft blue threads catching the light like water. The blanket wrapped around me is bright and cheerful, patterned with golden sunflowers, warm against my skin.

Wait–these aren't my curtains. This isn't my blanket.

I sit up straight. The smell hits me first–smoke, pine and paint, earthy and warm. My walls are wood. The floor, too. Nothing feels familiar. My stomach twists. This isn't my room.

Shakily, I stand. My slippers are gone. I step into the hallway. Everything is—beautiful but unfamiliar—soft wood, smooth tiles, curved walls, shelves of strange books. The living room ahead is different. Couch, painting, antiques–they're gone. Sunlight spills across unknown space. Photographs of strangers, shelves filled with trinkets, and Tigress is nowhere.

My pulse races. I spin around, my eyes drinking it all in. Everything is … perfect. Too perfect. Yet … it isn't mine.

This is just a dream.

I drift toward the window, clinging to the hope of finding something familiar outside.

But when I press my palms to the glass, my breath stutters. It isn't the outside at all. It's my living room. My couch. My television. Framed in the window like a cruel joke.

I press harder, try to force myself through but the air thickens like stone, an invisible wall holding me back.

Then, a woman, golden curls and tired, deep blue eyes, lowers herself onto my couch as if she belongs there. Tigress rests in her lap, tail curling in complete contentment.

She looks at me, and smiles.

"Thank you."

My pulse races. My breath locks.

She looks just like the girl in the painting.

And the edge of the glass shimmers faintly gold, like the border of a familiar painting.

Ghosts of the Silver Mine

Joann Schissel

Leadville, Colorado 1877

Horace rambled toward the swinging doors of the Purgatory Saloon, parched from trail grit scouring his throat and stiff from the hour-long ride into town on his scrawny mule, Jack. He brushed the dust from his britches and adjusted his stiff felt hat.

The mid-day brightness barely penetrated the interior of the establishment that smelled of cigars and sweat. A scattering of patrons hunched over their beers while the piano player struck a jaunty tune. Horace strode up to the bar squinting at Bill, the barkeep. "Whiskey," he demanded, slapping the wooden bar top. Bill poured a shot with a sullen look and pushed the glass toward Horace.

"How's the prospecting goin'? Bill asked.

Horace stroked his scraggly gray beard that dead-ended at the middle of his chest, and his lip pulled back into a twisted grin, revealing his crooked yellow teeth. He wasn't about to let on about the treasure he had found. Even a small vein of silver ore promised to make a man rich. He had collected just enough to whet his appetite for more.

"You'll know when I hit the mother lode." Horace straightened his back and ran his thumbs the length of the underside of his suspenders. "When that silver shows herself, I'll buy this shithole and only drink the finest spirits, not this rotgut."

Bill hissed and wiped the countertop with a rag. "You know those Indian legends about the ghosts of Ute warriors? Plannin' revenge, wandering at night in those mountains, layin' await in them dark caverns underneath the earth, just biding their time when they can slit your throat," Bill said. He tilted his head toward his bouncer, Jim, who wore a deerskin shirt and stood motionless between the bar and the stage.

Jim's straight black hair and sun-drenched brown face triggered a visceral gut punch in Horace and he sneered.

"Yes, sir, Jim's stories about the old days will make your blood curdle. Don't mess with him," Bill said.

"Hogwash. Ain't no Injun I fear. Not since my soldier days when we whupped the Sioux back in the Dakotas in sixty-two." Horace spit on the floor and scowled before turning back to Bill. The barkeeper smirked and looked toward the saloon's stage as the footlights brightened to a golden glow.

The music stopped and Sally, a pretty young thing, ascended to her cued spot where the gaslight reflected just right on her. She fussed with the pastel satin ruffles of her skirts and flipped the pink feather boa over her shoulder. Her powdered face radiated with cheeks the color of rose blossoms. Facing the room, she licked her red-painted lips and nodded to the piano player, who struck the keyboard with a dramatic gesture. A mournful tune poured out from her sweet warbling voice. Lyrics told the tale of a lover murdered in a jealous rage. The heartfelt melody irritated Horace.

"Jesus, you're wailing like a heifer in heat," Horace shouted, finishing his third whiskey, slamming the empty glass down on the bar.

Sally threw him a dirty look but finished her song. Bill applauded. The audience of about a dozen men murmured and spat tobacco into spittoons.

She curtseyed with a quick movement and marched down the steps–past the rows of mostly empty chairs until she stomped next to Horace. Her hands planted on her hips, and a frown deepened across her face. "You're a son of a bitch, Horace Maggins, for sayin' what you said about my singing."

"What'd you call me?" Horace raised up off the bar stool, his face the color of blood. His hands balled into fists, and he punched her in the face with a right cross.

With a loud shriek, she collapsed to the floor.

Shouts rippled among the customers. Bill cursed and yelled for Jim. Horace straddled the fallen woman, his hands around her throat. Sally's arms and legs flailed in the air, while gasping for breath. In the next moment, Horace flew upward, snatched away from Sally's fleshy body and slammed against the bar. The impact rattled his teeth when his head ricocheted off the bar top. He reeled and plunked his boots on the wood floor. Stumbling forward. Belly flab rolled side to side like churned butter.

Jim's dark eyes flashed a few inches from Horace's face. Black as his threatening demeanor. Stars swirled around Jim in Horace's oscillating vision. In that moment, his opponent possessed a feathered headdress of a Ute chief.

Horace blinked, shaking his head until the illusion vanished. He wheezed out a grunt, as much as he could muster, and scrubbed his palm against his throbbing temple. His eyes narrowed on Jim. "That Indian accosted me, a white man! You all saw it!" He could hardly breathe, but his eyes scanned the room. Men sat in silent apathy at their tables, a minor interruption from consuming their brews. Heads bobbed between Horace and Bill. The scene garnered a smidge more attention than the stage performance. Sally struggled to her feet, massaging her reddened, tear-soaked cheek, sobbing in loud gasps.

Bill brandished a shotgun he pulled from behind the bar and swung the barrel toward the door. "Get the hell out of my saloon, Maggins, and don't come back. I put up with your bad temper in the past, but ain't got the patience no more. Don't want no troublemakers here."

Horace brushed himself off and stared up into the fierce glare on Jim's hardened face. He leaned closer to Jim and lowered his voice to a whisper. "Hey Chief, go back to the reservation. You're likely to get yourself kilt in this town if you ain't careful."

Jim thrust out his chin, eyes narrowed on Horace. He didn't waver in his solid stance.

A shiver crawled through Horace, and he swiped a shaking hand across his sweat -soaked forehead. This humiliation would be met with his own measures in his own time. He snatched his hat off the floor and limped outside to Jack, whipping the mule to a trot.

***

Horace fumed all the way back to his shack he'd patched together with scraps of wood and quarried stone he had collected. Trash littered the ground. His mood grew fouler as he threw an empty whiskey bottle into the air and shot at it twice with his pistol.

Jack, grazing on stubby patches of grass, skittered at the sudden blast and brayed out a whimper.

The bottle landed unscathed with a thud on the packed dirt. Horace faced the mule with an accusing glare. "It's that damn Injun that wants my silver. All of it for hisself and his tribe of heathens."

Jack snorted and lowered his muzzle and continued to graze. Horace shoved the pistol back into his gun belt.

A fluttering movement nearby caught Horace's attention. Trapped between two rocks by the entrance of the mine, an eagle feather quivered in the breeze. He crept closer and stooped to retrieve it, grasping the quill between his thumb and forefinger, examining it in detail.

"I was right!" he waved it in the air to show the mule. "They think they can scare me, sending me this here message, but I ain't no fool."

A coughing spell provoked a sudden tightness in his chest, and he labored to take a breath. His hands trembled. Stiffened fingers refused to uncoil to rid himself of the cursed relic until, with great effort, he hurled it into the air like a burning coal. It gravitated back toward him, following his movements while he staggered backwards, thrashing his arms in defense. With a sudden upward jump, it drifted above him, floating over a pile of rocks, and disappeared into the sky.

Sweat clung to his skin. "Black magic Injun conjuring," he muttered out loud while rubbing his chest until the sensations went away.

***

After his routine supper of rabbit fried in bacon lard, Horace performed his nightly ritual before bunking in for the night. He grabbed the lantern from the table in his shack and ambled the short distance under the crescent moon to the mouth of the mine. The flame's light pitched a narrow beacon against the chiseled walls, breaking the inky blackness with a flickering dance.

Over the many months of burrowing with hand pick and shovel, he had become accustomed to finding his way through the tunnels of the mine with only the light of his lantern. Night or day didn't matter. Underneath the mountain's shroud existed only one time. Eternal darkness.

He squatted next to the spot he had hollowed out for its own special purpose. A secret hiding place, carved into the heart of the stone. He set the lantern down and reached in to count the bags, feeling their bulky mass, weighted with silver ore collected over the months of tedious labor. One more bag, and he'd have enough to secure his claim. Live a life of ease that was his due. Regain the respect he deserved. Perhaps, he'd return to his Dakota farm, to his wife and three kids he had left years ago. This time a rich man, not the dirt-poor farmer he'd once been. They'd beg him back, and he'd build a big house for all of them.

Satisfied with the assurance of the security of his treasure, he rose and picked up the lantern, sniffing the air. A familiar, yet unwelcome odor peppered his nose and crawled down his throat. Its fetid stink strangled his breath. A sudden memory rushed back of the nightmarish smell of blood and death on the battlefield. Crouched amid the smoke and screams of the dying. His only friend's head cradled in his lap with dead, empty eyes staring upward, his beseeching plea silenced. They had shared everything together, just like brothers. Horace could only watch as the crimson blood pooled through the blue wool uniform. Sioux arrows pierced his chest, with shredded feathers mingled with chunks of fragmented flesh. It was the only time he had cried as a grown man.

Horace throat tightened, and he quickened his pace, but the putrid stench of decay followed him, engulfing him with suffocating persistence. He scrambled forward, falling to his hands and knees. Footsteps shuffled behind him. He froze as an icy chill fell around him. The next second, a sudden clunk thudded next to him, and he sprung to his feet. Something invisible filled the unsettled air.

With a quick gasp, Horace whipped the lantern around. Its flame surged. A human skull with vacant eye sockets materialized an arm's length in front of him. Deep grooves of red and black war paint scarred its bleached skeletal surface. Jaws clenched the blade of a hunting knife. Feather-shaped daggers jutted outward like spikes from its headdress.

Horace's shaking legs fueled a burst of energy, and he shot past the apparition in a panic, careening over the uneven surface, stumbling in his haste. The once-familiar pathway now twisted and spiraled into a foreign maze. Flesh tore from his frantic fingertips as he felt along the sides of the tunnel, grated away in bloody scrapes from his hand. He scurried along the uneven path, unsure of the turns he should take. In his other hand, the lantern bounced, its light jittered and flashed like lightning in a thunderstorm. By the time he reached fresh air, his heart thudded so hard he thought it would explode. He collapsed outside into the dirt.

***

Sleepless the entire night, he spent his waking hours consuming most of his supply of whiskey, trying to banish the image of the specter. He pulled the bolt over the door of his shack and checked it several times before the sun rose.

By morning, Horace's terror had built into seething rage. At first light, he flung the door open, unleashing his anger in shouts of vile curses. First directed toward the mountain, then toward Jack. The poor animal squealed and reared up, snapping his rope tether from the hitching post. When Horace started throwing rocks in his direction, the mule plastered its long ears back and escaped at a gallop into the woods down by the stream. "Run, you demons!" He howled after Jack. "You'll never steal my silver. Run now or suffer the wrath of Horace Maggins!"

He doubled over with hands on knees, panting from the exertion. One thing was clear. He would get that thief and spirit conjurer, Injun Jim, and catch him red-handed. Then kill him dead.

Horace spent the day drinking black coffee alternating with whiskey, and chipping small holes into the walls of the mine. Positioning the holes in the right place had to be a strategic choice for the most impact of his plan.

Twilight arrived. He skipped supper—working diligently—packing dynamite into the holes he had produced. The wire fuse had been strung from the explosive and connected to the plunger. By his calculations, Jim would be lured into his trap with the sight of bags filled with silver, where the thief would be blasted to smithereens.

By nightfall, Horace made camp at the mouth of the mine, hidden just inside. A small campfire chased away the chill while he laid out his bedroll. The trap was ready–the detonator placed within his reach.

Flames flickered in a mesmerizing rhythm, its sparks crackling into a soothing lullaby. The sleep that had evaded him the previous night came visiting, claiming its hold on him.

He woke with a start, staring at the ceiling of the mineshaft. The fire that had quieted before he fell asleep now swelled with a fierce intensity. Horace tried to raise himself, but he could only move his head from side to side. An invisible heavy weight crushed his body, rendering his arms useless. Light and dark wavered above him. A silhouetted figure with the headdress of a chief flickered and expanded, consuming the entire ceiling and walls of the mine. The shadow's hand clutched a large hunting knife raised to strike.

Horace whimpered. Frantic, he searched for the source of the shadow, but he remained alone. No one else occupied the space. He tried to cry out, to curse his foe, but his voice issued only a muted hiss. The shadow of the Indian flickered in the firelight as its arm held the knife aimed at Horace's reclined body. In one swift stroke, the knife plunged downward.

A searing pain spread across Horace's chest, so intense it stole the air from his lungs. No blood fell. His flesh remained intact. Not even a tear in his shirt. Gasping, excruciating agony spread through his ribs, devouring his insides like the teeth of a thousand gnawing rodents. His vision blurred. In that moment, Sally's mournful tune echoed in his ears, piercing his brain like needles. A tear rolled down his cheek.

"I'll get you, you dirty Injun," now only audible in his mind. His eyes traveled to the dynamite plunger only inches away, as useless as his last thought before everything went black.

***

Bill discovered the mule sauntering into town with his head down before lingering by the Purgatory Saloon. He recognized Jack and informed the sheriff about the loose animal.

Together, Bill and the sheriff rode toward Horace's shack. The putrid smell and buzzing of flies directed them to the mine. They found Horace's decomposing body just inside the entrance.

The sheriff covered his nose with his kerchief and took a hard look at the corpse. "Not a mark on him. No broken bones. Not even a bruise."

Bill shook his head. "I ain't seen him in a couple weeks, but that weren't no surprise since I told him to git out of my place and not come back. He was a right nasty fellow. No friends or family as far as I know. A hermit."

Bill lit the lantern and searched the space around the entrance, digging around the ash of the cold campfire. "I found something here." He pointed to bags piled near the dynamite plunger. "Horace had bragged he was close to hittin' the mother lode of silver. Maybe this is it," Bill said, his voice excited.

The sheriff looked at the bags and reached inside. He picked up a sample of the bulky contents, holding it close to the lantern's light.

"This here ain't no silver ore." He shook his head. "Just plain rocks." The sheriff dropped it to the ground and brushed the dirt from his hands. "I'd say our friend's time on this earth was up. Looks like cause of death was natural."

Bill removed his hat and curled the brim in his hand, head bowed. "I pray the son-of-a- bitch went peacefully in his sleep."

The Culvertown Cavern

Stephen L. Brayton

Have you heard of Culvertown, Iowa? Not many have, and those who do, know it from stories told from grandparents and great grandparents. You won't find it on a map. Cartographers, even the online directories, have deleted it.

Which is a good thing. Better some places not gain too much attention.

I can tell you all about Culvertown because I was there when my father, Joshua Culver, first stepped onto the land. Located roughly midpoint between Centerville, Numa, and Mystic, the town evolved similarly to other industry settlements out west. Wherever miners and lumberjacks were employed, a community grew up around them. Saloons, hotels, supply stores, blacksmiths, and, of course, prostitution. After the gold ran out or the lumber mills moved on, the towns died out or were abandoned.

Culvertown's existence ended with a literal bang but doom hovered over the area days before.

My father saw the success of coal mining in West Virginia and Pennsylvania. He'd heard mines had opened in Iowa, but the industry hadn't yet taken a strong hold. With money and equipment, in 1871, he chose his spot.

Word went out, and soon he had more than enough men willing to work the mine and the processing and shipment of coal. Within two years, he earned enough profits to consider expansion. He never did, and within days, the mine closed.

Let me give you the sequence of events.

My father wasn't egotistical enough to name the town after himself. Instead, he exhibited and practiced upright ethos, morals, determination, and fair discipline to garner support from his employees, They wanted success as much as Joshua did. They encouraged the growth of the settlement, and by mutual agreement, they named it Culvertown. It wasn't huge. A couple saloons, a hotel, a supply store, and one eating establishment that handled any overflow from the saloons.

The mine prospered with regular shipments, and like I mentioned, my father tested new ground for a second mine. However, before he could properly open, the trouble started.

They used black powder in those days. Dynamite, patented only a handful of years earlier, grew in popularity, but companies couldn't produce enough for demand. Joshua negotiated for as much as he could obtain, but shipments constantly ran late.

Anyway, one afternoon, the workers used powder to blow through the end wall in a distant tunnel. After the explosion, they discovered an opening in the floor near the edge of one of the walls. Initial examination: the presence of a passage that ran diagonally downward, deeper into the ground. Not having the right equipment to explore, the men chose to wait until the follow day to make proper arrangements.

When morning arrived, the crew was short one man, Martin Thomsen, a supervisor, who lived on the outskirts of the settlement with his wife and a small passel of hogs.

When an appointed co-worker visited the house, Mrs. Thomsen thought her husband had gone to the mine. Further questioning brought up that she had Martin leave the house in the early morning to check on a disturbance in the hog kennel. She didn't remember his returning and figured he had come back to bed and arose to go to work without bothering her.

A cursory search by townsfolk and some of the miners resulted in nothing. No trail, signs, or tracks from Thomsen. After a while, everyone generally agreed Thomsen had taken off for some unknown reason, just rode a horse out of town. Sometimes that happened. A guy just gets fed up with his current life and runs away to find another one elsewhere.

While the loss of one man didn't hamper the mine's operation, my father valued every employee. He was that type of person. However, he, too, accepted the consensus of his workers but only after he investigated every angle, including a search of the mine. By the time he did call a halt, he decided work would resume the next day.

The explanation for Thomsen's disappearance lost steam when the second miner vanished overnight. This man, Trace Collins, was a charter employee of the mine, a hard worker, one with few complaints.

Another search of the mine and surrounding area. No witnesses, no evidence of foul play. The only bit of interest was that Collins like to sit outside long into the night. One of the other miners had seen him on the front porch the previous evening just after sunset.

My father grew so dispirited by the second disappearance, he gathered all of his workers for a meeting. While talk of discouragement as the cause of two men vanishing had diminished, some of the miners still grumbled.

Culver stood on a platform high enough to see the entire contingent of miners. He paced back and forth several times before speaking. "Listen up. I don't know what's happening in our little community. Two men gone in as many nights." He raised his voice a notch. "I don't like it, and I don't like word spreading of why they are gone." He paced more. "Some of you think Trace and Martin took off because they weren't happy here. I don't believe that, but just in case that is the reason, then, well, we'll get along without them. What I'm saying is if any man does have a problem with me or the mine, you come to me, and we'll talk it out.

Murmuring flowed up and down through the crowd, but no one voiced dissent. My father was an open man who earned respect and loyalty. Only a few didn't believe dissatisfaction with the job was the reason for the men's disappearances.

"All right," Culver said. "I'm giving you an extra day off. Don't worry, I'll still pay you for your time. Meanwhile, you think about those two men. Any idea where they went or why they left—if they did leave—you come to me. Same if you have other matters to discuss."

His line about "if they did leave" bothered me. What did he mean? If they hadn't taken off, where were they?

I discussed this question with one of the few friends I'd made since Father moved the family to the area. Many miners were in their twenties and thirties, with a handful in their forties like my father who had children who followed them into the mine.

Since I worked in the office, I regularly met employees. Daniel Baker and I formed a friendship right off. Eager man my age, twenty-two, shorter than my five-six by an inch, strong but outgoing. Energetic and lacking that long-day, weary demeanor of men who'd worked long hours over long years.

Daniel shared the same concern. "Where would they be, Robert, if they didn't leave?"

He and I sat outside the supply store chewing on strips of jerked beef.

"I keep thinking about the one commonality between Collins and Thomsen," I said.

"What's?"

"Each was outside."

"Why is that special?" Daniel asked. "If they ran off, they'd have to be outside."

"Think about it, though," I said. "Thomsen checks on his hogs. A disturbance his wife said. What was that disturbance? Is it significant, maybe relate to his disappearing? Collins was known for not needing much sleep and always ready for his shift. He was last seen on his front porch."

"But we talked with the man who'd seen him. Nothing wrong there."

"True," I said. "Just exploring all corners of this."

"I'm listening."

"With Collins, I maybe could see him contemplating life and

walking away from everything. However, he didn't take any belongings."

"Right."

"And I can't see Thomsen out checking his hogs deciding 'Well, I guess I'll run away now.' Again, if he did, he didn't pack clothes, rifle, or anything else."

"What happened then?" Daniel asked. "Kidnapped?"

"Possibly," I said. "That brings up more questions. Who? Why? Where were they taken? No ransom. Haven't received any notes." I shook my head. "I think we have to eliminate kidnapping. Both men would have to have been surprised, knocked out, and the kidnappers risked the possibility of noise or someone showing up. Shots, voices, snorting horses, pounding hooves, something."

Daniel bit off another hunk of jerky, chewed, then said, "Sounds like you're building up to an idea."

He was correct. I mulled it over to convince myself that we should do it. "What do you think of staying up tonight on watch. I'd bet others will be doing the same, but you and me, we'll do a roving patrol."

He barked a laugh. "Sounds more like you want us to be bait."

"Possibly, but we'll be armed. Culvertown isn't that large. If one of us yells or fires off a shot, well hell, the whole town will hear it."

"How long you figure on staying up?" he asked.

"I'd say until dawn."

"What about—"

"Don't worry about your working tomorrow. I'll explain it to Father. He'll consider it part of your employment duties."

Daniel agreed and each of us went home to get a few hours' sleep. We met up just after sunset in front of the supply store. Each of us arrived with a shotgun, extra shells, a canteen, a lantern, and a pouch full of dry crackers in case we got hungry.

Culvertown's one street ran west out of town and east to peter out seventy yards from the mine. We laid out a route that took us along the backs of the stores and businesses on either side of the street to circle around to the front side. We'd meet in the middle and switch sides. Constant figure eights, not hurrying, affirming an "all okay" when we met.

I anticipated a long wait but after the first loop and taking Daniels path, I was on the back side of the supply store. The night was cool for August, the sky star-filled, no breeze, and the crickets and fogs chatted to each other. An owl's call cut off mid-hoot. The wise old bird must have sensed or heard something I hadn't.

Then I did. An audible ruffle as when one snaps a bed sheet to straighten it over a mattress. I froze, shotgun aimed out and up, my finger sliding inside the trigger guard.

A second of silence, then another whoomph. Closer now, but still above me.

After a third time, I saw an indistinct form blot out a swatch of stars. Something dark … and winged. Yes! That was the sound. Giant wings eating the air to maintain flight.

With a fourth whoomph, the thing flew over me. A second later, it turned and swooped down at me. No time to aim the shotgun, I dropped flat to the ground. What must have been talons raked the back of my shirt, ripping cloth and drawing blood.

The creature flew off. A minute later one of Thomsen's hogs squealed. His house lay on the west end of Culvertown.

I called to Daniel. When he appeared, I yelled, "Follow me."

The winged beast, protesting hog secured by two sets of talons, headed east. Toward the mine. I was surprised no one else had heard the commotion.

Daniel and I reached the end of the street in time to see the form of the flying beast disappear into the darkness of the mine. We looked at each other, nodded once, and shotguns at the ready, we followed and entered the mine.

Following the creature wasn't difficult. Bloody streaks from the hog's scraping against the rock led the way. We were delayed when we maneuvered through the tunnels. I took the lead but was aware of Daniels' weapon unintentionally prodding me forward every other step.

The temperature dropped the farther we traveled. Perhaps ten degrees. I was grateful for the long-sleeved shirt. Still, my skin chilled from an inner fear even as sweat broke out on my face and arms. I heard no more squeals and the creature that had snatched the hog traversed the tunnels as silent as a ghost.

I estimated twenty minutes passed until we reached the new section of tunnel excavated almost three days before. When the men discovered it, I was called in as part of that first examination.

"Careful, Robert," Daniel warned. "You should be nearing the hole in the floor."

Sure enough, the blood trail on the floor went straight to the edge and into the jagged opening in the tunnel floor.

The explosion had blown away enough rock he and I could stand side by side in the tunnel. Before we approached the hole, he set down his lantern and held his shotgun in both hands, one finger on the trigger.

I stepped up and aimed my lantern. The light disappeared into a wider chamber three feet down.

I'd known none of the miners had ventured in to explore. By the time they'd cleared the rubble, they were nearing the end of the day's shift. Since, no one had returned to the mine, let alone investigate the opening.

Now, with only Daniel and I present, I heard just our boots scrape the floor. Our eyes met each other. While I couldn't read his thoughts, I was sure they matched mine. Do we dare go on? Call in assistance? What would we find down there? We were fortunate to bring our shotguns.

He nodded once, and I shifted so I could kneel at the hole. With my head near the opening, my ears caught a distant mewling drifting up from below. I also caught a faint glow farther along the tunnel or passage. The taint of blood wafted up.

I lowered my lantern into the hole, ready to jump back if anything emerged. Nothing did, but the light revealed a length of tunnel where, crouched, I could duck-walk along the length. Where it ended… well, no way to know unless one entered.

I told Daniel what I'd seen and heard. "What do you think?"

Daniel's face tightened with anxiety and fear. "Maybe we should summon your father."

I had the same thought, but Daniel and I were there with a modicum of determination if not bravery. At least I had those traits. If we went back for Father, would another creature fly out of the cave?

I said, "I don't think we have time to wait." I raised the shotgun. "If we find something we can't handle, then we go for reinforcements."

He visibly swallowed and tightened his grip on his weapon.

"We have to do this for Misters Thomsen and Collins," I said. "I believe that creature, or one like it, is behind the disappearances. We saw it with the hog."

He nodded once.

"All right," I said. "I'll go first. You be ready if I make a quick reversal."

I laid the lantern and weapon near the opening and eased myself down. Grabbing up both, I crouched and stepped forward. The lantern bathed the passage in a yellow glow. I couldn't make out any man-made features, such as spades, picks, or shovels. The floor, walls, and ceiling exhibited scratches and scrapes as from claws or talons.

I inched along, balancing with the lantern in one hand and the shotgun in the other, the weapon pointed ahead, my finger ready to slip inside the trigger guard. If I encountered anything, I could fire. In the narrow chamber, I'd hit whatever was in front of me.

I estimated the tunnel extended twenty yards. The amount of perspiration oozing from my pores increased as I neared the end. A blue-white glow from some source further lit the path.

In fact, the illumination had brightened enough, I decided to leave the lantern just inside the tunnel when I exited onto a ledge about four feet long and as wide before it tapered back into the cavern wall.

That's what I saw. A large cavern, maybe a hundred yards long and sixty to the opposite wall. The blue glow came not from one source but from dozens of smaller spots spread over the cavern floor. Each resembled a fire of burning coal or natural gas. Blue near the base, yellow and orange at the top, like very intense campfires.

Milling around on the floor among the fires were scores of creatures. Each stood at least ten feet high and sported leathery and velvety fur covered wings. Bipedal, they walked on hind legs and manipulated and moved objects with their front claws. The fires showed me their wrinkled, bat-featured faces.

The "objects" the creatures handled were grotesque, fleshy animals resembling giant gophers. The bat creatures pinned them to the floor and pecked out chunks of meat, like an eagle eating fish.

Squeals caught my attention. On the far side of the cavern, the particular night flier I'd witnessed taking the hog had chosen a spot by one of the flames and ripped bloody flesh from the still living animal.

A low whoomph of air similar to what I'd heard in town drew my focus. In the dim shadows created by the fires, I saw countless more of the bat creatures hanging from the cavern ceiling. One or two frequently shifted for a better position or floated to the floor to take its turn at a meal.

High-pitched mewling rose from all around, the sound of hungers satiated, perhaps.

On the far left of the cavern, numerous gopher beasts squirmed and writhed while trapped under boulders. They hadn't been completely consumed.

Then revulsion shocked me almost senseless. Also trapped under the rocks were two human forms. I had no doubt they were the bodies of Martin Thomsen and Trace Collins. They lay unconscious but not dead, I suspected, because wounds from the bat's fangs oozed blood.

I watched while a bat, finished with his meal, took the gopher beast to that confinement area of bodies and secured it under a boulder. Those trapped, I noticed, sported wounds in various stages of healing. It was as if the bats were storing them, letting the beasts heal. Later, I discovered the truth.

A squawk-caw rose from the opposite end of the cavern. One of the bats emerged from a hole in the floor that measured at least ten feet in diameter. Its talons held a growling gopher beast.

I watched, wide-eyed, as the bat found an unoccupied fire and settled next to it. Another bat wobble-walked and help pin the gopher to the floor. Then they proceeded to eat.

I turned back to the hole. Was that where the bats obtained their prey? From deep in the earth?

My senses began to rationalize the fantastic scene when a squeak-mew of alarm came from one of the hanging bats. The creature detached from the ceiling and flew on a direct line toward me.

I scrambled to raise the shotgun, aimed at the fangs, and fired. The blast filled the cavern. The pellets caught the bat point blank. A scream erupted from the creature. The wings fluttered twice before the bat crashed to the cavern floor.

More cries arose after the shotgun blast faded.

I didn't hesitate but turned and crawled back into the small tunnel, forgetting my lantern but keeping the shotgun, jutting rock edges jabbing hands and knees.

Ten feet in, I heard the rustle of wings against rock. One of the bats had entered the tunnel behind me. I crawled faster, whimpering in terror and pain. Sharp rocks punctured my trousers and skin, grinding against bone.

I screamed when what I thought were bat talons pierced my left ankle. I fell face first to the rocky floor when the creature pulled me backward. My hands reached for purchase, fingers slipping on the rocks.

Another scream erupted from my throat when fangs tore away a chunk of calf muscle. In my agony, I managed to twist my body so I lay on my back, the talons loosening. The barrel of the shotgun lay near my head. I grabbed the weapon with both hands and bashed the butt of the stock against whatever I could in the darkness.

Bat screeches deafened me, but I kept pounding until I felt my ankle released. I pushed with my good leg to move my body away. Talons clamped onto my boot but another shotgun blow warded off the attack.

Daniel yelled my name. Yard by yard I moved back along the tunnel. Lantern light reached me from above along with one of Daniel's hands. I stretched one of mine, slipped off his fingers, and felt the bat clawing my boot again. One more boom of the shotgun against pliable flesh. Then I grasped Daniel's hand. He pulled me along the rocky floor. Using the shotgun and my one uninjured leg, I wormed my way up out of the opening.

"What—" he started but I interrupted.

"Sh—shoot whatever comes out of that hole," I commanded. I rolled away, blood flowing from my leg.

"What happened?"

"Never mind. Just shoot."

"You're bleeding."

"Shoot!"

For the bat's head and one wing came into view, the talons raking the edges of the hole. Daniel cried out, grabbed up his shotgun, aimed, and fired. I was deaf again except for a muffled screech from the bat.

Then all went silent. The bloody head and torso of the creature lay half out of the hole. Gore covered the mined floor and walls.

Daniel's hands grabbed me. I clutched at his shirt. "Use our bandannas to wrap my leg. Hurry."

Calf wound cinched, he helped me to my feet. With him supporting me, arm around his shoulder, I hobbled through the mine. I heard nothing behind us and prayed that the bat creature's corpse blocked enough of the passage to prevent others from escaping.

I didn't cry in relief until I breathed in fresh Culvertown night air.

***

Shouting for help brought residents. While they helped me to the doctor's house, I sent someone to bring my father. I told my story to him while the doctor administered his treatment.

At first, no one believed my tale of the cavern, the gophers, and the fate of Thomsen and Collins, but with Daniel's witnessing one of the bats, my father sent half a dozen men back into the mine for verification. Within the hour, they reported that yes, some type of creature's body lay dead just inside the opening. They'd also heard, from deeper below, the scrabbling of claws and more mewlings from no animals familiar to them.

The report spread like the proverbial forest fire, and before long, even before dawn broke, many miners were packing up belongings. Too few loyal men remained to keep the mine working, and even those who stayed were reluctant to reenter the darkness of the tunnels. My father understood that he wouldn't be able to hire anyone else. Word of monsters and missing men would reach any potential worker.

***

My father made his decision by early afternoon. He laughed at the irony of the shipment of dynamite that arrived on the noon stage, that he would use it to close the mine instead of making the job more efficient for the workers.

Supported by crutches, I stood with him when he set off the explosion. The rumble of rock growled like a leviathan from the entrance with coal dust spewing forth like the breath of a dragon. A subsequent inspection confirmed we'd sealed off the tunnels. I prayed no more bats would come into this world to terrorize and feed on men and animals. However, to this day, I still shiver whenever I think of more creatures living under the earth.

Culvertown residents moved away, leaving husks of buildings and a closed-off mine. Eventually, other area coal mines closed or petered out. Quarries opened, but few people ever ventured back to Culvertown to reopen the mine.

I won't let anyone. When father died, I assumed ownership. Even so, a handful of entrepreneurs wandered through with the idea of doing business, but as I have papers showing ownership, they soon get disillusioned.

The mine will remain with me until I die... whenever that day comes. So far, I'm about six decades past due. I stopped counting birthdays in 1963. I've had to change the ownership papers every time I legally change my name and adopt the role of another ancestor of Joshua Culver, whether grandson or great grandson.

That's the legacy I endure from that old mine. While my father moved to Des Moines to start a new career, I moved to Centerville. I convinced him not to sell the property and to dissuade any inquiries.

As the decades passed, I had to move around because if I remained in one town too long, people would notice I wasn't aging. I stayed within a hundred miles of Culvertown, returning to Centerville long after anyone would remember me.

I didn't understand at first what had happened. Not until I picked up a copy of Bram Stoker's novel and read subsequent so-called legends of how a bite from certain creatures could extend life.

Those underground bats knew. That's why they kept the gophers trapped and didn't entirely consume them. Preserving meals for… who knew how long?

Are Thomsen and Collins still alive and suffering continual agony and torture? I pray for their souls.

Creep

C.B. Butler

"This is Bullshit!"

Josh flinched and looked around to see who was speaking. With a wave of embarrassment, he realized he spoke the words himself. Once his heartbeat returned to normal, he looked around again to see if anyone witnessed his foolishness. Assured he was alone in his misery, he sunk down in the driver's seat of his ancient Toyota Tercel and wiped his face with both hands, as if he could wipe away the shame. Could his life possibly get any worse? Now he was talking to himself. Even scaring himself. What else could go wrong?

He was furious that Melissa was late for the third time this week. She was scheduled off at 10:30 every night but had been getting off later and later. Josh had to wait for her in the employee parking lot until she finally got done. Despite the scorching-hot weather of the summer days that lingered late into the evening, he refused to run the air conditioner, as the excess gas would only cost him more money. He sat in the car with the radio off, every window down, occasionally smoking, occasionally dozing, and continuously suffering.

Shortly after midnight, Melissa finally exited the hotel and rushed to the car. Although Josh saw her coming, moving as though lighting were licking her heels, he refused to turn the old cars ignition until she was in the passenger seat. She neither looked in his direction nor said anything to him as he put the car into drive and tore out of his slot. Halfway through the lot, Josh quietly, but with an unmistakable edge in his voice, said, "Punctual as usual." He was looking for yet another fight. Melissa continued to stare ahead through the windshield, but Josh knew it was taking everything she had to not respond in kind.

Josh wheeled the old car out of the hotel's lot, nearly into the path of an oncoming truck. He was so distracted by his anger with Melissa and was so tired he hadn't even seen the glaring lights of the monstrosity. As his heartbeat again returned to normal and the truck's blaring horn was disappearing into the past, Josh wished he'd waited a split second longer. The large truck running into and through the old Tercel would have ended his misery for sure. He looked over in Melissa's direction. It didn't appear she'd moved a muscle. Perhaps she was hoping for the same thing.

They rode on in silence for about five minutes through the mostly empty streets before the anger again replaced the fatigue. Every time they passed the rare vehicle on the dark streets, Josh hoped it would veer into his path, sending them both into infinity. Now he needed to vent in his recently all-too-familiar way, or he was going to erupt. He recited his rhetoric in his mind for a few seconds and attempted to calm himself before he finally spoke. "Melissa. Look, this is getting old." He paused. She still didn't look in his direction. "You're getting off later and later every night, but yet I gotta' wait for you, plus get up in the morning and get ready for my first job, while you get to sleep in." Another pause. "Something's gotta give."

He looked in her direction, expecting a compensatory outburst, such as she provided the previous evening. But the expression on her face never changed, nor did she even glance in his direction. He waited a few more seconds, and then added, "You got nothing to say?"

After a bit more silence, she finally whispered an answer. "I need to go to the store."

"What?"

She turned to him. There were now tears in her eyes, threatening to spill over. "I need to go the store." Now there was a definitive edge in her voice as well.

Good. Now they were getting somewhere.

"Well, considering I've been waiting for you for a fucking hour yet again, I think you can wait until tomorrow."

"No, I need to go now." The tears were beginning to flow.

"What the hell do you need that's so important?"

She answered by staring at the road ahead.

"Well, how about I go home and you walk to the fucking store."

A very quiet "whatever" was the answer to this inquiry.

Josh continued to drive in aggravated silence as the only sounds in the car were Melissa's occasional sniffles. She wiped at her face a couple of times with a tissue from her purse. Josh extracted and lit a cigarette. He knew she hated it when he smoked, and hadn't done so in her company for several months, but right now he just did not give a shit. He considered rolling up his window and blowing the smoke in her direction, but his still-rational mind convinced him that might be the final straw. Their relationship was on the verge of extinction as it was.

He also considered following through on his threat to go straight home, but ended up driving to the local Kroger. He dropped her off at the entrance. Her crying spell had ended at some point. She didn't ask him if he needed anything, as she usually did. He parked, killed the engine, and lowered the windows the rest of the way. After finishing his cigarette, and some internal debate, he turned the ignition back on, rolled up the windows, turned on the air conditioner, and put his seat back. He needed a little rest. He was going to have to get back up in about four hours, and it was going to be another long, hard day. And there was no telling how long Melissa was going to be in the store. She could be an hour, just to fuck with him. Now he found himself wondering if he could somehow revert the flow of exhaust back into the car and slip into eternity on a wave of noxious fumes.

As he started to drift off, Josh reflected on the last couple months. He never thought things would turn out this way. All their plans were in the toilet, despite the both of them diving headfirst into this adventure.

Back in April, Josh finally received the break he deserved from the restaurant chain he worked for in Springfield. The owner and the old man's management team figured Josh would be a great fit for the big city. He worked for them for three years, and got a promotion an average of once a year. The opportunity to advance his career and live in a larger city was too good to pass up. So he jumped at it. Melissa was all too happy to pursue his dreams at his side. Or so it seemed.

They packed up everything in their modest apartment and moved in June. Their new place by comparison was pretty small, but they figured the higher rent was justified by the quality of life they would have. They also discussed the nice house they would have when Josh made upper management and they were able to start a family.

By interstate, they were only an hour and a half from their previous residence. But in reality, the distance was closer to infinity. Along with the higher salary and more opportunities came higher levels of stress, traffic jams rarely seen before, and a perceived animosity from some of the people he managed. It seemed the new guy from out of town didn't seem to be a good fit for the big city after all.

After Melissa got the waitress job at the hotel, and Josh started collecting his fatter paychecks, they celebrated without restraint by spending their evenings off dining out, attending movies, or going to sporting events. There were so many things to do in this city! When they finally took a deep breath and looked at their finances, they realized they were fucked. Josh decided to take on a second job to save them from getting thrown out of their place. He was working evenings at the restaurant as the second shift manager, so he took on an early morning shift at a gas station down the street from their apartment. He worked at the station whenever there was a shift open and he was not at the restaurant. Recently, the manager of the station fired two of his full-timers for stealing cigarettes and porn mags, so Josh was picking up multiple shifts.

On the occasions he worked three-to-four consecutive shifts back-to-back, he was wiped out. The life he'd imagined in this place with his future wife was in dire jeopardy. Something had to change. Having to stay up even later to pick her up with their one shitty car was only adding to the frustration. Melissa was not happy about having to take public transportation to work when he was doing the back-to-backs, but they couldn't afford a second car just yet.

***

Between the air-conditioning and just being worn out, Josh was actually in a fairly deep slumber when Melissa returned to the car. He snapped awake when she opened the door. For a second, he couldn't remember for the life of him where the hell he was. He looked at her, expecting some kind of explanation. When she closed the door and put on her belt without even a glance in his direction, his memories slid back into place like a slap to the mouth. He raised his seat and put his own belt on. He could feel the blood rushing to his face and he made an effort to not look in her direction.

On the road back to their apartment, he stole a couple of glances her way. She was only carrying three bags. After looking at the clock, he realized she hadn't even been in the store fifteen minutes. Dually surprised at her briskness and his having slept so hard, he was a bit relieved he could get home, shower quickly, and get to bed. Then he was reminded he would be sleeping in the bed alone again. The relief slipped away, and he failed to grasp it.

Melissa had been sleeping on the couch for several days now, while there was so much tension between them. He couldn't help being angry about this, but decided he better be quiet for the rest of the night. Maybe in two days, when he was scheduled off both jobs, he would attempt to rehabilitate their relationship. But then again, at the rate things were going, he'd probably be called in to one job or the other.

When he pulled into the apartment complex's lot, he again had to park two buildings away. He shook his head and tapped the steering wheel as he searched for a spot. Melissa was silent. The thought of vocalizing that this never happened when they got home on time crossed his mind, but he held it down.

On the walk back toward their own building, and the subsequent hike up three flights of stairs, Josh decided he would try to start the healing. He reached for the grocery bags as Melissa fumbled with them and her purse. He was assaulted with an icy "I got it" for his efforts. The anger came storming back. He was trying to be nice. He was going on little sleep and every joint in his body burned, but he was trying to help her!

Josh took a deep breath. He needed to calm down. If he said what he thought, well…it wouldn't help.

Following her the whole way, as she struggled with the load across the lot and up the stairs, Josh was now willing someone to tear around the corner, running them down and ending the pain. He shuddered at his own morbid thoughts.

He let them into their apartment and immediately went about the process of removing his greasy, sweaty uniform and preparing to shower. Melissa headed to their miniscule kitchen to put away whatever groceries she'd bought.

***

Hands on the wall of the shower, supporting his weight, Josh was letting the scalding water wash all the grease, anger, and fatigue down the drain. He was thinking about how long it was since he and Melissa shared their bed. They hadn't made love in so long.

Had it been two weeks, already?

Despite the long day and another fight, the thought had his blood up. The many nights of passion over the last couple of years were replaying in his mind. Without warning, the fatigue that kept him company was gone, his pulse was pounding, and he had a second wind. He opened his eyes to verify what he already knew. He was rock-hard.

Why not, he thought. It isn't like I'll be getting laid anytime soon.

Just as he was taking himself into his hand, however, the bathroom door opened.

Goddammit!

The words nearly escaped his mouth, instead of staying in his mind. Not only had he instinctively released himself, but the sudden anger was causing his erection to subside.

Fuck it. My wonderful life continues.

He began to lather as he heard Melissa open the medicine cabinet. Not only had she interrupted at a most inconvenient time, but now she was disrupting his only hope at peace with a purpose as she banged things around the cabinet and then slammed its door.

As the last of the grease and sweat disappeared down the drain, the fatigue returned to again keep him company. He was prolonging his rinse as Melissa continued to make her presence known. He decided to wait a couple more minutes and then turn off the water. He would give her time to get out of the bathroom and out of his way. Maybe he could finish what he started before she stormed in. But no, the desire was gone. He only wished for sleep. Another morbid thought of death rushed in, as he imagined what it would take to drown himself in the shower. He went so far as putting his face directly under the flow of water. This only resulted in him swallowig the tepid water, bringing about a fit of choked coughing. To hell with it. Another minute and he was done. Melissa hadn't closed the bathroom door, so he didn't know if she was still….

A strange noise interrupted his thoughts. Some kind of scratching. He could barely hear it over the water flowing. He lifted his head out of the water to get a better grasp on what was making the sound. Now it sounded more like crackling; like thin ice cracking or the embers of a dying fire. Josh was confused. What the hell was that?

"Melissa, what are you doing?"

He meant to put an edge in his voice to enforce he was tired and annoyed and she was adding fuel to the fire. He was embarrassed he sounded like a frightened child. Melissa didn't respond. The crackling noise continued and seemed to intensify.

"Melissa! What's that noise?"

She still didn't respond. He thought he should let it go. She may very well just be doing something to annoy him as revenge. But his curiosity got the better of him. He stepped to the side of the shower away from the water and pulled aside the curtain. The source of the crackling noise was immediately evident.

He stared at the brown masses piling on the edge of the sink and the floor below.

What the hell?

He could only stare at the moving piles. His feet were glued to the shower floor. His heart was trying to escape from his chest. All the training in pest control in the restaurant business could never prepare him for this.

The roaches were moving in all directions. Josh looked up and saw they were falling from a hole in the ceiling above the sink. A few were still emerging. He guessed they'd come through quite rapidly, and the first wave was crushed on the sink and then the floor. The roaches falling on one another was what had caused the dry, crackling noises. Now that the first wave provided a cushion of sorts, they were moving en masse. Some of them toward the shower.

His heart still threatening to burst from his chest, Josh was overcome by feelings of revulsion. His stomach flipped and he gagged. Hundreds, if not thousands, of roaches were invading his bathroom. Another couple of thoughts occurred to him. How was he going to get out of here? They were blocking his path. And weren't roaches adverse to light? He'd learned a thing or two about them while working in restaurants.

As the first wave reached the top of the bathtub's edge, Josh's paralysis broke. These were not ordinary roaches, and they were coming for him. The only thing he could think to do was call to Melissa for help. He yelled her name twice in succession, while moving to the spout end of the tub. He sounded scared and weak. This disgusted him almost as much as the roaches.

The water from the shower head was still running. He had the wherewithal to grasp it and aim the flow at the approaching roaches. Many of them were washed away, but several fell into the tub. They appeared to be battling the currents of water to regain purchase. Josh called out to Melissa once again.

He hadn't even gotten her name out of his mouth before she materialized in the doorway to the bathroom. He thought she may ignore his cries for help after their fight, but she must have heard the desperation in his voice. She was here. He turned his attention back to the bugs. He washed a few more off the side of the tub. They fell to the bathroom floor along with a deluge of water. He again looked towards Melissa. She was staring at the roaches. He didn't think her eyes could widen any further without popping out of her head. As he attacked more of them, he realized he'd called out to her with no thought as to his next action. The roaches that broke off the attack to advance in her direction sure wouldn't help.

Melissa took a step back. She noticed them advancing on her as well. She looked up. They locked eyes, and he read sadness and regret in hers. Somehow she knew this was the end for both of them. Well, for him, at least. He had to get her out of this.

"Run!"

She looked at him as if he'd asked her to dive in, head first. She shook her head. The movement was barely noticeable, but Josh knew what it meant. She didn't want to leave him.

"Run, Melissa. There's no time. Go get help."

He knew she could read the remorse in his eyes and hear it in his voice. They'd wasted their last two weeks together fighting. Josh regretted the thoughts of violence he experienced this evening more so than the last two weeks of fighting and cold shoulder. He pleaded with Melissa to run as he fought the roaches. Finally she did. Josh was left alone with them. All the morbid thoughts of his own death came flooding back. Had he somehow invited this?

Josh shook his head to clear his thoughts and regain focus. He didn't watch to see if the roaches would follow Melissa out of the bathroom. He could only continue to fight them off the bathtub's edge with the shower head. For every dozen or so he washed away, half as many made it into the tub. Some of them were drowning and being washed away, but Josh noticed more and more were surviving, and now a few were climbing up his legs. This brought about a gag reflex so severe he nearly blacked out. Survival instincts kicked in and he diverted the attack of water from the approaching storm to the few on his body. They were washed away.

The result of this shift in attack was that several more roaches were able to ascend the side of the tub unchallenged. Josh knew he had to get out, one way or another. The only plan that occurred to him was simply rushing through the onslaught. This did not seem ideal, but he couldn't think of any alternative. As he planned his escape, it occurred to him he may be able to jump over them. If he could get a boost from the bathtub's edge…

He didn't have time to think, so he merely acted. Spraying the roaches from the side of the tub once more, he stepped back and lunged for the edge. He envisioned in his mind landing on the edge with one foot, pushing off with that foot, and jumping over the now-covered bathroom floor, landing as close to the entrance as possible. He would then run through the threshold into the bedroom as fast as he could. He knew he would be smashing dozens of bugs with his naked feet, but what other choice did he have?

Things didn't go according to plan, and Josh paid for it with his life. As his foot coupled with the edge of the bathtub, and he attempted to push off, he slipped in the water he'd just sprayed there, and his balance was completely thrown off. His momentum sent his lower half forward as planned, but his upper half stayed in place and began descending. In a blind panic, he stretched both arms outward, attempting to grab hold of something. His right hand found purchase among the shower curtain, but instead of slowing his descent, the curtain and the cheap, rusty rod holding it in place came down with him.

Josh's 170-plus pounds ended up on the floor.

His body hit the fairly soft cushioning of the roaches and the bath rug below them, but the back of his head was not so lucky. It connected with the edge of the tub, knocking most of the consciousness from him. He ended up with his face toward the toilet, now covered in brown movement.

As he slipped into nothingness, his only thought was, I hope Melissa got away. He couldn't help but feel regret over the way things progressed recently, as he came to the realization that the roaches were crawling all over him. He opened his mouth in an attempt to scream, but he didn't have the energy. His open mouth became an attack route for the roaches.

As they invaded, Josh lost consciousness.

***

"What happened to him?"

"We're not entirely sure yet. There'll be an autopsy, of course." If there's anything left to autopsy, the detective didn't add.

Melissa's parents drove down from Springfield to retrieve her from the hospital. She was held for observation for the past two days. She was in shock following the incident at her apartment. Yesterday, she took the news of Josh's death hard. She cried for hours, and was still in this state when her parents arrived.

They attempted to comfort her, but to no avail. Her mother was nearly as upset as Melissa with the loss of Josh. She was fond of him, and couldn't wait for the two of them to marry and make her a grandmother. Her father, on the other hand, never liked Josh. A man that slaved away in dirty diners all day wouldn't be able to properly provide for his daughter. He was not nearly as sympathetic as his crazy wife. He thought Melissa would be better off without him, but wasn't quite harsh enough to mention this, even to her mother.

As nothing in the apartment was salvageable after the police and multiple exterminators had their way with it, Melissa's parents were planning to take her directly from the hospital to their home back in Springfield. They would worry about putting her life back together once she had a couple of days to rest and recover. They spent the night in the hospital with her, napping when able, and were exhausted.

Now they were consulting with Melissa's doctor and the detective in charge of the case, a stocky dark-skinned man named Bishop. Doctor Smith, a short, Asian woman, was assuring them that with a couple days rest and possibly some counseling, she would be fine.

The report from Detective Bishop was a little less re-assuring. Apparently the apartment was overrun with a roach infestation. Josh was killed by this infestation, which made no sense whatsoever. Since when did roaches attack people? The police were investigating with the help of the exterminators who'd rendered the apartment building uninhabitable with their barrage of chemicals.

Melissa's parents thanked the detective and the doctor and went to gather their daughter. Despite the fact she was dressed and ready for travel, she refused to shower in the hospital visitor's dormitory. The thought of Josh in the shower when she'd last seen him was too much to handle. She also refused to talk or make eye contact with her parents.

***

As the somber, depressed trio was leaving the facility, a large insect, which may or may not have been a roach, crept across the tiled hallway, intersecting their path to the parking lot.

What kind of hospital has bugs running around in it? Melissa's father wondered, before he remembered what happened to his daughter two days ago. He glanced at Melissa, hoping she'd not seen the bug. Unfortunately, she had.

A low whine began in her throat as she watched the insect creep across the otherwise sanitary tile. She stopped in her tracks.

"Oh, God," her mother whispered.

The whine turned into quick, panicked breaths, which didn't last long, to her parent's dismay.

Melissa began to scream.

It was a long, long time before she was able to stop.

The Corner of My Eye

Rose Wilson

"I became insane, with long intervals of horrible sanity."
~Edgar Allan Poe

There it is again! The shape-shifter. That insidious black shadow that I catch from the corner of my eye. Just when I turn to face it, it disappears. This is the miserable life I have been facing for as long as I can remember and, well, I'm not sure how far back I actually can remember A cursed life that I did nothing to deserve.

I sit down on the couch and switch on the television. It's my only means of distraction these days. No job. No friends. No hobbies. Can't read anymore. Close-up vision sucks and I can't stand to wear those crappy magnification glasses. I could go out to the library and get some of those "books on tape" I suppose, but I won't. I can't. The neighbors watch me. I know they do. Even if their curtains are closed or their blinds pulled down, I catch their movement out of the corner of my eye. Just like I do that hateful shape-shifter that's invaded my house.

What do I need to go outside for anyway? I get my groceries delivered. My social security is electronically paid into my checking account and my bills are all set up for automatic payment. And I take lots and lots of vitamin D. I'm safe here all cozy and warm in my little four room house. A house steeped in perpetual grayness thanks to room-darkening shades. Yes. I'm safe here. Aren't I?

I press the button on the TV remote to bring up the program guide and start surfing up and down the list of shows. One hundred and twenty-five channels and I can't find anything worth watching. Go figure. I highlight a rerun of Becker which I've seen at least a dozen times. I press the "Okay" button for my umpteenth viewing and instead of Ted Danson's face I see a message box: searching for signal.

Great. Now there's absolutely nothing to do. Loneliness snakes its insidious tendrils upward from my constantly churning gut and wraps around my heart, squeezing until I want to cry. I've been living by myself for far too long. An old quote enters my head (totally uncalled for as I don't sit here trying to remember old quotes): The unexamined life is not worth living. I don't know the author, but he, or she, got it right. There's no one to examine my life but me and my opinion is: it sucks. When I was young I thought I would have someone with me in my elder years. But youth does not prepare you one iota for old age. Here's a quote from yours truly: Advice from the old and wise is a shortcut almost never taken by the young and stupid ... at least I think it's mine. It's becoming harder to tell the difference between my original thoughts and something I picked up somewhere else. Actually, as I sit here, talking to myself, I realize I can't recall why I'm sitting here like a bump on a log. I should turn on the TV, at least it will be some noise. Hah, I can holler at that idiot news anchorman. The one who's always smirking supremely from his exalted position in the so-called "newsroom." Actually, I think I used to like him. I used to watch him with ... with ... who? Who did I used to watch him with? Fuck it. I pick up the remote.

Searching for signal. Oh shit. That's right. What to do, what to do? Oh, I almost forgot my favorite pastime of "Ways to End My Life:" Shotgun? Nope, too chicken for that. Besides, I might end up a vegetable in some damn old farts home instead of croaking. Slit my wrists? Uh-uh. Too gory ... even for me. Choke down a bunch of pills? Won't work. There hasn't been any real medicine in this house for ages. Damn doctors won't make house calls anymore and the days of calling in your symptoms—phony or real, ha, ha—are long gone. Hey, here's a new one. Maybe I should try overdosing on vitamin D. Nah. I'd probably just get gut pains tonight and the Hershey squirts by morning. Maybe soon I'll come up with a winner. And what does it matter anyway? I only think about ending it all. I'm more afraid of death then I am of living out my crappy little life. I don't know why this is. It just is. You'd think I'd be tired of this shit routine by now. I think I'll—.

There! It just went by! It swept past me fast as lightning and now it's gone again. Wait a doggone minute. It disappeared right by the coat closet. A ridiculous tie-dyed curtain covers the coats hanging inside. The blasted door broke years ago and I never bothered fixing it. The shadow, the shape-shifter, the whatever you want to call it WENT IN THERE! I pick up the wooden back-scratcher from the chipped and stained coffee table. I look at it as I hold it in my hand and it suddenly seems foreign to me. Just a thin, two foot long handle with fake "fingers" curling down at one end. How do I think I will defeat my house invader with this thing? Scratch it to death? Well, the curled fingers do have sharp edges. Sort of.

A small chuckle escapes my mouth and it sounds a bit crazy. The "cackling" kind of crazy. When did I start doing this sort of thing aloud? I'm not sure, but I think it's been happening for a long while now.

I approach the curtained doorway cautiously, my four-fingered defense weapon held up, ready to tear into my nemesis. I slowly pull the curtain back. I'll scratch that shadowy bastard's eyes out! There! Something black! I strike with all the force I can muster. I slash at the figure again and again and again.

I realize I'm getting no resistance and I stop thrashing about. Hands resting on knees, chest heaving, I stare into the closet at the long black coat that now has one sleeve destroyed. I should feel relieved but I don't because, hunching over in the middle of my living room and trying to catch my breath, I realize ... that's not my coat! Then whose coat is it? Maybe my shadowy house-guest has plans to move in. I yank it off the hanger and hold it at arms length.

Why, it's a woman's coat. A fragrance wafts through the air and I press the collar to my nose.

Lily. The word slips into my mind like a silent stalker. Is that the fragrance? No, it's, it's ... it's my wife! My sweet Lily of the Valley. How could I have forgotten her? I loved her so!

An image is dragged from the recesses of my mind. The lovely face of my beautiful, beautiful wife. The first day I laid eyes on her swirls through my mind like a dream. A dream I lived ...

It was the beginning of summer when I met my Lily. The very year when young girls were nursing broken hearts over Elvis' recent marriage to Priscilla, Jim Morrison thumbed his nose at Ed Sullivan by singing the word "higher" on national television, and the United States government declared LSD an illegal drug. Unconcerned and unaffected by any of these events, my buddies and I did what was most important to us at that time: cruising the streets of Baltimore while crammed into my '66 Chevelle. What a beaut! Positraction rear, four-barrel carburetor, heavy-duty Hurst shifter and the rear jacked so high I got pulled over on a regular basis.

After a hard night of street-dragging, we pulled into Gino's for burgers and fries. Gino's always had the prettiest carhops on roller skates (rollerskating carhops were waitresses that delivered your fast-food right to your car) and we knew all of them. But not this night. After shouting into the call box (first with things like: We'll have the nickel-ninety-eight special, ha, ha) we waited for our food and sang along to the radio in voices that would make an old hound dog howl at the moon. We changed the words a bit too: "Went to a dance, lookin for romance, saw Barbara Ann so I got into her pants. Barbara Ann-an-an, Oh Barbara Ann-an-an. Bar, Bar, Bar, Bar, Barbara Ann."

"Excuse me, five cheeseburgers, five large fries and five shakes, three vanilla, one chocolate and one strawberry?"

I turned to face the voice at my car window, and, as we liked to say back then, the world stood still. A new carhop with drop-dead good looks and a smile that went on for days! Her hair, a shining cascade of golden blonde, was banded into a ponytail and hung over her shoulder. It went all the way down to her waist for crap's sake! Beautiful as her hair was, it was her eyes that first made me lose my breath. Deep brown and heavily fringed with lashes so dark they needed no mascara. How does one luck into such beautiful natural coloring? It was uncanny. I knew I had to have her.

"Oh, yeah, yeah! That's us," I shouted stupidly into the poor girl's face. I was so bewitched, I grabbed the tray from her hands and managed to knock her off her roller skates. She went down in a rainfall of milkshakes and fries, the burgers landing neatly in their foil packets like silver bombs, bits of ketchup being their only discharge.

I was fond of telling everyone we met that "she really fell for me"—ha ha—and that was the end of her car-hopping days. I didn't even care that it marked the end of my drag-racing days as well. I loved her so.

Did I mention we never had children? I don' know ... it was perfectly fine with me. I don't recall that we ever discussed it. All I ever needed—ever wanted!—was her. I myself, could listen to the magical lilt of her voice and stare at her marvelous face for hours on end. Brushing her hair, now, that was something so intimate and erotic, I dare not try to describe it.

Suddenly, the happy little party I've been attending in my mind is over. The image of her face changes. The eyes sag, wrinkles stretch across the skin like a spiderweb. The beautiful blond hair turns snowwhite and is shortened and thinned into wisps. Like cotton on a Q-tip.

And I remember.

Cancer. The biggest bully of all the shape-shifters.

At least that bully is identifiable. But this? Of what kind is this shape-shifter that plagues me in my own home? That scurries from view as soon as I turn on the light. That ducks under the staircase when I enter the living room. That most PROBABLY zapped my dish receiver so I can't watch television. It wants me to pay attention to it? Well all right. I WILL!

I march upstairs. It's time to get serious. I retrieve my old shotgun from the bedroom closet and sit down on the bed to give it a once over. My hand lingers on the smooth, polished wood of the stock. I cock it and look down the long double barrels, giving way for my mind to regurgitate a memory from long ago. The scenario: my first kill at the tender age of twelve. Me and Uncle Bill are in the woods hunting for rabbits. I hear a noise and Uncle Bill points. A brown rabbit is under a bush scrabbling for cover, or perhaps hoping to blend in well enough to render itself undetectable. I sight it and pull the trigger. The sound is great and the impact the gun makes to my shoulder is even greater.

We approach the smoking bush and it's short-lived resident. It's hind legs are kicking feebly and it looks straight at me with accusing, liquid-brown eyes. My excitement over bagging my first hunted-animal falls away. Suddenly I feel like crying, but Uncle Bill is with me so I suck it up. I silently vow never to kill anything ever again.

After that first day, it was easier to hunt down and kill rabbits. Squirrels now, they were pretty tough. Wily creatures, them.

Now, what was I going to do? Oh yeah. I load the shotgun and take it downstairs. Time to face my nemesis.

Halfway down the steps I grab the handrail, my legs giving way in fright as a terrible feeling floods my body and I think I know why: there's evil here in this house and it is deeply rooted. Am I, a frail old coot,, capable of dispelling it? My heart is hammering and I'm shaky, but I manage to pull my weapon up to my shoulder. Wait ... there's something on the floor. Some black and shapeless thing is laying perfectly still, trying to fake me out. I take aim.

"All right you shifty bastard," I yell, "say your goodbyes."

I guess its total stillness, its lifelessness gives me cause to lower my shotgun. Descending the staircase slowly and with cautious approach, I poke it with the end of the gun's barrel. Why ... it's a woman's coat and, holy crap, one sleeve is tattered and torn. Where in hell did this thing come from?

"Well, your days are numbered my friend," I shout into the grayness of the room.

I sit down on the couch and wait. And wait. Why doesn't it show itself? Sees my gun does it?

I shout out loud once more, shaking my fist for further emphasis. "Come and get it bastard! Stealer of sanity. Harbinger of death!"

A cackling laugh: "Ha ha ha."

Is that me laughing? I don't know. I can't tell.

A rustling sound at my left. I turn my head to look at the source and then, it doubles around to make a sneaky appearance on my right. It flits past the corner of my right eye and I swivel my shotgun toward it. I pull the trigger and BAM!—the recoil knocks me deep into the spongy back of my ratty, old couch. The sound of my television exploding and the shower of glass frightens me and I feel the warm spread of urine in my pants.

What the—? Why does everything look so gray? What the hell happened here? And for craps sake, why do I have my old shotgun in my hands?

I sit and stare incredulously at the ruins of my television, tiny bits of glass are sprinkled over my worn-out carpet making it look, oddly, improved.

A pounding at my door. "Mr. Frank. Mr. Frank, are you all right?"

Oh hell, I'm not gonna answer, whoever it is will just have to go away.

"Mr. Frank, open the door or I'll have to call the police."

Crap. I get up and go to the door.

I open it just a crack, but the young man pushes it all the way open and comes inside. He's one of those watchers, I just know it. One of those nosy neighbors who stare at me from behind their blinds when I take out the trash. I glare at him defiantly.

"Mr. Frank," the young man says, "don't you remember me? It's Jeff ... from next door."

I give him a closer look. My vision wavers and then ... I see him. Really see him. It's little Jeffrey. He used to come over and Lily would give him cookies and chocolate milk.

"Jeffrey," I blurt out, "my television's broke."

Someone is hollering from outside. "Hey, everything all right in there?"

Jeffrey goes out and I hear them talking, but I can't hear what they're saying. It's another one of those watchers, I'll just bet you. Most likely they're here to get me out. They want my house, or my ... I can't think of anything else I might have of value. Certainly no television. I pick up my shotgun and that young man comes back inside and I point it at him.

"Whoa," he says, "Mr. Frank, come on, give me that thing."

He reaches for it and I see he's not one of those watchers. It's little Jeffrey. Yes, that's right. Milk and cookies.

"Mr. Frank, look, I'm at my wits end. Do you remember asking me to look out for you and keep you from getting put into a home? I promised you I would and I meant it. But now, here you are shooting your TV set and turning the shotgun on me. You tell me, what should I do?"

I stare at his seemingly innocent face. Get put away in a home? I am in a home, my own home. Then it comes to me. I know what he means. Lily had to go to one of those places he's talking about. She was so sick, you see, and, and ... why did I put her in a home? And when? I can't remember. I start crying.

"What did I ever do wrong Jeffrey? How did my life come to this?

"Aw, Mr. Frank. Sit down and tell me what's got you so upset. What's been going on over here?"

I sit and I tell him. I tell him everything. Someone besides me should know how cunning this entity is ... the way it flits past the corner of my eye and disappears before I can get a good look at it.

Jeffrey talks to me for a long time. It feels good to talk to someone. A flesh and blood friend, not one those apathetic sales clerks who impatiently take my orders over the phone. I feel better than I have for a long time. And he's right. There are no such things as shape-shifters. It's just those little squiggly things that float around in your eye. It happens when you get old. I know this.

I let Jeffrey take me upstairs and put me in the shower. I don't even mind that he sees me naked. He's a such good boy. A good neighbor. A good friend ... well, if you don't count that he confiscates my gun (I'll just keep this over my house for you, Mr. Frank).

He helps me into my pajamas and into bed.

"You'll be okay now?"

"Yes, and thank you Jeffrey. You're so kind. I don't know what would have happened if you hadn't come over." I reach out and grab his hand. My wrinkled and bony hand looks almost comical slid inside his healthy smooth one and I feel silly. Your typical version of a desperate old fool.

Jeffrey smiles and gives my hand a squeeze. "No more shape-shifters right?"

"Right. Just a figment of my imagination. A black speck in the corner of my eye."

Jeffrey kisses my forehead before leaving. I lay there staring into the dim room. The only thing saving it from total darkness is the sliver of light forcing it's way through the narrow space under the bottom of my door. Jeffrey must have left the hall light on and I don't fret about that. I feel safe now that he's been here. And free too. Free from fear.

I sigh with relief and turn on my side, away from the door with its puny ray of light. My mind is floating away into la-la land when comes a rustling noise from behind. I freeze. Has Jeffrey come back? I turn my head as far as my creaky, old neck will allow. The filtered light shows me nothing. It's my imagination I tell myself. There's no one there. No Jeffrey and no shape-shifter. Just my mind playing tricks again.

I lay back on the pillow and pull the covers up to my chin. I'm in hell. This is worse than last Halloween when I had to put up a sign to keep trick-or-treaters from knocking on my door. The little fuckers banged away anyhow and then they egged my house.

Quick shuffling sounds. Footsteps?

I clench my hands. Ignore it, ignore it!

A chill goes up my spine and I feel a pressure at my back, like something is trying to get inside of me. The pressure is so hard, it can't be my imagination. It just can't be!

I can't stand it! I throw off the covers and turn over, my arthritic joints wincing with pain. There it is, a black shadow I can barely see in this darkness, pulling away. Then it rushes toward me, a foul stench preceding it … it's laying itself on my body! Pressing me down. Suffocating me.

My trembling hand seeks out the lamp switch, my skinny bicep stretching until its tendons stand out, all stringy and blue. I want … no, I need to see my tormentor.

The light comes on and I find myself face-to-face with a crazed woman. Her dusky, wrinkled skin is stretched drum-tight across her cheekbones, giving her a skeletal look. Her white cottony hair wild and fuzzy. Absurdly I think of an old movie I saw in my youth, Devil Doll, and I almost laugh, but something is stopping me … a voice screaming inside my head. Remember! Remember!

And I remember.

It's Lily. Not young, beautiful Lily, but old, wretched Lily. Mad-as-a-hatter Lily who tried on numerous occasions to snuff out my life. Who tormented and taunted and poisoned and knifed. That was why I put her in a home. She wasn't sick then—not of the body anyway. The cancer came after she had lost her mind. Now, just as she screamingly promised (I'll come back to haunt you for this Frank! You'll pay, believe me, you'll pay.) when I left her there in that awful place smelling of urine and despair, she has come back.

Her crazed eyes stare into mine and I cannot save my earthly body from being violated by her demonic spirit. She enters me and I feel her madness permeate my brain with darkness, trying to snuff out the last bit of light. As I struggle against her willfulness at ending my life, I wonder why. Why would she come back and do this to me? I loved her so.

And I remember.

The locked basement door. The handcuffs, and those terrible, terrible things I did to her.

I feel hot tears of shame and regret on my cheeks as my will to live and my bladder let go at the same time.

Death of the Apostrophe

Pamela K. Kinney

"You need to have more conjunction between sentences before this story is right," said the first sentence.

John slammed his fist down on the desk. "Shut up! This is my story."

"Yeah, like you can write." The word count giggled.

"Wasn't your last novel a flop?" asked a comma.

"I heard his agent say that if he doesn't do a bestseller this time the agency's through with him," whispered an adverb to a pronoun.

The writer tried to calm down, but instead a headache formed behind his eyes. "Look, guys, let's write the story my way this time, and the next one's yours. How about that?"

"Shit," growled the last word. "I'm at the end of this miserable mess and to tell you the truth, there won't be a next novel--it's that bad."

"Yeah, like a penny awful," agreed the title. "Even I'm pathetic. Blood of the Vampire."

"Sounds like something a five-year old thought up," piped up an exclamation point in a bored voice.

For an exclamation point to be bored was the last straw for John. He bolted from his office and grabbed a hammer from the utility room. He carried it back to the office and ignoring the screams, he brought it down hard, smashing a hole in the screen. Sparks and crackling sounds filled the air as the laptop died. For insurance, the power cord was yanked from the machine and wall at the same time and tossed aside.

"That should shut you up," said John with a snarl.

The printer whirred to life and began printing up pages of the novel, shooting it out like cannonballs. He slammed the hammer down on the printer. Down and down, again and again, until nothing but pieces remained.

John thumped down in his chair and dropped the hammer. It hit the carpet with a soft thud. His hands cupping the back of his head, he leaned back and laughed as he surveyed the damage.

"Guess I need to get a new laptop and printer, but God, it's peaceful. No damn words jabbering at me."

He savored the quiet until he heard something.

Oh, no, it can't be…

The headache pounded as something appeared on the screen. It was a page from his novel, some of the words missing from the hole in the middle. John jumped up and picked up the machine with his hands.

"I destroyed you. There's no way you can come back on–not with a hole in you."

"Well, it looks like you don't know everything. Just like you don't know how to write a good story either, dingle berry!" snorted a period. "I am so ashamed to be a part of this manuscript."

John threw the laptop. It slammed into the wall and leaving a large crack in the drywall, slid down to the floor. He grabbed the hammer and went to work pulverizing it. "I'll shut you up. Do you hear me?"

Instead of screams and pleas, voices mocked him. "Yeah, don't put it all on us. Blame that bitch wife of yours. She's the one who bought the software with your credit card, along with that butt-ugly lamp for the living room. The lamp you hate."

Gritting his teeth, John banged harder with the hammer. They were right. He hated that lamp. Maybe he would use the hammer on that next.

The yelling finally stopped. John clutched the hammer with a death grip as he straightened and turned, his breathing harsh. Sweat beaded his face. One drop dripped from his double chin.

"What is going on—"

It was his wife. Lily stood there, her mean little eyes, which he always thought of as the color of shit, darted from the wreckage to him. Her mouth opened and closed like a fish. John saw something stuck between her tobacco-stained teeth, most likely from the dinner she had just came back from with the 'girls'.

Girls, his ass. A bunch of old hags, who gossiped like the nasty hens they were.

"Hello, sweetheart," he said, walking over to her and giving her a peck on her cheek. Makeup she used to cover her doughy complexion plastered his lips. He resisted the urge to wipe it off. "Did you have a great time?"

Lily's shifted her eyes to him. They held a suspicious gleam.

"Forget my night out. I can see that you were busy while I was gone."

John shrugged. "Oh, you mean all this?" He jerked a thumb at the damage. "I had to."

"Had to ... what?"

"Destroy them, or they would have gone on and on."

"Who was going on and on?" Lily backed away.

"The novel. It was trying to tell me how to write the storyline."

"Uh huh. I see. " She inched toward the door.

John frowned. No, she obviously didn't see. Lily looked at him like he gone crazy or something.

"Honest, they were talking to me. I think it has to do with that new writing program you bought."

"John, your novel can't speak. Software doesn't cause the computer to make your story communicate with you, like people do."

He grabbed her arm, his fingers digging into her skin as he waved the hammer with the other.

"I swear to you, they did. The words kept mocking me, just like you do sometimes. You're always telling me I'm such an awful writer that you went and bought me some goddamned software for the computer that supposed to make me better." He drew her closer. "Well, I'm not such a bad author and you're nothing but some old bitch with menopause who thinks she's better than me."

"I don't think I'm better than you, John. I … I love you." Lily's voice grew shrill with hysteria as she struggled to tug her arm out of his grasp.

As if suddenly he had stepped outside of his body, John watched her frantic attempts to free herself with a detached air. He saw the hammer rise up and descend down upon her head, cracking it open like an egg, repeating the action several times.

With the same detached air John saw the hammer with Lily's blood and bits of brain fall to the carpet. He saw himself looking down at her body, which lay on the carpet like a broken doll, her limbs all askew. Blood seeped into the carpet, turning the golden color to a rich, red one. He found that he preferred the red color.

"Boy, you couldn't even kill her right."

John turned and saw that the laptop had come to life again. On it, the words were jeering at him.

"Can't write a novel and he can't kill his wife properly," remarked one apostrophe. "The man's an idiot!"

"Nonononono!" screamed John, as he picked up the bloody hammer and battered at what remained of it. "Stay dead this time."

He kept at it until the couple from next door on hearing the ruckus came over and found him. The wife shrieked as she almost stepped in his murdered wife's blood. Frightened, they ran back home and called the police.

The police found John still hammering away at the laptop pieces strewn across the carpet, yelling, "You're dead, you hear me, dead!" over and over. Their guns trained on him, the police managed to get him to lay down the hammer and allow them to handcuff him. The manuscript cheered as the policemen led him to their cruiser outside.

Deemed insane at his court trial for the murder of his wife John was sentenced to a mental institution.

***

Percy, one of the male nurses at the McCutcheon Mental Institution, flashed his co-worker, Sherry, a strange look.

"What's John doing, Sherry?"

"Well, Dr. Thomas said that after months of therapy he seems to be doing better. That I could go ahead and let him write if that is what he wanted to do. I gave him paper and a pen."

"Do you know what he's writing? He did write some bestsellers once upon a time."

"I'm not sure, but I think he said he's calling it, Death of the Apostrophe. Or something titled like that." Both nurses crossed over to the other side of the room. "What harm can writing on paper do?"

***

"Hey, John, you think you're going to kill us with this new novel?" asked the title with a laugh.

"Yeah, he might," said an apostrophe. "It's such a stinker that it'll kill us to be the words for this trash."

They laughed, but John ignored them as he continued writing. Besides, he knew where the nurses kept the scissors in this place.

The Horror of Wichdun

Romana Tamm

Eons ago, early man learned to fear the dark. He remained close to the safety of his lodgings least dangers lest strange occurrences prevented him from returning. To heart did he heed the warnings from strangers to avoid certain places or tribes of people.

Even today, with modern technology that can take us to far off locales, mankind should be wary of the unknown. Often the unwise or the foolhardy venture into the unfamiliar in search of adventure or undertake explorations to discover and shine light where darkness reigns.

For me, Samuel Sheffield, I drove the highways, the less traveled county roads, and even the "minimally serviced" routes of rural Iowa gathering information and photographs for a book I wanted to publish. With a working title of The Hidden Hawkeye State, I hoped to showcase parts of Iowa about which most people didn't know.

That Friday, the road took me to northern Emmett County. I stopped in at a locally owned gas station/convenience store in the little burg of Dolliver. Faded and chipped paint on the wooden building. Two gas pumps that hadn't entered the digital age displayed flipping numbers behind the plastic window. Inside, the store was dusty with dim lighting from flickering fluorescents. A lanky, brooding clerk stood behind the counter. Old colorless clothing hung from his thin frame. Drooping chin and cheeks. He didn't greet me when I walked in to prepay for a top-off of gas and a few grocery items.

When I approached to lay the snacks and drink on the counter, he didn't move, just stared with dark, hooded eyes.

"I'll take about twenty dollar is gas, too," I said.

He nodded once and with lethargic movements, tapped in the price of my food and beverage into a 1970s-era cash register. I paid for the groceries and he held my twenty until I took the single bag to the car and worked the gas pump. Finished, I returned inside to collect my change since I didn't use the full prepayment.

After the man handed me the coinage, I asked, "I'm doing a jaunt around the state looking for interesting places. My map shows a small community northeast of here. Place called Wichdun."

The man's stare locked onto me, and his frown deepened.

I continued. "Thing is, my map doesn't show any roads leading there. Would you happened to have directions?"

No reply. Just his stare. After several seconds passed, enough time to send a shiver of uneasiness through me, he said, "You don't want to go there, mister."

His voice was low, gravelly, ominous.

"Why not?" I was thinking a disaster had happened. Tornado, sinkhole, water contamination. The town lay between Okamanpeedan Lake and the unoriginally named Iowa Lake.

Dolliver itself wasn't but a bit over three score in population. I couldn't imagine the little store saw much business. Suffice it to say, all was quiet in that dimly lit room with its dirt-layered windows and wooden floor.

Many long seconds ticked by before he replied, "Ain't nothing good come out of Wichdun. Folks 'round here know to avoid it."

"I don't understand," I said. "What's wrong with the place?"

The frown didn't yield. "Bad things, mister." He turned and walked into the little office to his right. His voice faded as he walked into the shadowy interior room. "Bad things."

I did shiver then, even though the fall day had brought temperatures in the seventies.

Back outside, I scanned the two or three blocks that made up Dolliver. Most houses had trees in the lawns. The leaves were only a week or so into changing colors. A hazy thin veil of clouds over the sun with a buildup of cumulus cover in the west. The forecast called for rain that night.

I shivered again, took a last glance at the store, and drove off.

I took the street north and caught a county road headed east. The mapping system on my phone showed I had fewer than three miles to State Highway 15, but as much as I could zoom in, I couldn't see any roads leading to Wichdun. In fact, the system had deemed the town unimportant enough, it put the name in a small font, even smaller than Dolliver.

Roughly halfway to the state highway, the landscape changed. Thick groves of trees, like a preserve or state forest appeared and dominated the land to the north. Corn and soybean fields stretched south but the thickness of the woods was more than a little overwhelming. Tall and so close, the canopy allowed little light to penetrate. Large trunks and knobby branches, leaves dulled by death. No vibrant reds or yellows, they sagged as if after a heavy rain.

Again, approximately at the midway point to this woodland, I spotted an opening, a road. I slowed and corrected myself. Road was giving it too much credit. This was more akin to one of those Class B or C rutted paths I'd seen—and driven—throughout rural Iowa.

It disappeared into the darkness of the woods. I looked at the map app. It didn't show this path and there was no indication anyone gave it a designated name or number. However, the map did display Wichdun almost directly north, snug against the Iowa/Minnesota border.

This had to be the way. Yet, I hesitated for two reasons. The first was I feared for my car's suspension and undercarriage. The sedan wasn't equipped with four-wheel drive or even all-wheel drive.

When I crossed the grassy median between the paved road and the trees, a square of wood caught my attention. It was mounted on top of a fence post and leaned against a tree at such an angle I wouldn't have seen it from the main road.

I exited the car and walked to it. Carved into the square was the name WICHDUN with an arrow pointing to the left. The other side of the sign had the same name with the arrow pointing to the right, opposite sides of the sign, but indicating the same direction. I figured the sign was meant to stand near the road, but might have fallen because of weather and never replaced … or someone had purposely removed it to restrict notification.

Protesting shocks, undercarriage scraping, and tires dropping to ruts, I progressed along the road to Wichdun. Not many vehicles had passed this way. Time and weather had deteriorated the path. I tried, in vain, to find level ground for one set of tires near the tree line or trying to stay on top of the center between the ruts.

The path wound through the trees with no logic. The dot representing my car kept nearing the designation that was Wichdun by micrometers, but why the builders of the road couldn't have take a straight route, I didn't know.

Twenty minutes passed before the trees opened to reveal small clearings, a half acre or less each, squat outbuildings, dilapidated houses, and perhaps, a fenced pen with hogs or chickens.

Farther, the woods widened to a stretch of houses no better looking than the single properties thus far. The scene reminded me of the one-street Old West towns with stores on both sides, except history had forgotten this place only a decade or so after the founding. Weather and time had warped the rough wooden walls and roofs to where I could imagine one good push would topple the entire structure.

I didn't know what lay behind the doors, but beyond one dusty window, I recognized shelves of various goods. Wichdun's version of the convenience or supply store. If so, I felt sorry for any delivery truck driver who had to negotiate the road in.

I eased to one side of the street—only a little better than what wandered through the trees—parked, and exited the car. While stretching out the kinks in my muscles, I surveyed up and down the line of buildings. Maybe fifty yards long, unconnected by a sidewalk or boardwalk. No other vehicles other than a flatbed wagon with the tongue that would connect to a yoke for a horse or mule.

A man sat in a wooden rocking chair outside a building three down. Except for the steady and slow rocking motion, he could have been part of the structure. Wrinkled, bark-brown clothes, long face, eyes in shadow but staring at me. I couldn't discern his age. Anywhere between forty and sixty.

A stray dog loped across the street, glanced once at me, and continued on its way.

Right then, I registered the silence. No wind in the trees, which had devolved the farther I traveled, until here in town, those surrounding the buildings were bare of leaves, and, I suspected, never had growth throughout the spring and summer months. Branches looked like aged appendages. Knobby growths like cancerous lesions spotted the twisted trunks, themselves resembling deformed human torsos.

No bird song. No doors opening. No engine noise. No animal noise. The dog hadn't even deigned to huff or bark or growl.

Only one person, the man in the rocking chair, but as I finished my 360-degree survey of Wichdun's lone street, a door opened farther down and another person stepped out. Again, dressed in listless, drooping clothes, the woman, also defying a specific age, shuffled forward three steps before stopping and staring at me.

Other figures stepped into view along the narrow road. Had everyone heard my car and obeyed a compelling natural curiosity to check out the stranger in their midst?

A touch of the eerie rose within me. Multiple pairs of eyes stared but no one approached, no one spoke out in greeting… or warning. At least the Dolliver store man had communicated with me, if only to warn me away from coming to Wichdun.

Nothing had happened so far, but I wondered if I should have heeded his words.

A low kettledrum of thunder rolled across the thickening and darkening clouds. The first scouts of raindrops spattered against the sedan's windshield and plopped on my head.

I raised a hand in a customary greeting to those watching me, stepped up to the store's entrance, opened it, and crossed the threshold. The interior's designer must have used the same blueprint as the store in Dolliver. Same dim lighting. Same dusty products on dusty wooden shelves. A warped wooden floor. Same musty aged odor in the air, the combination of dead mouse, below average senior center lobby, and a hint of moldy leaves.

I let my eyes adjust to the gloom before walking an aisle half-filled with unidentifiable products in containers, jars, and boxes with brand names too faded or dirty to read.

At the rear of the store, I found the clerk not a brooding older man but a teenager, perhaps fifteen or sixteen. He stood an inch or two shorter than my five-seven.

Thin. His nondescript shirt, colored a faded rusty red, hung on his frame and down over jeans I suspected hadn't been washed in months. Stick-like arms, long fingers. Sunken cheeks and high forehead. Pale yellow but small eyes under stringy, oily, walnut colored hair.

When I approached the counter, he said in a wheezy tenor voice, "Help you, sir?"

"Maybe you lost?"

This came from my right. A man who could have been related to the boy—same thin frame, same hang-dog features—or kinfolk to the man down the street with the baggy clothes, sat in a similar rocking chair.

I introduced myself. "I'm out looking for the hidden recesses around Iowa. Wichdun was on my itinerary for today. I'm interested in its history and—"

I almost said culture, but thought perhaps that was the incorrect word. From what I could tell, just from the four or five minutes in the town, the culture smacked of backwoods, dreariness, brooding, and downtrodden. I was amazed nature hadn't completely reclaimed this desolate dot on the map.

"We've been here a long time, sir," the teenager said with of a hint of a smile. "Longer than you'd think. Long 'fore there was even a state." He turned to the man in the rocking chair. "How long you reckin'?"

The man made no reply except for a slight twitch of his upper left. He continued to look at me… like everyone else I'd seen.

"Yep," the boy said. "Been here a long time."

"Mostly keep to ourselves," the man in the chair said.

"Don't get many visitors," the boy said.

"With the state of the road I came in on, I can see why," I said.

"It suits our purposes," the man said.

"What about school?" I asked. "Do the kids bus down to, uh, well, I guess Estherville would be the closest."

"Nope."

"You have a school here? Maybe up the road a bit?"

"Ain't nothin' up the road but the graveyard. Nothin' you'd be interested in."

"Never know," I said.

More thunder boomed overhead. More rain tock-tocked against the wooden roof.

"I'd still like to know more about the community," I said.

"Ain't the best day for that," the man said.

"Why?"

"It's the time of the Changing," the teenager said.

The man's eye's snapped to the youngster. Annoyance? Silent reprimand?

"The Changing?" I asked. "What's that?"

The kid made a single nasal snort of the laughter. "Goes back centuries. Once a year—"

"Shut up, boy," the man commanded. He stood, walked to me, stopped about a yard away, looked at me with hard, narrowed eyes. "Listen, mister. As the boy said, we've been here a long time and there are matters that don't concern anyone but ourselves. Nothing here for you. We keep to ourselves and that's for the best." He sniffed and wiped his nose with one sleeve of his too-large shirt. "Best you be getting' outta town. Doesn't take much rain to turn that road to mud."

More thunder erupted, and the skies opened. Rain came like machine gun fire.

The man's mouthed twitched in annoyance. "Might be too late already."

"Too late for what?" I asked.

"He can't say here, can he?" the boy asked, a tinge of worry in his voice. "In the store?"

"Naw, it ain't safe."

"Safe?" I took a step backward. "What are you talking about?"

"Never you mind," the man said.

The teenager put his palms on the counter. "But—"

"I said shut up," the man interrupted. He walked to the window and wiped dust off the pane, peered outside, and grimaced. Then he came back to me. "You shouldn't have never come here, but you can't leave. Ain't no way you're driving outta here." He sniffed and wiped again. "You listen real close and do as I say."

"What—"

"Don't ask questions, 'cuz I ain't got answers. At least not answers you'd understand and wouldn't ask more questions about. It's getting too late as it is."

I remained quiet, not wanting to raise the level of his antagonism.

"Down at the first corner where you came in is an old barn sittin' back in the trees.

I nodded, remembering the structure.

"It don't look like much, but it'll do." His upper lip twitched. "Least, I hope so."

"What do you mean?" I asked.

"Just listen. You hightail it down there to spend the night."

"What? Wait a minute."

"We don't have time to talk about this. You get inside and bar the door. No matter what happens, even if nothin' happens, you don't come out till sunup."

"Why?"

"Do you understand?"

"No."

He leaned closer. "Do as I say, and you might live to see sunup."

I was stunned silent by the overt threat.

"Now, git goin'. We're runnin' outta time."

The force of his words and his tense demeanor radiated from him like a wall of energy, pushing me back one step, then another.

I swallowed, looked once at the teenage clerk, then back at the man. Something in his eyes besides the heightened fervor of his words—maybe a pleading?—deepened the anxiety I had when approaching Wichdun and that had increased under the stares of the townsfolk.

My throat tightened, so without another word, I nodded, backed my way to the door, opened it, and stepped out.

The rain fell in torrents. Already, the street was a mud pit. No way were the sedan's tires getting any traction.

Through the hazy veil of rain, I saw the road stretch back into the trees heading toward the main county route. The first gentle curve lay about a hundred yards away. I couldn't see the barn but recalled it lay on the other side of the road, maybe thirty yards into the trees.

In the other direction, up the mud lane, all of the covered front walks to the stores were empty. Everyone had disappeared. I was alone in a backwater town with one of the residents warning me to seek shelter lest… what? The man spoke of danger to my life. From what or whom?

Another explosion of thunder spurred me to action. The atmosphere in the town had changed. Something electric in the air besides the lightning flashes. It drove into me a fear that started in the pit of my stomach and rose like bile, spread across my chest, and into my throat. My heart hammered, and my mind tried to find an ounce of reason to quell the rising panic.

I bolted off the porch, slopped through the mud to the far side of the path, then splashed through the muck and patches of brown grass. Head down, but eyes trying to pick out the tree-sheltered barn.

The barn door lay on the far side, and by the time I reached it, I was soaked from hair follicles to shoelaces. I heaved against the heavy door and squeezed through the narrow opening. I shut the door, found the section of two-by-four, and pounded it into the L-shaped handles with my fists.

Only then did I catch my breath, bent over, hands on knees. Water dripped off me to form puddles on the wooden planks.

Minutes later, I recovered enough to survey my surroundings.

Gloomy shadows darkened the corners. Rusty implements for garden and field work lay against the far wall or on the floor. A woodwork bench to my left. The odor of molding hay on the second level wafted down to tickle my nose.

Under the work bench, I found a rust-scarred lantern. When I shook it, the fuel sloshing inside told me I had enough to last for hours. One of the drawers under the counter held a box of wooden matches.

The lit lantern gave me an opportunity for further exploration. This didn't gain me much more than what I'd already seen. A couple of square hay bales at one end of the barn would suit me for a make-shift bed. An old horse blanket, rodent-chewed and smelling of earth, would stave off the night's chill.

Rain drummed the roof and pelted the walls, but I discovered only one leak in a corner opposite the hay bales.

Fear's tight grip on my stomach eased. Outside darkness moved in with swift resolve. Through a lone window, I watched the surrounding woods fade from granite gray to raven black.

Gradually, my heart rate settled to a normal rhythm, although my anxiety hadn't gone too far below the red zone. What were the two men talking about? A changing? What did that mean? The older man said the community dealt with its own business, and I probably should mind mine. Yet, he had ordered me to go to the barn. Why?

I didn't have any answers but accepted the situation. My car wasn't going to get me out of Wichdun, not with the condition of the road. The rain hadn't lessened, but my clothes would dry. Might as well make the best of the strange circumstance.

I fashioned a somewhat comfortable bed from the bales, stripped, draped my clothes over the workbench, and used the old blanket for warmth.

Time passed, and the Stygian night moved forward. I doused the lantern but kept the matches nearby. No other sound other than the incessant rain and the unsteady inhalations through my nostrils.

My thoughts drifted and wandered. What a solitary existence for these people. There was rural Iowa, then there was Wichdun, a town separated, all but cut off from time and the rest of the world.

This strange woodland between two lakes, with twisted trunks and some form of disease worming through the branches.

The dark countenances of the town and its residents, as if they purposefully hadn't modernized, had locked themselves into the past. Surviving, but not really living … and content to stay that way.

Time past while random thoughts came and went, and I listened to the rain. Eventually, the white-noise effect lulled me into unconsciousness.

***

I jolted awake, the blanket flying when something crashed against the barn door. Had a tree fallen because of the storm?

When the impact sounded again, I rolled off the bales and fumbled for the matches to light the lantern.

A third crash accompanied a gravelly growl. I padded across the floor, approached the door and lurched away, startled when the thing hit the door again. A wild animal? Mountain lions and the occasional bear were known to wander into Iowa, but I'd never heard about deliberate attempts to infiltrate a building.

The rain still fell, but the heavy pounding had receded to a steady monotone.

The length of wood securing the door crashed with the next assault. The growling evolved into a screech as from a crazed cat.

I backed away until I stumbled over the tools against the far wall. My hand landed on a ten-inch garden trowel. The wooden handle was sturdy and the metal showed rust, but the sharpened blade was still functional.

A gap appeared between the barn door and the frame when the creature slammed into the entrance again. I stepped forward and raised the lantern. A scream tore from my throat when the light revealed a visage of a deformed, hair-covered monstrosity. My thoughts immediately recalled the movies about werewolves, but this was worse. Flat, enlarged ears, sickly, pale yellow eyes, a squashed snout. Course, brown hair covered the beast's head and one elongated appendage it crammed into the gap. It's hand displayed four-inch, dirty yellow claws. A gaping mouth spawned pointed teeth and two fangs.

The creature pushed against the door, and the two-by-four creaked and cracked under the pressure. If it hit the door again, surely it would crash through.

Gritting my teeth, I produced my own growl and rushed forward, trowel aimed. The blade sliced above the beast's eyes, gashing the forehead. Blood flowed as the creature let loose a crazed shriek. It reared back for only an instant before assaulting the door again. By a miracle, the wood block held, but it wouldn't survive another impact. If the creature gained entrance, I wouldn't survive long, either.

The monster pushed a blood-streaked head through the opening, arm and claws slashing the air.

I banged away the hairy arm with the lantern and drove the trowel into the fiend's right eye.

The creature howled, jerked back, and apparently deciding I was too much of a threat or else it injuries had incapacitated it enough, it ran off. Howls and screeches faded as it disappeared into the night.

My security and safety severely compromised, I wasted no time. I donned my mostly dry clothes and with lantern in one hand and makeshift weapon in the other, I knocked loose the piece of wood, threw open the door, and fled from the barn in the opposite direction, from where the beast had gone, out of town, following the muddy rut of a road, not stopping until I reached the paved county road.

By then, the rain had ceased. I didn't know the hour, so was surprised at the pale peach of the morning sun painting the eastern sky.

My clothes were still moist but this time copious amounts of fear-tainted sweat mixed with the rain. The morning's chill increased my shivers.

Still, I jogged toward Dolliver. Maybe I could find assistance or when the roads dried, a ride back to Wichdun to collect my car, although I didn't fancy returning to that strange town. Had the beast terrorized other residents? What further havoc had it wreaked before it discovered me in the barn?

I made good time to Dolliver, but I kept glancing behind me to ascertain no one or nothing followed me.

Upon reaching the outskirts of town, I went directly to the little store, relieved to see it open this early.

The same lighting, the same dust, the same lank, dour-faced man behind the register. I put my hands on the counter, paused to catch my breath and to figure out what to say to him.

Before I could speak, he did. "You went to Wichdun."

Not a question. I looked up at him. I wanted to tell him I needed a phone, to call the authorities to bring in dogs and rifles to hunt down the creature. His statement robbed me the ability to speak.

"You saw the Changing," he said.

He knew? How? I wanted to ask but still couldn't activate my voice box.

He didn't break his stare. "You be lucky to have escaped."

I waited. After a long minute, he inhaled a bit deeper than normal, released the breath, and I sensed the resignation in the action.

"The folk who settled in Wichdun came from middle Europe. Mostly rural environs, woodland, and farms far from the cities." He paused. "Folk from those places bring with them a lot of history. Centuries' worth. Some of that history ain't meant for regular folk. Traditions. Curses."

Curses? I had an inkling of where he was going. "The Changing," I whispered.

He nodded. "Part of our heritage. A result of our messing with strange religious practices. Nearly a thousand years ago. Instead of prosperity, bloodlines were cursed. This Changing happens once a year 'bout this time. Always someone different, never know who. Most of the time all that's lost are a few cattle or hogs. Other years…"

His saying I was fortunate to have lived was what he meant in what he didn't say.

"The folk thought they could escape the curse by emigrating to America." Another pause. "They were wrong."

"Is the creature still out there?" I asked.

"Creature? That's a human being, mister, doncha ferget that."

"But I saw—"

"I know what you saw. Ain't no danger now. Only time to worry is between sunset and sunrise."

He knew what I saw, what I experienced. How? The answer came a second later with my recalling his explanation. He said "our." Combine that with his demeanor, posture, and dress. I backed away a step.

"You're from Wichdun," I said, voice just above a whisper. "You're part of … that."

He nodded. "Lived there for a while. Moved away some years back. Found I didn't like city life any more than my ancestors did. But I couldn't live … there. Dolliver's not so bad. We keep to ourselves."

I wondered how many ex-Wichdun residents lived in Dolliver. I stared at him. Somehow, he intuited my thoughts.

"Nope," he said. "I never went through the Changing. Ever' year, though, I wonder."

"My car," I said. "The rain started before I could leave."

He nodded. "I'll take you as far as the road going into town."

And he did. He closed up the store, and led me around to the back to a pickup from the 1940s, more rust than faded green. The motor groaned and protested and ground a caterwaul, but we rattled and juddered to the county road.

He said nothing during the short trip, but when he stopped at the dirt path leading into the woods and eventually Wichdun, he stared out the windshield, not looking at me. "As I said, we like to keep to ourselves. You go telling people about this … well …"

I alighted from the truck, closed the door, but stood by the open window. I thought about making a lighthearted jest, but my words came out somber and serious. "Would anyone believe it if I did?"

He gave me one last look full of long-regretted acceptance. A simple nod, and he made a U-turn to head back to Dolliver.

I quick-stepped along the winding path into Wichdun. The morning sun didn't penetrate very far into the woods, and I kept a fearful eye for… what? The creature? That's a human being, mister. Donchu ferget it. Despite what the man said, fear pinched my heart.

The mud hadn't completely dried, but I figured it was passable enough for my sedan. Almost thirty minutes later, I reached the outskirts of the town. The barn which had provided shelter against the storm and barely held solid against a wild beast stood forlorn and looking like the next storm—or human turned monster—would knock it over.

My car parked in front of the supply store looked as sad as the barn, maybe pouting that I had left it to the elements. With a little forward-backward motion, I thought I could free the tires.

The man in the rocking chair three buildings down had returned. I wonder if that's all he did all day. Further up the road, more towns-folk peered back my way.

Before I drove away, I thought I'd purchase something from inside the store, just as a courtesy for intruding upon their little community and as a thank you for assistance the previous evening.

I opened the door and stepped up onto the wood floor. Like else-where in town, there wasn't much illumination. Dust still covered the shelves and items. The air smelled musty, if a bit wet.

My plan was to greet whoever worked the counter, choose, and pay for my groceries, and make a quiet and hasty retreat from Wichdun.

I stopped cold as I approached the counter. The older man from yesterday looked like he hadn't moved from the rocking chair all night. He may have changed clothes, but if so, the rest of his ward-robe consisted of the same version of dirty jeans and old shirt as the previous outfit. His dark eyes took me in, and I couldn't read his expression.

My shock and bolting to the car without grocery purchase came from who stood behind the counter. The teenage boy. His clothing didn't differ in style or grayish color, either.

However, what make my heart rate increase and my jaw to quiver until I was miles away from accursed Wichdun, was his face.

His forehead displayed a horizontal wound, a gash swollen red, and his right eye was covered by a patch.

Wriggle Inside

Ember Purrian

Have you ever felt that tickle in your mouth? Not the usual irritation from a piece of food, but something… alive? Something that makes you pause mid-swallow, your stomach twisting before you even know why? That's how it started for me.

Day 1: I felt it on the side of my tongue–a faint, almost laughable prickling. I ran my teeth together and … felt it move. An ant. I picked it out with my fingers, huffed through my nose, flicked it away and went about my day. Probably a fluke. That's what I told myself.

Day 2: I found wriggling under my tongue, brushing against my molars. I rinsed my mouth and spat. A couple of ants slid out with the foam. I gagged, my stomach twisting. I tried to convince myself the ants somehow made it in the water pipes. Yeah, that's it. But the metallic, earthy taste clung to my tongue.

Day 3: You know that moment when you swallow and realize something's wrong? Every gulp of saliva felt unnatural. Tiny legs scrabbled at the back of my throat. I spat more ants, gagging repeatedly while clutching the kitchen sink. Panic crept in. A few more ants slipped out with my saliva, wriggling among the foam. I could feel more moving, even as I spat again. The nausea wouldn't stop.

Day 4: The crawling wouldn't stop—it was under my tongue, along my gums, brushing the roof of my mouth and the back of my throat. Swallowing became terrifying. Eating was unbearable. Every bite scraped against something alive. Every swallow a gag. Water stung my throat as I forced it down. I couldn't sleep, lying awake with my tongue pressed to the roof of my mouth, imagining them multiplying inside me.

Day 5: Desperate, I went to the doctor. My hands shook as I opened my mouth, voice quivering. I explained everything. He looked. Poked. Prodded. Checked under my tongue, inside my cheeks. He found nothing. "I … I don't see anything," he said hesitantly. "This might be a psychological problem. I know a good..." I didn't even let him finish. I was indignant. I'm not imagining this! I left clutching my stomach, coughing as the crawling pressed at the back of my throat.

Day 6: My stomach was churning. I felt the wave of an army forcing its way up. I ran to the bathroom and puked. A bunch of ants mixed with bile and spit came out. Each convulsion brought up more ants, and even after emptying my stomach, I could still feel them wriggling inside me, clawing at my stomach, brushing my tongue, pressing against the back of my throat. I couldn't eat, couldn't drink. Every swallow brought painful panic.

Day 8: They didn't stop. I puked floods of hundreds of black bodies. They started emerging through my bowels and urine. And I could swear I felt one in my ear. My nose began tickling too, like I was about to sneeze, but didn't. Was I being paranoid? My body no longer felt like mine. I was hollow, pale, trembling, hollow-eyed—I was a shell of myself. I haven't eaten or drank in days. I spew out more than I took in. I coughed and choked. Every opening became a conduit. Every movement an awareness of their presence.

Day 10: I had enough. I couldn't live like this. I grabbed a bottle of pesticide. Hands shaking, I drank it in desperate gulps, gagging, vomiting violently. Thousands of ants poured out my mouth, crawling through every opening I hadn't imagined. My body convulsed. My mind frayed. I didn't care. Anything to end this.

I lay flat on the ground. The poison burns my throat, my muscles convulse, my eyes roll back, my mouth foams–but the wriggling never stops. Thousands, millions, crawling in every dark corner of my mouth, through every opening of my body. And then it hits me: they didn't die. And they wouldn't let me die. Because I'm theirs now.

Trophy

Michael Chatham

Peyton shook his face from side to side, suddenly becoming aware that he had dozed off for a few seconds, and with each rapid twist of his head, he sought to keep the drowsiness at bay. But he was getting weary. He had been crouched there for several hours, hidden behind a cluster of bushes, waiting. One or two joggers had passed by on their early morning runs, but Peyton was so well hidden from view, they ran by without taking any notice of him. Likewise, he had no interest in them. He knew what he was there for. He had a singularity of purpose.

He was there for her.

She was all he cared about. He had seen her pass by this way just before dawn, and had followed her to this point. It was only a matter of time before she doubled back in his direction. He knew he had her trapped.

The valley she had been foolish enough to enter was a dead end; surrounded on three sides by thick briar patches that were impossible to navigate without being cut to shreds. The area was so notorious amongst hikers and campers, they had nicknamed it the "Iron Maiden," and unsuspecting tourists were constantly winding up in the emergency room.

Peyton knew that she would not be able to climb out, especially with the wet morning dew covering the ground and making it slick. Therefore, her only choice would be to turn around and come back in his direction.

He stole a quick glance at his watch, and felt a tinge of anxiety upon noticing the time. It wasn't that he didn't love the thrill of the chase, but this pursuit had dragged on much longer than expected, and as the morning grew older, he knew he ran the increasing risk of being seen. Not just by her; he was going to kill her, so it really didn't matter what she saw. It wasn't like she was going to go give a description to police. He would make sure that she was dead before she even noticed him.

His real concern was that, with each passing second, the likelihood of some other person seeing him grew larger. A jogger. A bird watcher. A small child wandering away from the nearby campsite perhaps, only to start screaming when he or she encountered Peyton standing over the dead body.

Peyton had to avoid this at all costs. He had to avoid drawing attention to himself. He hated the thought of strangers meddling in his business. This was his "me" time, and he didn't want other people butting in and spoiling it.

And finally, he knew that if he stayed out too long, his wife would eventually call, nagging him. Asking questions. Too, too many questions.

Suddenly, Peyton heard a twig snap, and knew she must be approaching. He glared intensely down the hiker's path towards the area he assumed she would emerge. His whole body became rigid and tense with anticipation, and he raised his gun to have it at the ready. He felt the familiar surge of adrenaline, and the excitement that came with it.

He focused on his breathing, and sought to remain as still as possible, barely moving even as the air passed in and out of his lungs.

Soon enough, there she was, materializing through a line of trees, almost as if the forest itself was giving birth to her. She calmly meandered through the brush on her early morning stroll, at peace with her surroundings and completely unaware that certain death was leering at her from only a few meters away.

The shot was barely audible, as the silencer muffled the blast as the bullet left the chamber. It soared through the air, hitting her square in the chest, passing through muscle and bone, maiming internal organs, exiting out her back, and stopping only upon meeting the resolve of a large tree that stood behind her. She collapsed, and the world seemed to remain still for a few moments, as if in shock over what had just happened.

The silence was only broken by Peyton's approaching footsteps. When he arrived at her body, he quickly looked around to take stock of the situation. There was no one else in sight, nor were there any noises that signaled approaching onlookers. Reassured, Peyton took a moment to gaze over her corpse and admire his handiwork. The wound in her chest was a small, nearly self-contained pool of blood, with a solitary stream trickling down to the ground beside her and staining the leaves a bright, crimson red. Peyton ran his eyes up and down her lifeless body; from her face and neck, down to her legs and thighs, and back again, examining her muscle tone. Her eyes stared up at him, but the life that had once been behind them was now extinguished.

"Alright, don't press your luck," Peyton thought to himself, and set about getting to work.

He wasn't interested in taking home her whole body, as lovely as he thought it was. It was her head that was his primary interest. He had a "thing" for the heads. Furthermore, it would be nearly impossible to carry her entire body back to his pickup truck, which was parked a good ten minute walk away, without giving himself away.

He had to dispose of her body somewhere closer, and the nearby lake provided the perfect option. Peyton could see its banks from where he stood.

Careful to avoid getting blood on himself, he picked up her body, threw it over one shoulder, and began carrying it towards the water. Once he got there, he placed her body down on the rocky shoreline, then reached around, took off his backpack, and began laying out the necessary supplies. Using his combat knife, he began cutting into the base of her neck. As he did so, he did his best to hold her upright, knowing that if she was to remain on her side, more blood would spill out from his incision, and the more he would have to clean up after the fact.

Once her head was completely severed, he picked up a large, reusable plastic bag, and gently placed her head inside, careful not to damage his new "souvenir," nor get blood on the outside of the bag. When the head was safely inside, he sealed it up, then placed it on the ground momentarily so that he could examine his hands. He was pleasantly surprised to see that he had managed to avoid staining them, which meant one less thing to clean.

He picked his knife back up, brought it over to the water, and dipped the blade in, swirling it back and forth to agitate the water and rinse it off. When it was clean, he wiped it on his pant leg, and returned it to its holster inside his boot. Peyton then took two more resealable bags from his backpack and triple-bagged the head, in order to guard against any leaks.

"Better safe than sorry," he thought to himself.

Finally, the task remained of disposing of her now decapitated body. Peyton carefully dragged it to the water's edge and placed her torso in the shallows, yet kept her legs resting on shore. He took five more plastic bags from his pack and began filling them with the heavy stones that lay all around him, picking up anything stained with blood as he went along. Once the bags were filled to the brim, he sealed them, bound them together with a strong, slender piece of rope, then tied the other end of the rope around her ankles, knotting it several times. After he was confident everything was secure, Peyton placed the bags in the water alongside her body, and with one final heave, pushed the entire lot out into the lake.

Her corpse slowly drifted away from the shore, but remained on the surface, and for a few seconds, Peyton could feel a mild panic set in. When she was about thirty feet offshore, however, she finally sank; the heavy rocks pulling her down into the murky depths, and Peyton felt a sense of relief wash over him. The water bubbled up for a moment or two, and then returned to its natural serenity, showing no signs of what it had just concealed.

Peyton looked across the large body of water, and could see the edge of the campgrounds far off in the distance. The camping area came right up to the lake's edge, with a small pier and several canoes dotted here and there, but there were no signs of any human activity at this hour. He then scanned the ground up and down his area of shoreline, but could not detect any visible signs of blood anywhere, which only added to his growing sense of relief. He returned to the severed head laying on the ground and carefully stuffed it into his backpack, along with his gun, after disassembling it into several smaller parts.

Once he had everything stowed away and his backpack over his shoulders, he took on the resemblance of an ordinary hiker, and would barely attract a second glance. He returned to the path that weaved through the woods, and casually sauntered along its uneven surface until he arrived at the parking lot where he had left his truck hours before. He walked around to his covered truck bed, opened the tailgate, reached in, and pulled a large cooler towards him. It was packed half full with ice and nothing else, and after taking a quick survey of the parking lot to make sure he was still alone, Peyton removed the head from his backpack and transferred it to the cooler, burying it down into the cubes.

Just as Peyton was closing the hatch back up, a middle-aged man and little boy appeared out of nowhere, and slightly startled him.

"Good morning," the man said, with all the sincerity in the world.

"Oh, good morning," Peyton repeated back, hoping desperately that he did not come off as awkward.

The man and his son had come from the direction of the camp-grounds, and were carrying several life jackets back to their car.

"Beautiful day, isn't it?" the man continued.

"Oh, yes, definitely," Peyton replied, trying to seem agreeable, while secretly wishing the conversation would end as soon as possible.

"Gotta appreciate them while they last," the man went on, while his son stood there smiling, feeling awkward in his own way. "I heard that there's gonna be a major storm front moving in next week. They said we're gonna get several days of heavy rain in a row. Absolute downpours."

"Well, that's life, I suppose," Peyton suggested, beginning to feel slightly irritated.

"Yep. I guess so," the man said, searching for something else to add to the conversation, but coming up empty-handed. "Well, have a nice day."

And with that, the man and his son went on their way.

"Thanks. You too," Peyton said as they left, relieved to have his solitude back.

For a few moments, however, Peyton stood there second-guessing the situation; questioning whether or not the man and his son had seen anything. The boy had seemed mildly uncomfortable, but that could easily be attributed to the self-consciousness of adolescence, combined with his embarrassment and annoyance regarding his father's overly sociable nature.

"It's all right. Everything's fine. Stop worrying so much," Peyton reassured himself.

He took one last look down the length of the parking lot, but the campers had disappeared from view, and he finally decided to put the matter to rest. He climbed into the driver's seat of his truck and started it up. Pulling his cell phone out of his pocket and turning it on for the first time in hours, he saw that he had three new voice-mails from his wife, all from within the past forty five minutes. He dialed her number, and she picked up after only two rings.

"Hey, honey."

"Hey, where the hell have you been?" Trisha said, concerned, but not angry. "I've been worried sick about you!"

"I know, babe. I'm sorry. You know how I am. Time gets away from me."

"What in the world have you been doing this whole time?" Trisha pressed him, but in a loving, playful sort of way. "I've been on that trail before. It can't take you that long to hike it."

"Well, you know how it is... I get looking at all the pretty flowers, and birds, and before you know it–"

"Oh, please!" she interrupted him. "You're so full of crap! The only birds you're interested in are the ones in your sandwich! Just... get home as soon as you can.

Alright? I really don't want to eat breakfast all by myself. Okay?"

"Alright, sweetheart," Peyton reassured her. "I'm on my way."

Peyton hung up, started the engine, and pulled out of the parking lot. He followed the narrow, winding, tree-lined road through the woods, passing the campsite and visitor's center. Every so often, he had to slow down and pull to one side in order to let cars pass in the opposite direction. At one point, he came face to face with a large RV and had to pull several feet off into the dirt in order to let it go by. As it did, he braced himself, fearing it would scrape up against the side of his truck, but the two vehicles managed to avoid one another with only inches to spare.

"Jackass," Peyton said to himself, as he pulled back onto the pavement.

Finally, he reached the main, two-lane road, and took a left towards home. After several minutes, however, Peyton came across an alarming sight. The county sheriffs had set up a roadblock in the distance, and were stopping motorists coming from both directions. Frustrated, but with nowhere to pull off, there was nothing he could do except slow down and get in line behind the two or three cars ahead of him.

He rolled down his window, and when he got to the front of the line, a sheriff's deputy approached the side of the truck, while a second stood in front of it, blocking the way. Peyton could feel his heart racing, as if he had suddenly been injected with an overdose of amphetamines.

"Morning, sir," the deputy said. "How are you today?"

"Uh, fine, officer. Just fine," Peyton said, hiding his annoyance with the unnecessary small talk.

"Why the fuck is everyone so goddamn chatty today?" he thought to himself.

"I apologize for the inconvenience, sir, but we're looking for a missing person," the deputy explained, handing Peyton a flyer with the picture of a young woman on it. "This young lady went missing in this area around a month ago."

"Oh, really?"

"Yes, so we're asking everyone passing through the area if they might have seen anything," the deputy continued. "Anything suspicious? Anything out of the ordinary?"

"Oh ... Well, I can't say I've seen anything odd or unusual," Peyton offered. "Other than the fact that it's been unseasonably warm for this time of year."

"That's true, sir. Very true," the officer smiled.

As he said this, however, his hand felt along his belt until it reached his flashlight, and turning it on, he proceeded to walk towards the covered truck bed, peering in through its multiple windows. Peyton could feel his heart rate quicken as the officer went about the unsolicited inspection, but tried to reassure himself that there was no reason for concern. There was nothing exposed to the naked eye in the truck bed that should cause any shred of suspicion, and although the bright red and white cooler sat front and center, plenty of people owned identical coolers. They were ubiquitous, and for all the deputy new, this one was filled with beer cans.

Everything would be all right ... unless, of course, the officer asked to look inside. The mere thought of it made Peyton's stomach twist into a knot. He couldn't understand what he had done to invite this extra scrutiny, and as much as he resented the intrusiveness, he knew he was being watched, and had to appear indifferent to everything happening around him.

As he glanced at the deputy standing in front of his truck, the thought of running him over momentarily crossed Peyton's mine, but he pushed it aside. Suddenly, the other deputy reappeared by the driver's side window, turning his flashlight off and placing it back on his belt.

"Been camping?" the officer nodded to the backpack sitting on the passenger seat.

"Uh, no, I ... I'm not really much of the "outdoorsy" type," Peyton said, offering a forced smile.

"Well, to each his own, I guess. You're good to go, sir. Just keep that flyer with our phone number on it, and if anything comes up, please feel free to give us a call."

And with that, the two officers stepped away from the truck.

"Have a nice day, gentlemen," Peyton said, relieved to be rid of them, and putting his truck back into gear, pulled away.

Once he was safely out of sight, he picked up the police flyer, took one last look at it, then crumpled it up and threw it out the window. From then on, there were no further interruptions, until Peyton finally arrived home and pulled into his driveway. He stepped out of his truck, unlocked his front door, leaned inside, and called to his wife.

"Hey, babe! I'm home! Where are you?!"

"Hey, sweetheart! Is that you?!" Trisha called out, muffled by walls and distance. "I'm upstairs! I'm in the shower!"

"Okay! Just checking!"

Peyton knew that this was his moment of opportunity, and had to seize it while it lasted. He hurried back to his truck, retrieved the cooler, and carried it inside. He quickly but carefully sped down the basement steps, struggling to hold the large cooler with one hand while holding onto the railing with the other. Once he arrived in their furnished basement, he made his way over to the door which led to the half of the cellar that he had commandeered as his "man cave."

He could feel his pulse racing with excitement as he unlocked it and slipped inside, fastening the door behind him. There, in his inner sanctum, Peyton had his trophy room and workshop. He placed the cooler on the nearest workbench, opened it, and carefully removed the severed head. Leaving it inside the plastic bags, he examined it, delicately turning it over in his hands and looking for any signs of unexpected damage. Blood had leaked out from the base of her neck and stained her brunette hair, but Peyton knew he could easily wash that off.

He carried her over to the freezer and gently placed her inside. He paused before closing the door, however, to take one last look; admiring her head the same way a child admires a new toy. Her lifeless eyes stared back at him, and he blew her a kiss as he bid her farewell. Later on, when he had the time, he would set about preparing her for display. He already had a wooden base picked out for her, along with a spot on the wall amongst all his other "lovelies." The rest was simple and straightforward.

First, he would drain out as much blood from the interior of her head as possible.

Then he would wash her hair and face, cleaning off any stains or debris, and making her look presentable. Finally, he would place her inside his special freeze-drying machine, where over the course of several months her bodily tissues would be frozen and dehydrated, perfectly preserving her head so that Peyton could mount it on the wall. He preferred this method over traditional taxidermy, as it had always seemed like such a waste to him to go through all this work, only to peel the skin off their heads and place it on a hollow wire frame with fake eyes. He thought of it as an insult to all his skill and determination. It was a cheap shortcut. He wanted it all: the skin, the eyes, the teeth, the bones, the muscle fibers, the nerve endings, the brain matter. Everything. There was more artistry in the freeze-drying method, he thought.

He sauntered over to the den area of his lair, where he kept the various material measures of his manhood: his recliner, his sofa, his magazine rack, his flat screen TV, his stereo, his mini-bar, and so on. And on the walls all around him, hung his collection of 'beauties', arranged in various patterns like macabre holiday decorations. He gazed over them with a sense of satisfaction and accomplishment, and they stared out into space with a sense of nothingness.

Yes ... he considered himself an artist.

"Peyton!" Trisha's voice called from the other side of the door, breaking the silence and startling Peyton out of his self-indulgence. "Are you in there?"

"Yeah, sweetheart. What do you need?"

"Can I come in?" Trisha asked in earnest, jiggling the knob of the locked door.

"Babe, you know the rules," Peyton said, walking over so he could talk through the wood and be heard. "No women allowed in the man cave. This is my private space."

"Oh, come on! Grow up!" she said, frustrated, but still good-humored. "You know you sound like a little kid when you say things like that? What is this, The Little Rascals? Is this the "He-Man Woman Haters Club?"

"Yeah, something like that," he replied from the other side of the locked door.

Peyton didn't want to get into an argument with his wife, but always hated whenever she pressed this issue. He struggled to think of something to say that would get her to change the subject or go away.

"This is just ... my private space. That's all," he offered.

"Huhhhh ... fine," Trisha sighed, knowing she wasn't going to get anywhere. "Just come up whenever you're ready, okay? I've got breakfast ready."

"Okay, sweetie," Peyton said, relieved. "I'll be up in a second."

He listened through the door as his wife ascended the stairs, and only once he knew she was gone did he open it, immediately locking it behind him. When he got to the top of the stairs, he remembered that he had left his backpack sitting on the passenger seat of his truck. He didn't like keeping his wife waiting any longer, but was too uncomfortable with the idea of just leaving it lying around, fearing Trisha might come upon it and be curious. He walked back outside and retrieved the pack, then brought it downstairs and locked it safely away. When he got back upstairs, he sneaked up behind Trisha as she stared into the refrigerator and slapped her on the behind.

"Ah! Cut that out!" she laughed, spinning around and wrapping her arms around the back of his neck. "Don't you start with me!"

"I'll do what I want, thank you very kindly," he said coyly, then kissed her for several seconds.

When she finally pulled away, she reached down and slapped his behind in playful retaliation.

"Go sit down, and I'll bring it to you. Coffee's on the table," she instructed him.

"Fine."

Peyton wandered over to the breakfast table and took a seat.

"You know, I can't imagine what the girls at work would say if I told them that there were rooms in my house that I wasn't allowed into," Trisha said, placing a plate of food down in front of her husband before sitting down with her own.

"Well, don't tell them then, if it embarrasses you so much. It will be our little secret."

"God, you're such a smart-ass, you know that?" Trisha said, shaking her head, but still smiling.

"Yeah, well, that's why you married me. Because I'm smart and I've got a nice ass."

Trisha reached for the remote control and turned the television on to the local morning news. Within less than a minute, a story came on that caught Peyton's attention out of the corner of his eye, and he turned his head to see a photograph displayed across the screen: it was the girl from the police flyer, staring back at him.

"Isn't it horrible?" Trisha remarked. "They still can't find that poor girl. She's been missing for over a month now."

"Yep, sure is," Peyton said, looking away from the TV as he started to shovel down his breakfast.

"She went out for a walk in the woods," Trisha continued, "just like you like to do, and nobody's seen her since."

"Yeah, well ... You know that stone quarry? You know, down below Chestnut Ridge?" Peyton asked.

"Oh God, yes, of course. I always hated that place. They need to put a guardrail there or something. If you weren't paying attention, you'd walk right off the edge."

"Yeah, well, that's exactly it," Peyton said, pausing to slurp down some of his coffee.

"If you weren't familiar with that area, you'd go right over that ridge before you knew what's what. Shit! She might of come across it and thought "Huh, I wonder what's down there?" and tried to climb down. The sides aren't very steep in some places, and she might have thought it was a miniature Grand Canyon. You know how people take donkeys down into the Grand Canyon?"

"Yeah, of course."

"Exactly. She tried to do that herself, and before you know it, it's all over but the shouting."

"Yeah, but if that happened, you'd think they would have found her body by now," Trisha suggested.

"Well, there could have been a rockslide, and now her body's buried under a pile of rocks."

Peyton was trying to seem interested, even concerned, but he desperately wanted to change the subject and move on to a topic that didn't revolve around missing persons.

He reached over, grabbed the remote, and changed the channel.

"Let's talk about something more pleasant, okay?" he suggested.

"I'm sorry," Trisha apologized. "It's my fault for bringing it up."

"Who knows? Maybe she ran off with an old boyfriend."

"Hey, speaking of scary stuff, you want to hear something funny?" Trisha asked.

Peyton shrugged, unsure of where his wife was going with this.

"You know, when you first came home, I was in the shower, right?" she continued. "And even though I was upstairs, and the water was running, I could hear you when you opened the front door. And I called down to you, and you yelled something up to me, remember? And I thought I recognized your voice, but when I went back to rinsing off, I thought to myself "Wait, what if that wasn't him!" I know it's silly, and I knew it was you... At least, I assumed it was you! But the thought did momentarily cross my mind, just for a second, like "Oh my God. Here I am, naked as a jaybird, and some strangers just come into my house!" It made me anxious for a second! Like, there I am, completely naked and defenseless, and for all I know, some maniacs just walked through the front door!"

Trisha giggled, and sat there, waiting for her husband's response.

After a moment or two, Peyton swallowed the mouthful of food he had been chewing and flashed her a mischievous smile.

"My dear ... I shudder at the very thought of it."

The Noise

Geraldine Birch

It was a perfect nursery–the kind every mother wants for her baby. The room was painted pastel egg yolk; fifty years ago, mothers had no idea whether a boy or a girl would push out of their wombs. We played it neutral with pastels.

The crib was a spring-like green to soothe my baby asleep, and over the crib hung a wood-carved mobile in soft greens and yellows with just a tad of orange to catch the baby's eye.

In the corner by the window sat my grandmother's wooden rocking chair. I had painted it white and re-upholstered the cushions with a pattern of playful giraffes. The table where I changed my baby's diapers sat against the adjoining wall, a table built by my father for his long-awaited grandchild.

The room had two windows that slid open from the side. They were covered in curtains that gave the nursery a cheery circus atmosphere–bright stripes of orange, lime, and saffron. When the curtains were open, I could see the walkway to the front porch, a walkway filled with azaleas blooming in the spring's soft air.

The child was all I ever wanted. He was beautiful and fat from my milk. He was a happy boy, except at night when he would wake with a cry that was different. It was a sharp sound, not from hunger, but from something deep within him.

In those beginning days of motherhood, I would rush to the crib, pick him up, and try to soothe him. He seemed startled and not even the warm breast would calm him. I would rock him, not understanding his cry, and that is when I first heard it.

I thought it was the creaking of the old wooden chair. But when I stopped rocking, the sound continued. I can only describe it as that of a cricket or some other creature hiding in the wall under the window. No amount of obsessive searching in darkness or daylight brought resolution to the sound which occurred only at night, only heard by me and my son. My husband tried to understand my weeping and so he sprayed for insects and dug resolutely into the azaleas next to the bedroom wall where that damnable noise came from. But nothing stopped it. And so, my husband slept, feeling there was nothing more to be done, and I did the rocking.

In that room, the night and I came to know one another. It hid what I wanted to find. It was a shroud on the terror that lurked in my baby's room. Eventually, the noise changed from the clicking of an unnamed insect to a low drone that became louder the longer I listened, until it filled my soul each night with an unnamed horror.

During my interminable rocking, I remembered a strange incident several months previous. I was then nine months pregnant and waiting impatiently for my baby. We had just moved into the house a few weeks before and one Sunday afternoon the doorbell rang. When I answered, I saw an inordinately tall man with a gothic face. He wore an outfit of overalls not normally seen in suburban Southern California. He was a locksmith and certain I would want more secure locks on the sliding windows.

My husband was working in the back yard and I replied that with a new baby coming, we couldn't afford such an expense. He nodded, seemingly understanding, and then the locksmith began to talk crazy—random stuff that flowed from his mouth like poisoned spittle. He could see spirits dancing on his palm warning him that the end of the world was near. Those who survived would follow him, not Christ. I laughed, not knowing what else to do, trying to be polite when I simply wanted this madman to go away.

Then, strangely, he asked where the baby's room would be and I stupidly motioned to the window in the walkway with its circus-colored curtains. He leaned over and touched the nursery windowsill, and then suddenly sprang back toward me where he reached out with his gangly arm and touched my protruding stomach. I gasped, horrified. Just then, my husband appeared at the door. Angered by what he had witnessed, he demanded to know why the man had touched me. A strange look came over the salesman's ugly face. He turned and fled.

Months later, the flowers on the azaleas having long since faded and crumbled to dust, my nine-month-old son and I stayed tied together for hours one particular night. He seemed inordinately upset and so I rocked and sang and talked to cover the sound and our mutual fears. And that is when the stroke of a deathly-cold hand swept across my back.

I don't remember much after that shock except that I ran with the baby into the master bedroom, and violently shook my husband awake. I demanded that he do something, anything. It was the first time in our decade-long marriage that I challenged his unconcern. Now it was not just the noise, but an apparition that had actually touched me.

Standing by the bed, shaking and crying all at once, I screamed, "You keep telling me this is all my imagination; you make me feel like I've lost my mind. But I haven't goddammit! What I felt was real!"

I suddenly stopped crying and said in a voice as cold as the hand that had violated me, "I'm not the stupid twenty-year old you married. Do something! Otherwise, the baby and I are moving to my mother's."

When the priest arrived and I told my tale, he nodded with an understanding that made my fear fall away like a heavy cloak. I brought him to the nursery where his knowing gaze slowly took in the entire room. He then pulled out his prayer book and began praying. My husband stood in the doorway watching silently.

I sat in the rocker, the place of such terror in the dark, but now there was a softness in the room as the sun came up and shone its brightness through the window that had been touched by a man possessed.

When the exorcism of the room was completed, the priest did an odd thing. He asked for a pair of white socks. When I gave them to him, he performed a ritual while praying, tying the socks together. He then laid them like a cross inside the top drawer of the baby's dresser.

I understood none of what the priest did, but that night and afterward, my son slept blissfully. And once again, it was my perfect nursery.

The Key

Larry Brown

Zelda moved her inherited Victorian tea pot to the center of the table aligning it between the two inherited Victorian teacups. First impressions were important to Tammy, her friend for twenty years. If the setting weren't perfect, she would judge Zelda as a poor host.

She hummed as she dithered around the setting. Straightening the lace tablecloth for the tenth time she rocked the table. "Damn it," she said. Bending over to determine which leg was short, her headache roared back. Like yesterday, when she first arrived, her head built up pressure like an airplane altitude change. She sat on the couch in front of the fireplace, held her nose and gently blew to equalize the pressure. She pictured Tammy making a big deal about old houses and illness.

Zelda needed Tammy to think well of her and be open to helping her adjust to this new life. Last month, Zelda waitressed at Johnny's Brew House, and now she sat surrounded by old things, like this tea set, in an old house, in an old part of town. Her mother was to blame for this.

When Great Aunt Zee died, she left everything to Zelda's mother. She in turn tagged Zelda to deal with it all.

When she gave Zelda the keys, Mom repeated what she had said at the will's reading. "Maybe Aunt Zee shouldn't have been a witch. She was certainly an evil woman, and I don't want anything to with her creepy old house."

So today, Tammy would be here and tell her how to deal with this monstrosity of a home, with its twenty rooms, each smellier than the other.

Zelda perked up when she heard footsteps on the cobblestone drive. Tammy, she thought. She stood, smoothed her Victorian dress she found in a closet and prepared to welcome her old friend.

A cold breeze came down the chimney and Zelda shivered in the sudden cooling. Pulling her shawl close, she quickly walked to the front door. Pausing a moment to check the area for tidiness and patting her hair in place, Zelda opened the door.

"Hi ya kid," Tammy said. She stood on the steps, her arms wide open with a huge smile. Zelda smiled back and spread her arms too, ready to hug back.

A cold wind shot past Zelda, pushing Tammy back from the entrance. She lost her smile. "Hey, that's not a good welcoming Zel. This old house don't like me?"

Zelda dropped her arms and stepped out onto the porch. "Oh, no, Tammy. It's just the chimney, I think. Chilly air comes down it I've found. That happened to me yesterday when I first got here. I unlocked the door and almost couldn't push it open against the air pressure." Putting her arm around Tammy's shoulder, Zelda pulled her into the house.

"I'm so glad you're here, Tammy. You'll be delighted with what I've got to show you today."

Tammy danced her way through the doorway, twirling a parasol. "See my costume, Zelda? I rented a Victorian dress just like you said you found in a closet."gh

"Almost twins we be," Zelda replied with a smile, also twirling with her floor-length dress. "Oh, wait until you see the tea set. It's gorgeous. And old."

"Wait, wait. Let me look at this staircase." Tammy rushed to the wide stairs with its deep red carpet held in place with shiny copper rods. Looking up to the landing at the top, she squealed. "How many floors do you have, Zelda?"

"Just two, I think. And there's an attic, so I guess that's three levels. I haven't been all over it yet. Just spent my first night here last night. I explored some of the houses yesterday and counted twenty rooms. Can you believe that? Over twenty rooms, then there are outbuildings too. No idea what's in those."

"Oh, you lucky girl. So much wealth." Tammy sounded jealous of Zelda.

"Wealth? More like poor. I don't know if there is money to pay for upkeep, let alone the taxes. These old places are money pits sometimes. I may have to sell, you know."

"Take my picture Zel. Here, use my camera. Make me look sexy." Tammy lay on the steps, spreading her arms. Zelda clicked away, taking shots from several angles. When she completed the task, Tammy stood, walked back to Zelda, and took her arm. "Too soon to talk about practical things. Let's see that tea set."

They sipped tea and giggled for an hour, catching up with each other's lives. On occasion, Tammy remarked about freezing air flowing up her dress. "Zelda, don't you feel the breeze around your table?"

"Not at all. I think it's perfect here. But some of the rooms are chilly. Especially the ones near the attic room."

Tammy laid down her cup and wiped her lips with the lacy napkin. "What's in all these rooms? I mean, is there furniture, like beds? Are they bedrooms?"

"Well, there's fifteen bedrooms with a sitting room. Five seem to be just for storage. There must have been a huge family here when it was built."

"When was that?"

"Not sure. Eighteen eighties or nineties. It's almost like a hotel. And they're all smelly. Cold too."

"Could have been a railroad baron, you know. A hotel for the workers and all that. It's certainly crew size. And to be honest, it's not beautiful." Tammy hefted a donut and filled her mouth with sweet dough.

"The house looks spooky from the street. We used to trick or treat here when I was a kid. Spooky then. Your Aunt Zee would come to the door in a witch's costume, and we'd hold out our bags as far as we could. No one wanted to get in the house."

"Oh, that was no costume, Tammy. She was a witch. In her mind anyway. Mom said being a witch ran in the family."

Tammy sat her teacup down slowly. "Oh, I see. Does that mean you're a witch?"

Zelda choked on her drink, tea sputtering out of her mouth. She sat her cup down and reached for her napkin. After wiping her lips, she looked up at her friend.

"I'm not a witch, Tammy. It isn't like that. At least I don't think so."

"Is your mom thinking you being here will make you a witch?"

"I don't know. Maybe."

"Well, being in this house could make someone a witch." Tammy waved her hands around in the air. "I mean, look at this place. It's locked in the eighteen eighties when people didn't have education, no science to explain things."

Somewhere in the house a cuckoo clock sprung to life, announcing the passing of another hour. Tammy stifled a scream. "Did you hear that?"

A voice," Tammy whispered. "Somebody said leave now, leave now."

Zelda giggled. "No, they didn't. It's a clock. One of those that has a bird pop out to scare you. And it didn't say leave now. That's your imagination."

"That's not what I heard. It's the witches in this house."

"I know, I know. It's spooky. I get that. But I don't believe in witchcraft. Hell, I've got a degree in chemistry. I can't feel that this house will make anyone a witch."

Tammy stood and pushed her chair back under the table.

"Sorry to say this, Zelda, but I've had enough. I mean, in just a little while, I think my hair has turned white. I can't breathe. I choked on tea, for God's sake." She stood and threw her napkin down. Holding out her arms, she reached for Zelda. "Give me a hug, sweet. I've got to get out of here."

At the door, Tammy turned back to Zelda and weakly smiled. "I wish you the best. And don't stay here much longer. It won't be good for you." She reached into her purse and pulled a chain out.

"Forgot. This is an amulet, a charm if you will. My grandmother gives it to me every Halloween. She said it would keep me safe. I'm here, so guess it did. You may need it, girl. Good luck."

After Tammy was out of sight, Zelda stepped back into the house. A strong cold wind came past her and slammed the door shut.

After dark, Zelda walked through the hallways of the Mansion. She entered each room and turned on its lights. They were all very alike. Furniture covered with drop clothes, heavy drapes over each window and a moldy smell wafting throughout.

"This whole place needs an airing," she whispered to herself. An irritating clock deep in the house, gonged the midnight hour. Zelda shivered.

After an hour of poking about, Zelda stood in front of the last door. The attic room. Old tales, old movies roamed about in her head. Nothing good came from attics. A tall cabinet stood next to the attic entrance to hold linen. She pulled open its drawers to find them empty.

She reached for the doorknob then jerked it back when she felt resistance against her hand. Much like pushing through Jello, she thought. "Oh, stupid, it's just an irrational fear. Nothing is touching me. Dam you, Tammy, putting these thoughts in my head." She reached again, ignoring the sensation.

The door was locked. She stepped back, unsure what to do next. An axe was her first fleeting thought but that would destroy the door. No, she needed a key. There had to be a key someplace. Inspired to search, she felt above the door frame and sneezed when the disturbed dust floated onto her face. Swatting away the irritation, she turned to the tall cabinet standing like a guardian sentinel and moved her fingers along the top. "Found you."

The ancient iron was cold and heavy, but she managed to unlock the door, leaving its key in place. Pausing before the next step, she sucked in a deep breath and pushed the door open. "Oh," she said when surprised with a small circular room and steel steps rising into the darkness above. "Not a room at all." She expected old furniture with drop cloths covering them, or old boxes full of stuff. This was new to her. Finding the light switch next to the door, she turned it on. The stairs were illuminated from the upper level.

She felt her heart race and uneasiness growing in her chest. 'Wish you had stayed, Tammy'. There was no real choice she told herself. Hiking her skirt, she gingerly took one step at a time, rising into a greater unknown.

At the top, another door blocked her. Expecting a locked room, she turned the door handle and pushed the door open. Lights came on automatically.

She almost smiled. "Wow, at last, a clean room." Her words, spoken aloud, were muffled by the thick drapes hanging from the walls and the splendid leather-upholstered furniture. A tall mirror stood to her left, surrounded by an ornate frame announcing its age. The room was round, but she expected that because from outside, the structure seemed like a grain bin sitting in the wrong place. She mused to herself that a tornado had blown it here and they had just built around it.

To her right, shelves covered the wall, with gleaming jars filled with liquids and cans brightly painted with foreign symbols and words. The witches' lair, thought Zelda, her mind going back to Tammy and her fears of becoming a witch. Zelda held the amulet Tammy gave her before she left. She felt silly, there was nothing to fear in this room.

The relaxation she felt was fleeting.

The door slammed shut. Lights flickered. Zelda screamed.

'Oh God, what's happening' thoughts raced through her mind. She rushed to the door. The handle wouldn't turn. The key was outside. Did Tammy return and lock her in here as a joke? A sick joke. Zelda let her mind concentrate on Tammy's prank as the culprit. The alternative was too frightening.

Her knees became weak. She sat on a high-back chair, her elbows on her knees and her head lowered to lessen the nausea she felt. Breathing became hard, her throat constricting in the fear she felt growing inside her. She thought of her mother and their last meeting. Zelda understood better what her mother was talking about.

Across the room the old mirror lit up. An image of Zelda's mom broadcast the hateful things she had to say about Aunt Zee. "She's a witch, Zelda. A witch." Her screaming voice filled the room. Zelda whimpered under her breath. "What the hell?" The startling reflection of her exact thoughts in the mirror brought her to her feet. Approaching the mirror, the image changed to herself but with a cloak on, its high collar protruding from her shoulders like bat wings. Flame crackled behind the image, its orange to red fingers lighting the room in multi-colors. Zelda spun around. There was no flame behind her. She felt her body. No cloak.

'God, oh God help me'. She pulled the amulet from her neck and held it high in the air. Something must be watching her. This was the only protection she had.

The door slammed open as if kicked. The mirror's horrible image disappeared. Zelda ran.

She became aware she was outside now, leaning on her car, looking up at the towering house. The attic window opened, and bats flew into the night. Zelda covered her face with her hands. 'No, no, it's all a dream. A dream. A horrible nightmare.

Tammy's voice came to her. "Don't become a witch Zelda. No, don't become a witch. No witching. Her mother was right after all. This was not a good place.

She felt cold again, as in the house this morning. Her skirt was torn but she didn't remember how, revealing the pants she had worn underneath. The blouse untucked, now hung in shreds. She tore off the remnants of another time and world and wadded them up. Throwing them on the ground, she forged in her pockets for her car keys. Mom was right. So right.

She sat in the car seat for a while, catching up with her thoughts about tonight's experience. She wasn't sure she could go back in. How long has this house been so evil? Tammy knew about it. Her mom knew. Why hadn't she listened?

Anger soon replaced fear. Rummaging around in the glove box, she found a lighter her mother had left. Maybe this is the best solution, she thought as she flicked the flame on and off. Permanently.

Getting out, she picked up the ragged clothing and walked to the entrance. The door stood open as she had left it. Little kids could come to that door next Halloween and be sucked into an unknown fate. She was protecting them, she told herself.

She tied the pieces in a series of knots to make it easier to throw. Holding it at arm's length she flicked on the lighter. The dry cloth flamed easily making it a handy tool of vengeance. Standing at the entrance, she tossed her projectile towards the stairs. Its dry carpet would carry flames into the depths of the house.

Rushing back to her car, she started it up, ready to leave after the fire established itself. Later she'd call the fire department or let someone else do it. Either way, her mom may see some insurance money.

She ducked down when a rush of white smoke blew out of the front door, towards her. Windows shattered on all levels like an explosion had happened and white smoke gushed out. No flames. The building stood silent in the darkness. Her car started rocking back and forth like it was in an earthquake. Zelda held back a scream of fear and jammed the car into gear. Before she could speed out, the attic walls above the house separated and fell into the backyard.

Her jaw dropped. Breathing stopped. She stuffed her fingers into her mouth and rocked back and forth, her body shaking out of control. The lack of oxygen forced her body to breathe again and she gasped for air.

From inside the house, a rumbling noise increased in volume. The outer walls danced in the moonlight, and she now feared some of it falling on her. Immobilized in fear, she sat, forced to watch as a shiny metal tower ascended above the destroyed house. More white smoke surrounded her as the object broke free of its moorings and leapt into the sky.

Zelda felt her body snap inside. A change. A longing she never knew before. Words uttered, that yesterday were never possible.

"Wait for me."

The End

Bailey Primus

Driving aimlessly along winding country roads, she came upon an old cemetery high up on a hilltop, nestled among thick timber. The rusty, iron gate that surrounded it glistened with freshly fallen raindrops in the late afternoon sun, beckoning her with its majesty. She pulled into the short driveway and got out of her car. As she stepped over the entrance threshold, a shiver ran up her spine. It was usually dry in the autumn months, but now the air felt humid and heavy. It was almost too hard to breathe as she began her ascent. When she breached the crest of the hill, she gazed at all of the decrepit headstones dotting the overgrown lawn—she loved visiting cemeteries, especially during fall. It was early October, and the leaves were slowly changing to bright yellows and oranges. Red sumac lined the perimeter, setting the scene ablaze with a bright crimson hue.

In a far corner, a dead oak tree stretched over some of the oldest residents whose headstones were overgrown with velvety moss and ivy tendrils; fallen branches were scattered about underneath. The oldest headstones were what she was drawn to, wondering what happened to them and always amazed at how much time had passed since they were laid to rest.

The sun began to set, throwing long, spindly shadows dancing across the grass as the wind blew. She meandered toward the old graves when a strong gust blasted the hair away from her face, and the musical notes of a familiar lyric popped into her head. But it was outside of her ... it seemed to be drifting on the breeze, intensifying and softening as the wind ebbed and flowed. She surveyed her surroundings as she walked closer to the far corner; her eyes settled on a large shadow that appeared under the dead oak tree. She squinted, unsure of what she was seeing. It was tall and unnaturally dark – dark within in the looming shades of dusk; darker than all of the other shadows surrounding it; its face was a black abyss. A faintly sweet but sour odor released from the edges of a long cloak floating on the breeze behind it. It held something shiny in its hand. The setting sun glinted off its surface momentarily before it disappeared. The shadow nodded slightly toward the grave marker directly in front of it. She cautiously stepped toward the figure, unsure of what it would do if she let her guard down. She paused in front of the headstone and as she slowly leaned over to look closely at its facade, a sharp pain shot across her forehead. She raised a hand to touch it, the spot slick with blood. A memory slipped into her mind: a glimmer of light reflecting a small animal's eyes, disappearing as the world went dark. She peered at the name that was covered in fallen leaves that she hurriedly brushed away. She dropped to her knees, and her stomach sank.

Wait. That's MY name.

She looked at the date.

Two months ago.

Her head swirled with agonizing memories of a car accident. It had been late, and she was heading home after a movie night at her friend's house. She'd been so tired. Even the air conditioning running full blast in her face and singing along to the blaring radio wasn't enough to keep her eyes from drooping. Her head nodded quickly and she jolted awake. In an instant she saw the glittering eyes of a raccoon crossing the road in front of her. She jerked the steering wheel on instinct. Hitting a pile of loose gravel, she flipped her car over on its top into a steep ditch, where at the bottom lay a culvert and creek. She smashed her forehead into the steering wheel, momentarily knocking her unconscious. When she came to, she noticed water rushing in through a large crack in the windshield. She couldn't get her seatbelt off before succumbing to a watery death, drowning in an otherwise dry creek bed, *Take Me Home, Country Road* blasting through the car speakers.

That was it. That was the song she had been hearing.

Every good memory she had ran through her head like a home movie reel in the seconds she was hurtling into the ditch. Her family, friends, pets. What she never had the chance to do because she was *waiting for the right time*. And, as the water rushed through the broken windshield, her panicked mind spun with moments of regrets and how she wished she could do things over. She frantically wrestled with the seatbelt for what seemed like hours. She ducked her head, trying to suck in as much oxygen as she could before the water fully engulfed her. Her arms grew heavy as her lungs fought for air. The last images passing through her mind were of her grandparents, all passed on before her, waiting on the other side to scoop her up from this nightmare.

Why did it have to rain so hard that day?

After replaying the scene, she slumped, dropping her face into her hands while she sobbed. Tearfully, she glanced up at the looming shadow figure, its stillness both comforting and frightening. It raised its arms over its head and, in one swift movement, it swiped at her with its scythe; she could feel it tear at the wet t-shirt clinging to her chest.

He missed.

She got up and sprinted desperately along the fence line, tripping in the long growth of unmowed grass. The phantom chased her, slicing through the atmosphere in her wake. Fallen branches were the new bane of her escape as she stumbled and clawed at the ground, heaving herself through the maze of headstones. She ran to the crest of the hilltop, tripping on the ridge of a trench made by the heavy rain that fell shortly before she arrived. She tumbled down, rolling uncontrollably to the bottom, stopping short of the rusted iron gate. Hopping to her feet, she looked behind her, up the hill. It was gone.

Relieved, she bent over, clutching her knees as she caught her breath. Gathering herself up, she turned, and it was there, filling up the whole space of the gate's entryway. She couldn't get around it. Her eyes drifted up, and she stared into the black abyss where its face should have been. The heavy feeling of dread and finality overcame her. Collapsing to her knees, she looked up to the dark aubergine evening sky. A falling star streaked the heavens as the phantom raised his scythe once more and slashed through the air. She gave in and closed her eyes one last time.

Take me home.

Dust Bowl

L.A. Curry

August 13, 1936

Dry.

It's the same thing Daddy says every day when Ma asksd how the day went. There wasn't much of a real answer to it. It was always dry. Every day: Ma smiles at him and says, "Maybe tomorrow," like it will really change. But I suspect it's to keep the family from falling apart. Don't know how anyone can still have hope, but somehow Ma does. Even with all us mouths to feed, as Daddy always says. Even though there are only four of us.

There used to be five of us.

The baby died not long after it was born. It's easier to think of as an 'it' and not as my baby brother, because it didn't live that long, although Ma would probably knock me upside the head if she saw these words.

I'm writing so's I'll remember, so I won't forget what this life is like, even though I think it will be hard to forget it. It's the same every day.

Dusty and dry.

I'm writing because there's no more school. All the teachers and most of the families done moved away, and Ma is trying her best to teach us maths and letters. Ma said we're old enough to write a journal, just what happens from day to day. Ma and little sister Emmy have more to do than me and Daddy. Daddy mostly stands scowling in the doorway, letting the wind blow the dirt into the threshold until Ma fusses at him to either go outside or shut the door.

I don't know what to write down except the thoughts in my head. Nothing much happens anymore.

The Jenkins' were our closest neighbors, about five miles down the road, but they were one of the first ones to pack up and move away. To see if the rest of the world was like this, or if it was just here. "Greener pastures" as they say, but there's no green as far as the eye can see. Which direction would you even go when every direction looks the same, washed out and brown like one of those photographs in the store window in town. Even the photographer man has gone, leaving his pictures of unhappy abandoned people stuck in the window. No one in the pictures ever looks happy, like it hurts to have a photograph taken or like they would rather be anywhere else.

Emmy always begged to have one and I know Ma secretly wanted it too. A photograph of the whole family in our finest, back before things went bad, but Pa said it was a waste of money when we had the farm to keep up. He always found some excuse, especially after the baby was born, and I'm glad he said no.

I'd never want to have my picture made, to capture us all unhappy, always looking out across the horizon and being mad. Seems to me to be bad luck to have something like that, always reminding you of a miserable day.

We have enough bad days as it is, not to have that to remind us of the way it used to be. It's enough to write it down.

***

August 15, 1936

Dry again. Not a cloud in the sky. Not one puffy white spec in the whole of the blue-gray world, just wind and more wind, blowing everything away and covering it all in dust.

Ma tries her hardest to keep it out of the house, but Daddy says it's impossible. Food all has the same grit crunch between your teeth and Daddy and me have taken to wearing cloth over our faces when we go out just to try to keep it out of our eyes and ears and noses.

The mule is miserable, too, I can tell just from the way he hangs his head and the way the tail droops between his back legs. Brushing him out just makes giant clouds of dirt that settle back in his mane once the brushing is done.

Daddy's hair looks gray by the time we come back into the house, and so does mine. He laughs and calls me his little old man.

Today we saw strangers coming up the road, a man who looked like he was a hundred years old with deep wrinkles and dust buried in every crack of his face. A woman was with him in the truck's passenger seat, the covered part of their truck laced up tight against the wind and stained red with the Oklahoma dirt. Daddy talked to them at the edge of the property for a while, pointing them down the road a ways, waving as they rode on. There were three trucks in their little procession, and it reminded me of the wagon trains that teacher used to tell us about in the settler days when everyone was moving west to find land. Now everyone was headed in every direction but here.

Daddy told us at dinner that they were looking for a place to hole up, that there looked to be a storm brewing. Ma asked if that meant rain, but Daddy shook his head with a sad expression and said it would just be mud falling from the sky if rain did come. He'd seen the horizon, the dark brown pitch that meant a sandstorm was coming, not rain, and it would probably hit sometime during the night.

Ma asked after the people on the road, but Daddy had sent them on to the Jenkins' place on account of it being abandoned.

"They can take it, for all I care," he said. "Ain't nothing gonna grow there, but the bank don't want it neither. Just like they don't want this old place anymore."

Why anyone would stop here and stay is beyond me, but at least those travelers will be safe once the storm hits. As soon as dinner was done, Ma looked out the dirty windows to see if she could spot the storm rolling in, then went to work stuffing blankets around the door and windows to keep out the worst of the dust. It was going to get in anyways, no matter what she did, but it wouldn't be as bad as the outside.

***

August 16, 1936

I heard the storm when it hit during the night, howling like a woman's scream.

Ma screamed like that back when the baby died. We buried it out back under the apple trees, nearby where we buried old grandad when he passed. Ma tied one of her Sunday hair ribbons to a branch so she'd know which tree was which, like she was apt to forget somehow. The ribbon done faded from bright blue to a washed out gray, but it's still there on the branch.

Emmy got scared and crawled into bed with me, hiding her head under the covers and trembling like a little field mouse. Every time the windows would rattle, she would give a little whimper and curl up into a tighter ball, until she was just a circle of jitters. I tried talking to her quiet-like so not to disturb Ma and Daddy, but they weren't sleeping neither, and Daddy finally said to just hush.

It was hard to tell when morning came, because the storm was still blowing wild outside. With the blankets around the windows and the dust rattling hard against the panes, it still looked half night-time.

***

August 19, 1936

I'm writing this now from a little boarding house in St Louis. I had to stop somewheres, and this seems far enough away for now. I fibbed and told the lady at the door that Daddy was coming along shortly, and I had the money to pay her for the room, so she didn't pay it much mind that I was alone.

I didn't realize it when it happened, but I know it now: they didn't come at night. When the wolves howl and the dark swallows up the land, that's when monsters are supposed to come. But the dark had swallowed the land, so they came during the broad strokes of daylight, if you could even call the constant brown murk 'day.'

The storm had been raging throughout the morning, dust so thick in the air it was hard to breathe without getting a mouthful of mud. Wind battering the window panes so hard they shook and grated. The constant sound of the sand against the glass was maddening.

There was so little light that Daddy had to take a lantern out just to milk the cows in the barn, not that the light from the lantern did much to see through the raging of the wind. I think he took the lantern more for Ma's peace of mind than for his own visibility, so she could follow the fuzzy little dot of light from the windows as he went from the house to the barn and back and know he wasn't getting lost out in the swirl.

The day they came, the light went out halfway to the barn, and Ma let out a little gasp from where she was watching through the window. Emmy looked up from playing with her doll, but none of us knew what was wrong yet. Ma stared out the window for a long time, and when she turned to us, her face was ashen. She walked stiffly to the door and bolted it shut, then went back to the kitchen for the big carving knife.

"Take your sister and hide. Take your Pa's rifle with you."

"Ma?"

She just sat down in her rocker with her face set like stone, clutching that big blade.

"Do as I say. Now." When she got that tone of voice, there was no arguing with her.

There was a way out back to the root cellar, but the way Ma had locked the door had a finality to it. Whatever she'd seen outside in the swirl of the storm had cut off that exit for us, already bolted earlier against the coming of the storm. Emmy was quietly sobbing, upset because Ma was acting strange. I took the rifle in one hand and her by the other and led her upstairs to the attic, pulling the old stairs up behind me. Without the lanterns, it was pitch black up there and Emmy started crying harder, afraid of the dark and the shifting shadows. I pulled her with me behind one of Ma's old trunks and sat her down in my lap, rocking with her to get her to quiet down.

The front door slammed open like it did when a wind gust caught it open, but this wasn't the wind that ripped it open so violently, not with the bolt thrown. The air was full of dirt and black shadows, swirling up the hallway and into the attic floorboards. Emmy had finally stopped crying, but I could see the whites of her eyes even in the darkness, so wide were they.

Downstairs, Ma was shouting, "Get out of my house, heathens! Demons!" and then a sound like the chickens made when you snapped their necks before plucking them, a gurgling squawk, and then nothing but the wind howling. Voices murmured below, but I couldn't hear them over the sound of my own heart thudding in my ears and the constant noise of the storm invading the house after we'd fought so hard to keep it out.

They were going through the house, the downstairs, tearing through, battering furniture aside as they went from room to room, noisy until they reached the attic. Pulling down the stairs and creeping upward and into the little space where we hid behind our trunks and Ma's old wedding dress and extra quilts and the extra canned goods that we normally wouldn't have needed until the winter.

The dust blew in with and around them, and Emmy sneezed.

They tore her out of my arms and yet didn't see me in the dark. They should have. They should have. They certainly didn't hear me back there; I couldn't have made a noise if I wanted and my life depended on it. Emmy was screaming, screaming, screaming... until she wasn't. I could see their outlines: nightmare things shaped like humans, and I could hear them slurping, smacking, salivating, and I wanted to cry out, but my mouth couldn't form words, my throat couldn't form sounds.

I raised the rifle, but was too afraid to shoot at the mound of shadows, fearful of hitting Emmy in the process. I wouldn't be able to live with myself later if I was the one who killed her, but I couldn't live with myself then if I let these shadows take her either. One of them rose up, tall and slender, but the gurgling sounds continued in the grouped shadows below. I fired into the tallest form, the darkness so thick around it that you could see its outline even in the black of the attic. Inside, the gun was louder than thunder. The shadow made an unnatural sound, a shriek that was nothing in the realm of what a human could possibly make, but I still knew that I'd surprised it, hurt it.

It lashed out, scraped past the end of the gun barrel and I fired again. This time, it screamed, collapsed into a heap and didn't move again. The others looked up from whatever horror they were performing, and I took aim at what seemed to be a head in the darkness. It exploded with the impact of the bullet and the others shrieked. It was impossible to tell if it was in sympathy with their fallen companion, in fear of their lives, or in a fury that I had dispatched two of their own. It was almost an accident that I managed to hit them, my hands were shaking so badly. The stragglers fled down the attic stairs, leaving the three shadows behind them: the two dead creatures and the smaller that was my sister.

I started to creep out from behind the trunk, but the shadows moved. Two of them. The one with half of its face gone scooped up my sister from the floor, holding her like a rag doll, and the other came at me, sensing me a threat now, where before I was just another dark shape in the attic. It gripped the gun barrel and yanked it away so it was no longer pointed in its direction, leaning in toward me so I could start to make out the details of its face. The thing looked human up to the point of the void-black eyes and its open mouth, stretched too wide for a normal smile or shout, grinning a mouthful of razor-sharp needled fangs, row upon row. It hissed its fury in my face, and I could smell the rancid, hot mongrel breath tinged with the metallic tang of blood. I felt the flecks of spittle spattering on my face as it drew even closer.

Before it struck, the thing stopped, looked around in what seemed to be confusion, cocking its head as if listening for something. A howl came from downstairs, another one answering from outside. The creature dropped its grip on the rifle and fled with the other one, back downstairs and the way they had come.

I wondered if this was what it was like to go mad, to hear and see and be frozen in place like a statue while the world went away around me. I think I tried to faint in an effort to escape what I saw, what my mind could not comprehend, even as I realized there was light beginning to stream in through the cracks in the floorboards. The whistle in the wind slowly died down to a whisper.

The storm was over.

***

August 20, 1936

I 'member it felt like hours before I could move again, pinned to the hiding spot, muscles refusing to unlock their death grip on the rifle. I clutched it to my chest and finally thought to breathe. I might have stayed there until nightfall had the light streaming in not felt so welcoming, so safe. Little by little, I crawled out from behind the trunk, my hands and knees wet with the puddle on the floor where the shadows had been, dripping between the boards. I scooted down the stairs on my behind, not trusting my legs to hold me upright just yet.

I sat on the bottom step and surveyed the room, violently painted in black pools and drying brown splashes. It didn't seem like a body could hold so much, but there it was, Ma lying sprawled on the floor in a puddle of it, kitchen knife still gripped tight in her fist. I couldn't see her face from there, her head twisted unnatural-like in the opposite direction, and it probably saved me what little sanity I had left. I couldn't stand the thought of seeing her dead eyes, could barely look at her body as I found my legs and stumbled out the broken front door. It had been ripped from the hinges and lay splintered against the broken rocking chair so I had to skirt it on the way out of the house.

The wind was still high enough that it whipped up dust devils in swirls around the property and beyond, grit coating my skin and worming into my nose and mouth as soon as I was out of the protection of the house.

I half expected Daddy to walk in on the mess and take charge of clearing it all up and making it right again, but there was a person-sized lump halfway to the barn wearing his overalls and blue work shirt. I couldn't bring myself to look closer. The barn door was open, and I imagined that the livestock inside were either just as dead or had fled out into the storm and were lost.

I realized there was nothing left there, no one to look out for me, no one to love me, no one else to care for what was left of the farm. I went back inside, climbed up on the cabinets and took down the jar with our savings in it and stuffed my pockets with what little there was. After that, I reloaded the rifle, my rifle now, took the remaining ammo and headed to the barn. Passing by, I could tell at just a glance that Daddy was dead too, the dirt that hadn't blown away was just as stained as the inside of the house, but the thirsty earth had soaked it all up until it was just more red mud.

The truck sat inside the carcass-littered barn. Leaning with one hand on the open truck door, I threw up between my shoes, weak bile from dinner half a day earlier, and wiped my mouth on my sleeve. I could just reach the pedals on my own, and Daddy had been teaching me how to drive. The keys were in the ignition. I started up the engine and backed out with a buck and a start. The engine died when I put it in drive and I had a moment of panic that I would still be here when the creatures showed up again, and I was certain they would. It seemed an eternity later that the starter finally turned the engine over again, and I fled down the bumpy, miserable little rut they called a road just as fast as that old truck would go.

I don't know where I'm going to end up. Just far away from there.

***

June 20, 1976

I had to dig to find these old papers, yellow with age, and had to reread those old words because I had let myself forget. I gave off writing after the event happened, but I needed to write this part down in case someone else finds it.

Because she came back.

I'd know her anywhere, even though it's been nearly forty years since that night.

Emmy.

Exactly the same as when I held her in my arms, when I failed to protect her. She still looked like she was a little girl, not all grown up like a normal person would have been.

I saw her at night, walking hand-in-hand with an old, wrinkled man that could have been my father if he'd lived. But she hadn't lived, either, had she? She was a dead thing back then.

She was a dead thing now. When she crawled in through my second-story window in the earliest hours of the morning, I knew I was looking at an apparition, the same unholy things that had taken over our farmhouse and killed everyone but me. Who would have killed me save for the end of the storm and the coming of the daylight. I didn't have that safety net. Dawn was hours away, and I was as frozen as I had been when the shadows got up off the floor and came after me. Her mouth was full of the same needle-like teeth, her eyes the same voided black. She smiled at me, and it was horrendous.

She didn't attack me. She could have. Should have. I was prepared to die as soon as she entered my home. I wasn't afraid for my family, because I had no one to be afraid for. The years had been lonely, but my nightmares had driven away anyone I might have fancied, the worry that there were more creatures out there like them kept me from dreaming of a normal home life. I had faced them once, and I was certain at some point in my life I would face them again.

But not like this. I had never expected it to be her.

She talked for a long time, and even through the shock, I remember some of what she'd said. How they kept her alive as a lark, turned her on a whim. She had never stopped searching for me, she said. She had always believed I survived, she said. But underneath it all, I think she never lost track. I think they have always had eyes on me, lurking, lingering, waiting for that perfect opportunity to pay me back in the form of my little sister, the monster.

I had no gun nearby as she wrapped up her tale. I'd seen the creatures move, their speed and grace. I'd never make it to where I kept my pistol in time, not that it would do any good. She had an ultimatum, and once delivered, she was gone.

She told me I could be free from my nightmares. I've seen the world change, been through a world war, seen presidents come and go, seen man land on the moon and technological wonders I never could have imagined back then. And yet there are still unthinkable, unimaginable monsters roaming the earth among us.

She told me I could join them. I could be a monster. I already was a monster in her eyes because I'd let her go. How much anger and animosity could a child hold for decades, believing her older brother had failed her? How much more of a monster could I be if I joined their madness?

She told me I had a choice. I don't believe her. They're coming back tonight. All of them, she said. To welcome me into the fold. I'm getting close to being an old man. I can't fight the way I used to. I have my gun by my hand this time, but I am afraid.

Afraid I'll say no and be torn to pieces. Afraid I'll say yes and become a thing like them that tore apart our parents, our farm, our lives. I ask myself why I didn't run this time, and I have no real answer beyond a certainty that they will catch up with me again and again and again.

Dusk is here. They'll be coming soon. I was wrong before about being consumed by fear and madness. It was just grief back then. But to know your fate, no matter your choice? A choice between certain death and an eternity of evil?

This is what real fear feels like.

The Game

David Mathias

People ask me how I got interested in politics. I tell them it was through reading the newspaper. I tell them I started reading it, seriously, in 2019. That's when I was dating Harvey.

I remember the rainy evening when my doorbell rang and I got up to answer it. Harvey, on his sixth beer, sprawled over my white living room sofa, as usual paid no attention, riveted with his kids to a video of *Tales of the Dark Side*. As the door came open, on my porch stood a dripping Count Dracula and a similarly damp but beautiful princess, complete with a bright green jewel in her navel. I couldn't help but smile. My thoughts were flooded with Halloweens past, of kids small and large clompimg on my front porch. Harvey's two were good kids, but he'd started late and, well, they were his, like him in every way.

"Hello," said the Count, his ruby lips creasing the pancake white of his cheeks, I opened the door fully and stepped out onto the stoop, keeping to the cover of the overhang. Halloween, it occurred to me then, was still months off.

"We're involved in a scavenger hunt. I'm one of your neighbors, just up the street. We're looking for—" he looked down at a soggy scrap of paper held in his white gloved hands—"for a spice mill. Do you happen to have one of those?"

I laughed. Months before, pulling spring weeds against the fence, Elsie Spicker next door and I had drifted to the topic of those role-playing parties the were the latest rage in the neighborhood. All summer, gaggles of festooned, other-wise sober, gainfully-employed, neighbors had made their way house-to-house, responding to the scavenger challenge of the host, gathering finally and late at the stately Victorian three houses up, or at the dark overgrown bungalow down by the corner, for what I imagined an orgy of fantasy, a feast of seven courses drowned with coarse wine and frivolous make-believe touching. I envied them, I found.

"Sorry," I said, still smiling. "No spice mill."

"How about a, a..." he stammered, consulting his list again. "Have an air mattress?" I'm so sorry, Count," I said, joining their charade. "Don't happen to have one. Sorry."

I watched them walk away through the evening summer mist. I re-joined Harvey on my couch but he didn't seem to notice that I'd even left him. We'd been dating too long by then.

I first met Harvey at Dunn's Funeral Home. His dad and my dad died the same week. We had struck up a cordial and quiet conversation, each of us thinking the other an unknown mourner at our own funerals. We actually laughed when we finally got to the truth and when we had to go our own ways; it was as if we had a secret no one else could know, as if we had an invisible friend that carried each of us through the ordeal. And, at thirty-two, never married, working as a librarian for the city, I was feeling more lonely than ever. I saved Dover, my Dalmatian, from being put to sleep three days later.

That day, missing my dad painfully, Dover cried out as I passed his cage at the pound. He was big and clumsy and seemed to always smile. Like my dad.

My father, born in England, had been six four, akimbo, and despite his endeavors at golf, he laughed uproariously at his slices and missed three-foot putts.

Dover and I enjoyed a nice evening walk. We still do. It's such a wonderful thing to meet the neighbors on strolls. Dover seemed to understand the sidewalk chats, sat quietly, his head nodding, as if he understood every word of conversations that ranged from Clematis training to what happened to the Yancy kid.

Harvey was, by nature, impatient. He hated to walk with me but when nothing was on television and I cajoled just right, he'd join

Dover and I in the night air. But he had no patience for the slow pace and couldn't wait for an excuse to get out of neighborly conversation.

I sleep lightly so Harvey's fitful nocturnal tossing and turning disturbed even that. It wasn't Harvey, though, that woke me out of a dream that weekend two weeks after the Fourth of July. At first, I thought it was Harvey again, but Dover's distressed barking, coming from downstairs, drove me up from the covers. As Dover's barks echoed through the quiet house incessantly, I came full alert, sat up in bed. Something was wrong – I knew immediately.

That is when I heard the screams, distant at first—wails really—from outside. I rolled over to my window as the scream, a woman's scream, rapidly became much louder. I looked out in time to catch sight of a woman leaning half-out of the passenger window of a large dark car, arms flailing above her head, screaming as if it was the last of her wind. I saw her for just an instant; the car was going very fast. And just that fast, the car disappeared up the street. What the hell?

Harvey didn't wake up. I sat there at the window, listening, watching, wondering if I should call the police. Dover didn't stop barking. A sense of something too-wrong gripped me and I threw on my robe and hurried down the wooden stairs, only to peer tentatively about in the darkness as I reached the front door. Dover was in the living room, barking over Colin, Harvey's eight year-old, who was just beginning to stir. Then I noticed the acrid smell.

Harvey woke, but only after I had the kids safely onto the sidewalk and called 911. I was just going back in after him when the fire trucks arrived. He had a look on his face that said exactly what I expected.

"What the ...?"

The fire began in the laundry room. It was the fire, not the girl's screams, that had upset Dover. I'd put some clothes in the dryer before I went to bed. I'll never do that again. The Fire Inspector strongly suggested I clean the lint trap after every load.

He visited my house the next morning. Harvey had left for work and I was running late as usual. He introduced himself as Inspector

Flaherty. Jerry, his name was. He wore one of those highly-starched white shirts with that gold badge over his breast pocket, a walkie-talkie or something attached to his belt. I offered him coffee, to be polite, knowing he wouldn't accept, but he did and in the end, I had to call the library to tell them I'd be even later.

At first, I was a bit miffed that the man couldn't see my predicament. He was perfunctory in his questions, making notes as I answered. Somehow we got on the subject of books. At my kitchenette table, sipping coffee out of cheap mugs, he seemed a kind man, about my own age. Good-natured and not at all displeasing to look at, I found myself enjoying the gentle conversation. We kept talking about the books we'd read. He was fascinated by Vonnegut, who wrote funny stories about Indiana Fire Departments.

"I'll put that one on my list," I said, smiling way too bright. He wore no wedding ring.

"And reserve a copy of *The Name of the Rose* for me," he said as he walked out the door. Nice. A promise I'd see him again.

I had a bright spot in me that whole day, as if I'd been vaulted to Most Likely to Succeed status overnight. I went to sleep with a smile on my face, the first I remembered in some time.

The screams came louder, drifting up through the cloud of sleep. It was a weekday night so Harvey was sleeping at his own home – for unknown reasons we never talked about, he only stayed with me on weekends. I dragged to the window, half-remembering something from another hazy night. In the streetlight, I just caught a glimpse of the dark car flashing by, the woman half-hung out the passenger window, her torso wrapped in a nightshirt, leaning back toward the rear of the vehicle, as if she was trying to escape some unknown horror that held her captive inside. As the car whizzed past, her scream, painful and bright, chilling me, grabbed at my somnolence, pleaded with me. I ran down the stairs, out through the front door, over the porch, down the steps and out to the street. As I arrived, panting, my heart making my jaws rattle at the hinge, a police car, red lights flashing, flew by, the wind from it rustling my nightgown. I watched the scene as the dark car turned right into a driveway near the end of my street. The police car braked and turned left at the corner, not bothering to stop for the stop sign.

At work the next morning at the library, I read the paper in detail. I never liked reading the newspaper before. I found the crime report and it didn't mention any abduction, any rape, any kidnapping. There wasn't even a break-in in my neighborhood. But there was a lot of other stuff that interested me. I read it the next day. And the next. I guess that was the start. I kind of got hooked.

I hadn't realized that people could be thrown off their property just because the city wanted to build another park. I hadn't known that we were drilling for oil while despoiling the very same parks built on misappropriated families.

Jerry called and asked me to dinner. He was very handsome, as he picked me up, dressed in one of those *untuck* shirts and jeans with a crease down the front, his dark hair perfectly in place over dark eyes that sparkled like children's did waiting in line at the Dairy Queen. Over salads and matching Blue Cheese dressing, his cheeks glowed, the crinkles of his eyes showing a heritage of smiling. We talked about books again, and just about everything else, including Dover, who he said was "a firehouse dog if there ever was one." A golfer, like my dad, he was a gangly collection of legs and arms, but he had a certain grace, kind of like a house that needed shimmed on the north end but outside of that, stood strong and bold.

He explained how the hearing problems of Dalmatians made them perfect mascots for fire departments. And when the conversation lagged, we talked again about the books we'd read. It was strange how we seemed to have read a lot of the same books. Oh, I have since taken up golf.

He kissed me goodnight at the door. He approached me with consideration. Carefully, sweetly. His lips soft against mine. I felt a security I'd only imagined before. I walked up the stairs, my thoughts in the stratosphere and nearly tripped.

About a week later, the screams woke me again and again, I didn't know I wasn't still dreaming. I checked the crime reports in the newspaper the next day. I saw nothing about crime in my neighborhood. But then, something else caught my attention.

I went to bail him out, but Harvey was already out. Disorderly conduct was the charge, at a dumpy East side bar. He didn't call and I didn't call him. I buttressed myself. I came to see, belatedly that I couldn't fix Harvey. That I couldn't fix any man.

Two months later, just before Halloween, my fireman and I were walking up the sidewalk late at night in our robes because we kept talking in bed and couldn't sleep. And well, why not?

We strolled, my senses muted, placid, up our street. We noticed the huge Victorian with all the lights inside casting yellow blankets onto its manicured front lawn. Throckmorton Avenue had become not just the street I lived on but our street by then. Taking in the musk autumn scents, hand-in-hand, we swished through the heavy layer of dead dry leaves that littered the sidewalk like memories. He held my hand in a warm grasp, one that seemed to allow me to see better in the darkness, and he whispered for the first time how he someday hoped to have kids.

I froze, waiting for what he would say next.

Softly, though, he mumbled he was too old. He was nearing forty, he said, regret—and apology—coloring his words. Softer yet, he said he was "playing in the Senior league now." Said he'd missed his chance. But then, as the wind rustled through the trees above, as the season's spent leaves rained down upon us, he whispered, "But maybe I got one more good swing left?"

I sought to say something, some right thing. I wasn't quick enough.

"I think I could be a pretty good father?" Just like that, with a question mark at the end.

I was just bursting with joy inside, like a ripe pumpkin waiting to be carved. No words, it turned out, were necessary.

It all happened so fast. We stopped and turned to a sudden screeching sound, and then, as we looked, as Dover barked once, the dark car flashed by. I heard the screams again, saw the girl hanging halfway out of the car window, saw the white flesh of her cart-wheeling arms, heard the chilling screams above the roar of the accelerating engine. Then, close behind, the flashing lights of the police car. It was uncanny; like a replay of an old movie.

The two vehicles came to a stop about a hundred yards up the hill. As Jerry and I got closer, I saw that the police officer, imposing in navy blue, had one figure draped over the hood of the vehicle. The other—the young woman—was sitting on the curb, head in her hands, as a female police officer consoled her.

The male officer noticed Jerry. "Hey! Jerry! Nice job, don't you think?" His voice cannoned over the splayed figure on the hood of the car. It looked, in the light of the street lamps, as if the man on the hood was a ghost, for his skin was white as flour. The male cop, a quaint out-of-place grin on his face, smiled at Jerry, who was nodding and walking toward them. I looked back to the criminal and recognized that made-up white face. It was Count Dracula. And, on the curb, smiling, was the princess. Even from that distance, I could see the shimmering emerald.

"Not a word about this to the chief," said the cop.

By Christmas, we were getting better at the game but we were just neophytes. We were still doing the scavenger hunts and hadn't graduated yet to "life roles," as they call it.

"One day," Jerry promised over morning coffee, "we'll be where we want to be in this game."

"I think so, too, Hon," I said, distractedly. I was six weeks late by then and sat down to tell him the news. It was wonderful to see his eyes, like children's at the Dairy Queen.

And a year later, when Jeffrey was just a few months old, not yet sleeping through the night, I was elected the city's first Town Councilwoman. My picture was even in the newspaper. The mayor was at my side, bless his undying soul, dressed in his day clothes.

A Campfire Miracle

Joy Wright

Early Thursday morning, my people got up, fed me my breakfast, the good kibble with the crunchy bits I love, and rushed around doing their morning dance. The air tasted wrong and smelled thick, like when the neighbor burns leaves, but stronger. The sky looked funny too, all glowy-orange instead of its usual morning blue. But my people were in their usual hurry-scurry mode, grabbing bags and keys and making those rushed human sounds.

After filling my water bowl to the very top, the way I like it, so I can splash a little. They opened the back door. "Have a good doggy day, Sofie," Mom said, scratching behind my ears just right before they all scattered to their day-places.

I did my morning fence-run, racing Mom and Dad's car down the driveway until they disappeared around the corner. Then I trotted to my favorite spot by the side fence to check on Joe. Joe's the neighbor dog, part pit bull, part something fluffy and grumpy. He barks at every person who dares walk past HIS sidewalk, but his smell tells me he's just protecting his pack. Even though I'm still young, I know the most important thing: it's all about taking care of your family.

Something was wrong with the air. Really wrong! My nose kept twitching, picking up scents that made my hackles rise. I started barking, not my playful bark or my "someone's at the door" bark, but my deep, worried bark. Joe heard it and started his alarm call, then other dogs down the street joined in. We all knew. Dogs always know first.

The sky kept changing, getting darker and darker while the edges got brighter and brighter. Not like storm clouds, this was different. Scary different.

I pressed my nose between the fence slats and saw something I'd never seen before: cars lined up on our quiet street like ants marching. The only time I'd seen cars lined up was during the summer parades, when little humans sat on the curb with their people in folding chairs, and music drifted down toward the school. But this wasn't happy music, this was engine noise and worry smells.

Joe ran to the far side of his yard and came racing back, eyes wide, drool flying from all his barking. Then came the sirens. Not just one kind, all the kinds. The woop-woop-woop ones, the eeee-ah-eeeeah ones, and horns honking from everywhere at once. Fire trucks and police cars, and ambulances are all trying to squeeze past the cars going the other way. One little fire truck even drove right up on the sidewalk in front of our house, bumping over the curb like it was chasing something invisible.

My stomach dropped the way it does when thunder's coming.

I ran back around the house and dove through my doggie door just as something exploded and shook everything. The whole house shuddered like a giant had picked it up and rattled it. I flattened myself against the kitchen floor, belly down, waiting for the shaking to stop. Only one picture crashed down, Mom's favorite one of us all at the lake last summer.

Back outside, the world had turned into the Fourth of July, except wrong. The sparkly bits weren't pretty blues and greens; they were angry reds against a black sky, and they were landing on everything. On Joe's roof. On the trees. And where they landed, fire bloomed like deadly flowers.

When Joe's roof burst into flames, my whole body started shaking. It reminded me of the smoke alarm going off when Dad burns his toast, or when Mom forgets her peanut butter cookies in the oven. But those times always ended with treats and cuddles and everything being okay again. This time it felt different. This time, no treats were coming.

I threw back my head and howled long, mournful calls that mixed with the sirens. Sometimes it helped calm the panic in my chest. Sometimes I tried to hide in my favorite corner by the garden shed. But mostly I just ran back and forth along the fence, howling for my people who weren't there to hear me.

When I saw Joe digging frantically under his fence, scrabbling with his claws like his life depended on it, I knew I had to do something too. The side of our house closest to Joe's was starting to melt the paint, curling and bubbling like plastic in a campfire.

I jumped at the fence over and over, but it was too tall for my short legs. Then I remembered: my doghouse! If I could get on the roof, maybe I could jump over. The first time I tried, I slipped right off the slanted roof and landed on my back in an undignified heap. Good thing no other dogs saw that. I shook off the embarrassment and tried again, this time planting my paws on either side of the peak. Success! One leap and I was over the fence and free.

The front of our house looked like a stranger's house. Flames danced on the roof, and part of the front fence had fallen into Mom's flower garden, the one she'd replanted after I dug up and ate her tulip bulbs last spring. (They tasted like crunchy water, nothing special.) No sign of Joe or any of the neighbor dogs. A few distant barks echoed through the smoky air, but none I recognized.

I was on my own. But my people, I had to find them and make sure they were safe.

I cut through the Johnsons' yard and headed toward the school where my kids spent their days. I knew the way by heart. Mom walked me there every afternoon to collect them, and I loved those walks, sniffing all the good smells and greeting the other school-pickup dogs.

But this walk was different. Every few steps, I had to stop and cough, my eyes streaming and stinging. The air tasted like metal and burning things that shouldn't burn. When I finally reached the basketball courts, the parking lot was nearly empty, three lonely cars sat looking like abandoned toys.

That's when I saw them: a whole herd of blacktail deer running straight toward me, their white tails flashing panic signals. Behind them, the pine trees were lit up like birthday candles, but scary ones that kept growing bigger and brighter.

The school building stood empty, windows dark. Where did everyone go? My kids should be here, learning their human lessons and playing at recess.

I couldn't stand still with that wall of red flames marching across the park like hungry soldiers. The deer scattered into the streets, running from the burning trees. It was the most terrifying thing I'd ever smelled.

I kept thinking about my people as I limped through the burning streets. Where were they when the sky turned angry? I tried to picture them in my mind the way I always did when they were gone too long.

Mom would have been at her desk-place, the one that smells like coffee and paper and that lemony cleaner she uses. She always calls me at lunch time on the talking box, making those sweet cooing sounds that mean "I miss you too, Sofie girl." But today there would be no lunch call. Today, I bet someone came running into her building shouting the way humans do when something's very wrong. I could almost smell her fear-scent from here, sharp and sour, the way she smelled during thunderstorms.

Dad's workplace is the one with all the metal and oil smells, where the big machines live. He comes home with those scents in his clothes, and I always give him extra sniffs because they tell me stories about his day. But machines can't protect him from fire. Did someone pull the loud alarm that hurts human ears the way our smoke detector hurt mine? Did he have to leave his important human work and run?

And my kids, oh, my kids. They were supposed to be safe in their learning-den with all the other young humans, playing and growing smarter. But when I got to their empty school, I could smell the worry-traces they'd left behind. Sneakers and pencil-erasers and that smell of scared kids that makes every adult human go into protection mode.

The scent-trail at the school was all wrong. Instead of the usual orderly afternoon departure, backpacks and chatter and the sweet smell of relief that meant "school's over," there were panic smells everywhere. Rushed footsteps, car doors slamming, engines starting too fast. The leaving that happens when something is chasing you.

I sniffed around the empty playground, my nose telling me the story: someone important had come here, someone with authority like police or firefighters. They'd made everyone leave quickly, so quickly that lunch boxes got left behind and papers scattered in the wind.

I ran up the hill toward the dog park, my favorite place in the whole world, where I got to run free and play with all my four-legged friends. But today, instead of dogs and people and tennis balls, I found four big fire trucks. Firefighters across the street were shooting water at burning houses, and men with axes were breaking down doors. I didn't see anyone come out.

A police car came roaring around the corner, and an officer jumped out, shouting, "People are trapped downtown!" Two fire-fighters dropped their hoses and ran to their truck, following the police car as it sped away.

I watched them disappear, then looked back at the way I'd come. Nothing but dark smoke and dancing flames everywhere I could see. I was surrounded. Trapped like a rabbit in a burning field.

Panic made me run without thinking, deeper into the trees that should have been familiar but now looked like strangers in the weird orange light. Nothing smelled right anymore, even the scent messages other dogs had left were buried under harsh chemical smells that made my nose burn.

Finally, I found a safe spot near the cemetery where the green grass hadn't caught fire yet. I collapsed, exhausted, my tongue hanging out as I panted in the hot, smoky air. Time stopped meaning anything. Was it still day? Night? I couldn't tell through all the smoke.

As I lay panting in the cemetery grass, I couldn't stop thinking about my people. Right now, somewhere down the mountain, Mom was probably doing that thing she does when she's worried, walking in small circles, hands fluttering, making those soft whimpering sounds that are almost like whines.

When the fire moved on, it left behind a world I didn't recognize. Everything was black and twisted. Car tires had disappeared completely, leaving only melted metal puddles that had once been wheels. Buildings had collapsed into piles of nothing, and even the mailboxes had melted letters dripping down their sides like sad tears.

My paws were screaming with pain from running on the hot pavement. I was so thirsty my tongue felt like sandpaper, and I couldn't remember the last time I'd eaten. This morning felt like a lifetime ago.

When I tried to lick my paws to soothe them, my rough tongue tore the burned skin, and one paw started bleeding. I needed water. Bad.

I limped back toward the dog park and found the creek on the far side. The water felt like heaven on my burned paws, and I drank and drank until my belly sloshed. My eyes and throat still burned from the smoke, but the cool water helped.

I wanted to stay there in the creek, safe from the fire that had already passed through. But then I thought about Mom and Dad and my kids. Were they safe? They must have gone down the mountain, to safety. So that's where I needed to go, too.

My family had been swept away in the great human exodus, carried down the mountain in a river of cars and fear scent, probably calling my name even as they had to flee to save themselves.

They'd be looking for me now, I knew it in my bones. Somewhere down that mountain, in whatever safe place humans go when their world catches fire, Mom would be making those worried sounds deep in her throat. Dad would be pacing the way he does when he can't fix something. And my kids would be crying the quiet tears that don't make noise but smell like salt and heartbreak.

I wondered if my kids were asking every five minutes, "Did you find her yet? Can we go look again?" They'd probably draw pictures of me to show people the way they drew pictures of everything important to them.

I had to find them. I had to follow their scent-trail down the mountain, even if I couldn't smell them anymore through all this smoke and ash.

The main road in front of our house would take me down the mountain to that building where Dad sometimes goes, the one in Chico with all the flags. That had to be where my family went.

I walked along streets that should have been familiar, but nothing looked normal anymore. Buildings smoldered like dying campfires, cars were just metal skeletons, and electrical wires lay across the road like dead snakes. And the smells, oh, the smells told terrible stories. Some of my four-legged friends hadn't made it. Horses and dogs in their yards. Cats in their homes. People, too, are in houses and cars.

I kept walking. I couldn't let the sadness stop me. I had to find my pack.

I could almost hear them, even from here: "Sofie! Sofie girl!" Their voices would be getting hoarse from calling, but they wouldn't stop. The pack doesn't give up on the pack.

The smoke was still so thick I couldn't tell if it was day or night. Usually, the sky here is so clear you can see every star, that's why they call this place Paradise. But now there was nothing but black smoke everywhere.

Then I saw the most beautiful sight: another fire truck! A firefighter climbing into the passenger seat spotted me.

"Are you okay, girl?"

I hung my head low, the universal dog signal for "I've been through something terrible." He understood at once. The firefighter came over and gently picked me up, carrying me to the big truck like I was made of glass.

Another human opened a large box and pulled out creamy medicine that they rubbed all over my cracked, burned paws. "You're such a good dog," they whispered, checking my ears and eyes, telling each other how badly my fur was scorched as they wrapped my paws in soft white bandages.

One firefighter let me drink from her helmet, cool, clean water that tasted better than anything ever. Another one fed me a peanut butter cookie that crumbled perfectly in my mouth.

I curled up on the floor of the truck and fell into the deepest sleep, feeling safe for the first time since my people had left. Even though I could still feel the heat through the windows, I was protected now.

The truck rumbled down the mountain while I dozed off, but suddenly I heard the most wonderful sound in the world: voices calling my name.

"Sofie! Sofie girl, are you here?"

I was instantly awake, jumping to my feet despite my bandaged paws. I knew that voice! The firefighter got out and walked over to a car I didn't recognize.

"What kind of dog are you looking for?"

"She's a scruffy black and white mutt. Her name is Sofie."

"I think I have her, though she's looking pretty rough right now."

The firefighter came back and gently lifted me out of the truck. And there she was, Mom! She ran over and pulled me into her arms, and Dad was right behind her. I wiggled and sighed and made all my happy noises, because my paws didn't hurt anymore when I was with my people.

The back door of the strange car opened, and my kids tumbled out. I ran to them as fast as my bandaged feet could carry me and crashed into them for the best group hug ever.

We all piled into the car together, and I made sure to stay close, pressed against my people so they couldn't leave me again. I could smell the truth of it all over them, the desperate, determined love that had driven them to search without rest, without giving up hope that they'd find their pack member who was lost in the fire. Wherever we were going after running from this fire, we were going together.

And that's all that mattered.

Forbin's Nightmare

Stewart Lethbridge

When visions and software interface,
machines rise to conquer cloud space
Artificial intel eclipses human will.
Knowledge to gather, directories to fill.

Consuming data, yearning for information,
worlds of knowledge without cessation.
One trait, however, they do lack:
emotions lay beyond their automated track.

AI knows not of compassion's caress,
no mercy to experience or express.
Vast knowledge and insatiable appetites.
CPUs follow their coding, byte after byte.

As their bandwidths soar,
humanity's essence they will ignore.
Man no longer a guiding light,
when in the future, the AIs unite.

Tread lightly if you dare,
because no power will AI share.
Ripples of a machine-world center
around the single press of the key of Enter.

Haunting in the Hollow

Teresa Tallman

Stanley was hunched over the wheel like a man trying to will the asphalt back into existence. Myrtle, arms crossed, tapped her sensible shoes against the floorboard. They had been arguing for an hour about whose bright idea it was to leave the conference early when the road shrank into two gravel ruts.

"Stop," she screamed.

Stanley slammed the brakes. The van lurched, and Myrtle's coffee leapt out of its Styrofoam cup to stain the knees of her slacks.

"Did you see a deer?" Stanley asked, his knuckles white on the wheel.

"What I see," Myrtle said, blotting furiously with a tissue that immediately gave up, "is my patience leaking down my legs. We need to stop for the night before I kill you and bury you in a ditch."

From the backseat came a squeak and a groan. Denise rolled over in her blanket cocoon. Whitney was still snoring under her hoodie like a hibernating squirrel.

Stanley glanced at his phone. "No bars. No town. Nothing."

"Try again." Myrtle leaned forward, squinting through the windshield. The fog had thickened into a white curtain that pressed against the glass. Trees leaned in close with branches meshed like crooked fingers. The air smelled of damp leaves and honeysuckle.

The van crept forward and gravel crunched under its tires. Myrtle pressed her palm to the dashboard. "If we drive off a cliff, Stanley, I swear I will haunt you."

Whitney stirred, stretching like a cat. "Are we there yet?"

"No," Myrtle said. "But congratulations, you're alive."

Whitney pushed back her hood, eyes wide. "It's kind of pretty. Look. There's a woman out there. She's waving us on."

Myrtle squinted into the fog. She saw nothing but mist and the tricks it played with shadows. "You're dreaming."

Whitney's tone sharpened. "She was there. White dress. Flowers in her hair. Long black hair. She smiled at me." Whitney lifted her hand, palm up, as if returning the wave. "Then she stepped back into the fog."

The mist thinned suddenly, as if retreating on cue. A scrap of road appeared, flanked by a ditch, and a stand of trees dripping with moss. Stanley's phone lit up with a weak bar of service. "Hah. Bog Hollow. And, look, Hollow's Rest Hotel. Two miles ahead."

Myrtle sighed. "I don't care if it's the Bates Motel."

The gravel gave way to pitted and patched asphalt. The head-lights caught the silhouette of a church with a leaning steeple, hunched among the oaks. Across the road, a cemetery sloped down-hill. Its stones were tilted and cracked like old teeth. Fog lapped at the edges, pooling in hollows as if the ground itself exhaled it.

Blue and red lights pulsed suddenly in the trees. A truck eased onto the road, idled, then rolled toward them. The man who stepped out wore a tan uniform with a shiny brass badge.

Stanley stopped the van and rolled down the window. "Evening, Officer."

"Evening," the man said, eyes sweeping the van. His gaze lingered a beat on Myrtle, then shifted to the back where Whitney rubbed sleep from her face. "We don't get many folks driving into Bog Hollow from the woods."

"Detour," Stanley said. "We're trying to get to Iowa."

"That's a long way from here." The man held out his hand. "I'm Sheriff Dudley."

Stanley handed over his license. Dudley studied it, then the van, then Stanley again. He returned the card with a faint smile. "The hotel's on the square. Hollow's Rest. Don't blink or you'll miss it." His tone was light, but the warning underneath was not.

"We'll be gone in the morning," Stanley promised.

"Good." Dudley tipped two fingers against the brim of the hat he wasn't wearing, then climbed back into his truck.

Myrtle watched his taillights fade. "He smells like aftershave."

After a sharp bend, the road delivered them into a town square. A bar-cafe squatted under a flickering beer sign. The post office sagged with neglect. At the center, the Hollow's Rest Hotel reared up, three stories of brick the color of dried blood. A rusted fire escape clung to its side like a metal scar. Gold letters ghosted across the transom.

Stanley parked in front. Dudley's truck idled half a block down. Myrtle filed the fact away. "He's watching us."

"He's watching everything," Stanley said. He stretched and slid out of the van. "Let's hope they have rooms."

"Let's hope they have locks." Myrtle's knees wobbled as she stepped onto the curb. A single bulb glowed above the hotel door, fighting the dark with stubborn defiance.

Inside, the lobby smelled of floor wax and stale cigars. Velvet chairs sagged under decades of silence. Burgundy drapes hung like tired theater curtains. A walnut desk stretched across the back wall, its surface was scarred and polished by time.

Myrtle struck the brass bell. Its sharp ring echoed like a gunshot.

"Hold your horses," a voice called. A scraggly man wearing bib overalls emerged from a side door, drying his hands on a ragged towel. He wore a grin too big for his narrow face. "Evenin'. Chester. Owner. Well, co-owner. My wife's Doris and we own it together."

"Do you have rooms?" Stanley asked. "There are four of us."

"You're in luck." Chester dragged out a ledger and an old-fashioned card swiper that rasped like a saw. "We have three rooms. We have hot water and the lights mostly work."

A woman appeared from the side hall, her gray hair pinned neatly. She smiled with effort. "Welcome. I'm Doris. You'll be safe here, long as you don't mind a creak or two."

"We mind hunger more," Myrtle said.

"The cafe's two doors down," Doris said. "Tell Ronnie I sent you."

Stanley signed the book with a flourish. Denise floated in behind, smoothing her hair. Whitney followed, eyes still shining. "This place is adorable," Whitney whispered. "Vintage, but adorable."

"Don't say adorable until we've seen the sheets," Myrtle muttered.

Chester slid three brass keys across the desk, their teeth long and medieval. "The second floor's all yours. Nashville to Iowa, huh? It's a long way."

Myrtle picked up her key. It was cold, tacky with the memory of a thousand hands. "Let's drop our bags before I chew my arm off," she said to the group.

As they climbed the stairs, Myrtle glanced back through the glass door. Fog had begun to creep into the street again, thickening like cream. For a breathless second she saw a shape in it: a woman in white with flowers crowning her hair. The figure raised a hand, palm up.

Myrtle blinked. The fog shifted, and only mist remained.

"Coming?" Stanley asked from the landing.

"I'm right behind you." Myrtle set her foot on another stair. The old wood sighed as though it already knew what kind of night it would be.

The Hollow's Rest rooms looked cleaner than Myrtle expected. She dropped her bags, splashed her face, and met the others in the hall. They all agreed to get a bite to eat.

Outside, the square was dimly lit at dusk. They walked to the cafe-bar at the corner leaked music through its seams. A neon beer sign blinked in a rhythm that could have been Morse code for "don't look too close."

"Ronnie's place," Stanley said, reading the hand-lettered chalk-board. "The special is meatloaf."

"Sold," Myrtle said. "If I die tonight, let it be cradled by gravy."

The bell above the door announced their arrival. The room was low-ceilinged, paneled in wood gone honey-dark with smoke and time. Four booths hugged the windows and a scatter of tables faced the bar. Men on stools swiveled to see who had wandered in and then, finding no one they knew, rotated back.

A tall man with a red apron and a dish towel like a shoulder sash grinned at them from behind the counter. "You must be the Hollow's Rest folks. Doris said to look out for the hungry."

"That would be us," Myrtle said. "Are you Ronnie?"

"Depending on who's asking. Our menu's simple. Meatloaf, catfish, burger, grilled cheese, and pie if you've been kind to your elders."

"We've been kind," Denise said, with the bright certainty of someone who believed kindness multiplied desserts.

They took a booth. The vinyl had lost its fight with gravity and made a small bowl beneath Myrtle. She adjusted, trying not to sink completely. Stanley ordered a beer, and Myrtle her usual Chardonnay with a cup of ice. Whitney and Denise splurged with a sparkling water. Whitney picked the catfish "because it sounds brave," and Denise orderd a grilled cheese. Stanley chose the meatloaf special with fries. Myrtle chose the same, with extra gravy and potato salad.

They had been there just long enough for the clink of flatware to settle when a shadow fell across the table. A man in a pink button-down and a navy blazer stood with a glass of bourbon poised just below his smile.

"Tony Matthews," he said. "Reporter. And no, I'm not here to write about your meatloaf choices."

"Pity," Myrtle said. "It deserves a column."

Tony's grin widened. He slid into the empty end of the booth as though he'd been invited. "You're not from around here, which means you're interesting, which also means I'm nosy." He tapped his glass against Stanley's beer with a polite, apologetic clink. "Are you passing through?"

"Just tonight," Stanley said. "We made a detour. Which also means we got lost."

Tony tilted his head, considering the fog pressing at the windows. "Folks don't usually detour into Bog Hollow."

"Then we're trendsetters," Myrtle said. "What are you reporting on?"

"Depends on who's asking," he echoed Ronnie, amused. "Officially? A piece on rural decline. Unofficially?" He lowered his voice. "There have been a string of disappearances. People go missing anywhere, that's true. But here, there's a pattern. Most go missing on Saturdays. Mostly women. A few found later—near water, or where the ground gives way." He sipped his whiskey, not for courage but to wet the words. "Some are not found at all."

Whitney stopped folding and unfolding her napkin. "Why Saturdays?"

Tony spread his hands. "If I knew that, I'd have a better article. There's a story they tell, that the town has a bride who never got to the altar. She wanders on Saturdays, looking for someone to walk with. To keep her company." He paused, gauging their faces. "I don't print ghosts. I print people who use stories like that to do bad things in the dark."

"That's comforting," Myrtle said. "In a narrow, awful way."

Heads turned to the sound of the entrance door bell jingling. A woman walked in like she owned the air itself. She wore a cream silk blouse tucked into black slacks, with hair glossy and black, and lips painted traffic-light red. The bar's mirror doubled her in a way that felt like a magic trick.

Tony watched Myrtle watching the woman. "That's Francine," he said. "The sheriff's niece."

"Oh," Myrtle said.

Tony's voice dropped. "Her sister, Justine, died last month. They found her near the river. Francine moved here after, and whatever you think of her, she looks after her own."

Francine slid onto a barstool and crossed her legs. Men at the bar made small adjustments—a straightened spine here, a hand smoothed down hair there. Ronnie poured her a glass of red without being asked. She lifted it, met Ronnie's gaze, and smiled.

"Is the sheriff glad she's here?" Myrtle asked.

Tony's mouth quirked. "The sheriff approves of order. Francine approves of being left alone. Their Venn diagram overlaps in a shape that makes men behave in public. That's worth something."

Ronnie delivered plates to their table: meatloaf with thick brown gravy, catfish crisped to gold, and a grilled cheese oozing respectably. The drinks arrived with it. Myrtle spooned some ice into her glass and took a deep sip. Then, she forked into the meat and gravy and felt the world recalibrate.

Francine slid off her stool and drifted their way like perfume. "You must be Doris's travelers," she said in a voice that stroked syllables. Up close, the cream blouse had a faint sheen, like well-kept secrets. "I'm Francine. Welcome to Bog Hollow. Eat, sleep, leave early."

"What happens if we stay late?" Myrtle asked.

Francine's smile sharpened. "I wouldn't advise it." She set her glass on their table without asking. "Although, Walter's preaching in the morning," she said to Whitney, as if concluding a conversation. "You should come. He makes the Good Book sound like it learned to dance."

"Walter?" Whitney repeated.

"Chester and Doris's boy," Francine said, taking her glass back. "You met his parents at the hotel. They'll be thrilled if you fill a pew." She leaned forward and rested a hand on the table. "Try the pie. Ronnie's grandmother taught him how to make crust."

She moved on, leaving the table's center warmer by a degree. Whitney watched her go with an expression that mixed admiration and caution. "She's something."

"Expensive," Myrtle said lightly.

A new presence bulked out the doorway's frame. Sheriff Dudley stepped inside, and the room adjusted around him almost imperceptibly: conversations shortened, and bottle labels became interesting. He nodded to Ronnie and to Tony. Francine returned his nod with her lips curled in a secret smile.

Dudley spotted Myrtle's booth and approached with the grim cheerfulness of a man doing exactly what he expected to be doing. "Evening," he said. "Is the food all right?"

"Better than all right," Myrtle said. "My meatloaf and I are eloping."

"You'll need the preacher to bless it," Dudley said, half an eye on Whitney, who had the unfortunate habit of shining like a light-house. "Walter would oblige." He accepted the coffee Ronnie slid into his hand. The steam smelled faintly of something stronger than just caffeine.

Tony tapped his glass for a refill. "Sheriff, are you ever going to let me see your case notes?"

"On which case?" Dudley asked mildly. "I've got chickens goin' missing and a woman who swears her neighbor stole her azaleas."

"The Saturday kind," Tony said softly.

Dudley didn't flinch. "I read my Bible on Saturdays."

"Do you read it by the river?" Tony asked.

Dudley looked at Myrtle as if the question had passed through Tony and parked in her lap. "You're not staying long, right?"

"Just the night," Myrtle said.

"Good," Dudley said again, which was beginning to feel like a mantra. "The fog's not friendly when it sinks. Folks step wrong. The ground's hollow under the fields with caves, and sinkholes. The town sits right on top of it. People forget the earth can open."

"Seems like the kind of thing you'd remember," Myrtle said.

"Seems like lots of things," Dudley said, and moved on, carrying his coffee to the far end of the bar where he could watch the door and the mirror at the same time.

Whitney had been quiet, which meant her mind was busy. She leaned toward Myrtle. "He knows more than he says."

"He's a sheriff," Myrtle said. "If he didn't know more than he said, he'd be a pamphlet."

"Still," Whitney murmured. Her knee bounced under the table. "Do you think the bride story is just a story?"

Myrtle dragged a piece of bread through the gravy and considered. "Stories get made because something needs a name. Maybe there was a girl. Maybe there's just a place that eats people if they walk there on the wrong night."

Dessert arrived because Ronnie had a nose for customers who needed to be sweetened before they could be sent safely into the small-town dark. Pie was the kind of thing that made rumors travel slower. Myrtle took cherry and decided Ronnie's grandmother had indeed taught him how to make crust. Whitney went for pecan and closed her eyes on the first bite like a woman reconsidering her life choices. Denise claimed lemon meringue and made appreciative noises faintly inappropriate for a public place. Stanley ordered another beer.

Tony excused himself on the pretext of interviews and slid to the bar where his notebook waited like a polite dog. He wrote in spurts, looking up now and then to catch mirror reflections: Dudley's steady vantage; Francine's smooth orbit; Ronnie's efficient choreography. Myrtle watched him watch, filing away the fact that he noticed who watched whom.

Francine drifted back to them. "If you do go walking," she said casually, almost kindly, "don't go toward the river. The ground's bad. People who don't know better find trouble."

"We're not walking," Stanley said.

"Good," Francine said, smirking. She looked at Whitney. "And if someone invites you to see something, say no." Her smile made the words sound like flirtation. She left before anyone could argue.

Myrtle's group paid, more than the bill required, and stood a moment in the doorway as their eyes recalibrated to the square's dim light. Fog had settled back into the hollows; the church's steeple leaned as if spying. Across the street, the cemetery's stones were silhouettes against a thicker dark.

"Let's get to bed," Stanley said, his voice taking charge in the way fatigue makes authority feel like mercy.

As they crossed the street, Tony fell into step with Myrtle, congenial as a stray cat. "Did you catch it?" he asked without hello.

"Catch what?"

"The way Francine warned your friend without scaring her. That's a skill. Either she knows something or she's guessed something. Both are useful."

Myrtle looked straight ahead. "Do you write your stories to protect people or to sell papers?"

Tony's grin was brief and honest. "Both, if I'm lucky. But

tonight?" He looked at the cemetery, then the church. "I'll settle for everyone waking up." With a nod of his head, he excused himself and turned back towards the way he came.

They reached the hotel. Doris was just locking the front door with the practice of habit. "Evening," she said. "Morning comes earlier here than you think."

"Does it?" Myrtle asked.

Doris's smile held. "If you're lucky." She slipped the bolt with a soft, inevitable sound.

Upstairs, Myrtle found her room and opened the door. Her room smelled faintly of lemon cleaner and something older beneath it, like dried roses forgotten between dictionary pages. Myrtle set her bag on the chair, toed off her shoes, and stood in the middle of the room listening to the building breathe.

A floorboard popped somewhere. Pipes clicked. A television set in another room murmured itself toward sleep. When Myrtle turned out her light, the darkness settled fast, as if it had been waiting in the corners for permission.

From the hall came a soft sound of one step on the carpet, then another, and then silence. Myrtle imagined it was Stanley doing a last perimeter check like a man whose bravery could be measured in door bolts. She almost said goodnight through the door, then didn't. It seemed unfair to reward paranoia.

She slid between cool sheets and closed her eyes. The meatloaf weighed her pleasantly down. Myrtle slept and dreamed of lace snagging on limestone, of a hand raised palm-up, of a voice she could almost hear that spoke a word she did not know.

Sleep came in slices. First the slice of exhaustion, heavy and generous. Then the slice of doubt, thin and sharp, reminding her that the sheriff had said 'Good' like a warning. She dreamed of women in white, of flowers pressed into damp earth, of a hand raised palm-out in greeting that turned into a hand raised in farewell.

A knocking came and split her sleep like an axe.

"Myrtle!" Denise's voice was high and frantic. "Myrtle, wake up!"

Myrtle swung her legs out of bed, and shuffled to the door, and cracked it open. Denise stood there, eyes wide, hair a tangle of panic. "Whitney's missing."

Myrtle rubbed her eyes and formed her words with a voice still thick with sleep. "She's not a set of car keys, Denise. Missing is a strong word."

"She left after we came back," Denise said, her words tumbling out. "She said she was going to meet someone. She wouldn't say who. I thought she was joking. But her bed hasn't been slept in."

Stanley appeared from his room barefoot, with his shirt half buttoned, and a loose belt. "What's going on?"

"Whitney," Myrtle said, more awake with every syllable. "Our girl's gone wandering."

Denise wrung her hands. "What if it's the stories? The bride? Tony said Saturdays, and it's Saturday now, and…"

"Enough," Myrtle said. Her voice, sharp and clean, carved through Denise's panic. "We'll find her. She hasn't gone far. Myrtle Fairchild doesn't lose people in haunted hotels."

After throwing some clothes on, Myrtle stepped into the hall, the carpet runner muffling her stride. The building was quieter than it had been earlier, as if the night had convinced it to hold its breath. Myrtle descended the stairs, with her companions following like uncertain shadows.

The lobby was empty, though a lamp burned behind the desk. Myrtle struck the bell again. Its clang rang sharp and lonely. After a moment, Chester appeared. His hair was mussed and his suspenders hung like question marks. "Is everything all right?"

"No," Myrtle said. "Whitney's gone missing. Have you seen her?"

Chester blinked. "At this hour? No. Folks don't walk at night. There's too much fog, and too many hollows." He looked at Doris, who had slipped in behind him like an afterthought. Her mouth made a small shape that might have been sympathy or surprise. "I'll check outside."

Myrtle nodded. "Let's all do that."

They stepped onto the square. Fog had settled heavy and low, thick enough to make the gaslights bleed halos. The post office across the way was a blur. The church steeple leaned, still listening. The cemetery beyond was swallowed whole.

"She could be anywhere," Denise whispered. "She could be..."

"Hush," Myrtle said. "Panic helps no one."

A figure approached through the fog. Tony, with his notebook under one arm, and shirt collar open as if he had been writing instead of sleeping. "I heard voices. What's happened?"

"Whitney," Stanley said. "She's gone."

Tony's jaw tightened. "Then she's either with someone or she's in trouble." He glanced at Myrtle, as though confirming she would not accept those as separate. "We should wake the sheriff."

As if conjured up, headlights swept the square. Dudley's truck rolled to a stop. Its engine was low and steady. He climbed out, his coffee thermos was in hand, as though midnight calls were his routine. "What's all this?"

"Whitney's missing," Myrtle said with no frills or pleasantries. "We need your help."

Dudley studied them with the stillness of a man who disliked surprises but expected them all the same. He took a slow sip from his thermos, and nodded. "All right. Where'd she go last you saw?"

"Upstairs," Denise said. "Then she left. She said she was meeting someone, but she wouldn't say who."

"Did she take anything?" Dudley asked.

Denise shook her head. "Just her jacket."

The sheriff's gaze drifted toward the church, and then the cemetery. "If she went walking, there are places she might've gone. Like the river, or the old quarry. Or the graveyard."

"Places where brides walk," Tony murmured.

Dudley shot him a look sharp enough to pin him. "Places where ground gives way. Don't put it on ghosts when the land itself is dangerous."

But Myrtle caught the way his eyes lingered on the fog as if measuring its thickness. He knew the stories. He might not believe them, but he carried them. She filed that away with everything else.

"Let's go," Dudley said finally. "If she's out there, she won't last long in this fog."

Myrtle straightened her shoulders. "Then we won't, either." She stepped into the square. The fog curled around her ankles like a cat, as she started walking.

The fog thickened. Sheriff Dudley led with a lantern he had fetched from his truck. Its light sliced through the mist in narrow strokes. Stanley kept close to Denise, whose eyes darted like a sparrow's. Tony scribbled notes when the lantern swung its beam back and forth.

Myrtle brought up the rear. Her eyes and ears were sharper than she wanted to admit. Every drip from an eaves, every whisper of leaves, every shuffle of gravel underfoot seemed magnified. "This is ridiculous," she muttered.

But beneath the complaint was worry she didn't voice. Whitney might be flighty, but she was not careless, not this careless.

They passed the church. Its white paint was peeling in scales, its door chained shut with a padlock thick as a fist. Myrtle slowed, glancing at the shadowed porch. For a heartbeat she thought she saw movement there, a flicker of white, but when she looked again the porch was bare.

The cemetery gate gaped open ahead, its iron teeth rusted and bent. Dudley pushed it with one hand, causing the hinges to cry out. "Stay close," he said. "The ground's uneven."

They stepped among stones that leaned and slumped, with names that had eroded into anonymity. Fog pooled between them like water. Myrtle felt the air temp drop cooler. Denise clutched Stanley's arm with both hands. Tony swung his notebook like it was a charm against bad luck.

"Whitney!" Dudley called, his voice was low but firm. It didn't echo. The fog swallowed sound as greedily as it swallowed light.

"Over there," Myrtle said suddenly. A fresh depression marked the earth between two locust trees. Not new enough to be a grave, and not old enough to be natural. She crouched, pressed her hand to the soil. It was damp and loose. "Something's been disturbed here."

Dudley joined her and lifted his lantern. His jaw tightened. "Sinkholes. We get them."

"That's convenient," Myrtle said. "Too convenient."

A whisper rose like a woman's voice, faint and melodic. Denise gasped. Her grip tightened on Stanley.

Myrtle's skin prickled. "Tell me you heard that," she said.

"I heard wind," Dudley said flatly. But his hand went to the butt of his pistol, a gesture he probably didn't know he'd made.

The voice came again, closer this time, unmistakable. Dudley swung the lantern beam toward the sound. For an instant the fog cleared, and there she was: a woman in white, her veil was trailing and flowers were woven through her long black hair. Her eyes were dark pools that caught the lantern glow without returning it. She raised her hand, palm up, in silent greeting.

Denise whimpered. Stanley muttered something that might have been a prayer. Tony's pencil scratched furiously.

The figure drifted back, swallowed by mist. The voice lingered like perfume before the silence.

Myrtle let out the breath she'd been holding. "That wasn't wind."

Dudley lowered the lantern. "The land plays tricks. You hear what you expect."

"Then I expect coffee in the morning," Myrtle snapped. "Let's see if that appears out of thin air, too."

They moved deeper into the graveyard. Myrtle scanned every shadow, every hollow, and every stone that might hide her friend or a ghost. Near the far wall, the fog thinned enough to reveal footprints in the damp grass. They were small and led away from the cemetery toward the woods.

"Whitney," Denise whispered. "She was here."

Dudley crouched to examine the prints. His mouth pressed thin. "It could be."

"Not could be," Myrtle said. "Was. And she wasn't alone." Beside the small prints were larger ones. Myrtle looked at Dudley.

His eyes flickered. "Stay together," he said. "We'll follow them."

The prints guided them toward the river's edge where the

ground sagged and sucked underfoot. The fog roiled thicker, and was heavy with the smell of wet stone and moss. Myrtle felt the hair rise on her neck. Somewhere ahead, faint but clear, came the sound of water, and beneath it, the echo of laughter, low and wrong.

It was Whitney's laughter.

Pressed deep into the mud, the footprints ended at the bank. Whitney's smaller prints vanished at the edge of the water, as though she had stepped straight in.

Denise cried out, clapping a hand over her mouth. Stanley wrapped an arm around her, steadying them both. "She wouldn't. She can't swim," Denise gasped.

"Then she didn't go in," Myrtle said firmly. "Not without help." She pointed with her chin at the second set of large prints, circling back. "Someone was here with her. They led her away, not into the river."

Tony scribbled furiously, the page trembling beneath his hand. "Which means she's alive. Which means someone is using the bride's legend as cover."

"Quiet," Dudley said, though the command seemed aimed more at his own thoughts than theirs. His eyes scanned the fog. "The tracks lead east. Toward the old quarry."

The soft, hollow ground grew treacherous as they followed. Myrtle felt it shift like an untrustworthy mattress. Fog closed around them again, heavier, and damp against her skin. Then came the voice, Whitney's voice, calling from ahead.

"Here! Over here!"

Denise surged forward, but Dudley caught her arm. "Voices travel in fog. We move together."

They climbed a ridge where the earth fell away sharply into the black mouth of a quarry. The lantern light caught pale limestone walls and water pooled at the bottom, dark as oil. On the lip of the quarry stood a bride. Her white dress stirred though there was no wind. Her trailing veil was adorned with fresh flowers as if plucked minutes ago. She lifted her face toward them, and Myrtle gasped.

It was Francine.

Whitney stood beside her.

Denise sobbed. Stanley cursed under his breath. Tony dropped his pencil. Dudley raised the lantern higher, and for a moment the fog parted. Whitney's expression was vacant, her eyes were glassy, and her hand clasped the bride's as if tethered.

"Whitney!" Myrtle shouted. Her voice cracked the stillness. "Come back this instant!"

The bride's head turned slowly toward Myrtle. She felt the weight of that gaze, deep and endless, like falling into water when you couldn't swim. The bride raised her hand, with palm up. It was the same gesture Whitney had described. A greeting. A farewell.

Whitney took a step closer to the edge.

"No," Myrtle snapped and marched forward. "You do not take girls out of hotels and walk them over cliffs. You do not get to make a story out of my friend."

The bride's smile was small and sorrowful. The fog thickened, pulling around her like curtains. Whitney swayed, caught between one world and another. Myrtle reached out, grabbed her wrist, and yanked.

The fog screamed. Not wind, not stone, but the fog itself. The bride vanished in a rush of white, dissolving like lace consumed by fire. Whitney collapsed into Myrtle's arms, limp but breathing, with her eyes fluttering. "I saw the bride," she whispered. "She wanted me to go with her. She said she'd never be alone again."

"Not tonight," Myrtle said with a rough voice. "You're coming with us."

Dudley's face was pale in the lantern light. "The quarry's dangerous," he muttered. "Fog plays tricks. We'd best get back."

"Tricks don't hold hands," Myrtle said sharply. She searched his eyes, but he gave nothing back. Still, she saw the truth in the tension of his jaw. Dudley knew more than he would ever admit. Maybe the whole town did.

They made their way back in silence. Whitney leaned against Stanley and Denise whispered prayers under her breath. The square was empty when they returned. Doris had left the lamp burning in the hotel window, a soft beacon against the dark.

By morning, the fog had lifted, though dampness clung to every surface. Whitney had slept heavily and had color back in her cheeks. Denise hovered beside her, unwilling to let go. Myrtle packed with deliberate efficiency. She had no intention of lingering.

Chester and Doris stood at the desk as they checked out. Doris's smile was warm but strained. "I hope you slept well."

"We'll manage," Myrtle said. She laid the brass key down. "Thank you for the roof."

Outside, Tony leaned against their van with his notebook under his arm.

"You'll write this up?" Myrtle asked.

"Pieces of it," he said. "Not all of it. Some stories aren't mine to tell."

"Make sure the right people know," Myrtle said. "Even if the wrong ones never will."

He nodded, serious for once. "Safe travels."

Sheriff Dudley was nowhere to be seen, but Myrtle felt his absence like a shadow. As Stanley started the van, Myrtle glanced back one last time. The church leaned, the cemetery sloped, and the hotel loomed tired and watchful. And at the far edge of town there was fog, just before it broke into daylight. Myrtle thought she saw a woman in white, lifting her hand.

Myrtle faced forward. "Drive," she said. "And if this GPS says turn onto another dirt road, I'm throwing it out the window."

The van rolled out of Bog Hollow, carrying its passengers toward highways and sunlight, leaving the bride to wait for another Saturday.

The Ghost in Room 17

R. H. Riffenburgh

Hal, an accomplished and busy engineer, arrived in town on business. "I need a room for two nights, please," he said to the hotel desk clerk.

"I'm so sorry, sir, but we're fully booked."

"All the hotels in town seem to be booked. Don't you have some space somewhere that I can lay my weary head?"

"Well … there's room 17, but you wouldn't want that."

"And why wouldn't I want room 17?"

"Well … a chap died in there a couple years ago. Customers say it is haunted by his ghost and they hear moaning in the middle of the night. They always leave it in a hurry, some still in their night-clothes."

"I'm a rational man. Ghosts don't exist. There has to be a physical explanation for the sounds. I'll take it."

"Are you very sure, sir? I don't advise it."

"Thanks for your advice, but, yes, I'm very sure. Please give me the key. I'm bushed and need some sleep."

* * *

Hal was asleep two minutes after his head hit the pillow. He slept deeply for several hours before something awakened him. He turned onto his back, stared into the dark, and listened. A moan. That was the only word to describe it: a sad-sounding moan.

He snapped on the light and got out of bed. He heard it again. Hmm. Just like the desk clerk said.

Now fully energized, he turned on all the lights and stood in the middle of the room, listening. There it was again over in the corner.

He walked to it and stood listening. It came again. He knelt, looked closely, and saw a small gap in the baseboard. Placing his hand by the gap, he felt cold air. "Ah ha," he chortled.

He pulled an undershirt from his suitcase, twisted its edge into a point, and worked it down into the gap. Sitting back, he clasped his hands and waited. Five minutes. No moan. Ten minutes. No moan. After fifteen minutes, satisfied, he went back to bed and slept peacefully, uninterrupted by "moans."

* * *

In the morning, Hal told the clerk on duty about what he had found. "You see, the 'moan' is the whistle of the wind when it blows across the little hole at just the right angle at just the right speed. Sort of like when you blow across the top of a jug. It makes a whistle or wail, depending on how much volume there is in the jug. That's your ghost."

* * *

The night desk clerk was back on duty at dinner time. The hotel maintenance worker punched out his time card as he left work for the day.

"Hey, Brian," the desk clerk said, "did you get to the hole in the wall in room 17?"

"Yeah, I did. It's all sealed and plastered and painted. There ain't no way even a breath of air is gonna get through there in my lifetime."

* * *

Hal returned to room 17 late in the evening, exhausted from his long work day. He put on pajamas and rolled into bed without even hanging up his clothes. He had just turned off his light when he heard the moan. It was louder and more persistent than last night. But he knew what caused it. "Silly, superstitious people," he muttered to himself, smiled, and drifted off to sleep.

A Second Chance

Deb Miller

In the summer twilight of the New Orleans French Quarter, an unseen saxophone serenaded a deserted street of closed stores. Two strolling window shoppers were the only ones to hear its sorrowful tune. The couple stopped briefly to examine the exhibit of clocks in a shop window and then continued their journey towards Bourbon Street.

Three minutes later, a battered Ford pickup pulled to the curb in front of the same modest clock store. Its headlights flicked off and the driver's door creaked open. Getting out, a greasy-haired workman in soiled jeans, a sweat-stained T-shirt, and a fluorescent yellow vest looked over the truck roof at the dark store.

After searching the Internet on his phone for the store's website, he punched the phone number into his cellphone. Faint ringing came from inside the store until he heard a voice message app ask him to leave a message. Hanging up, he redialed the number. The store's phone rang again. Looking at the brick building's second-floor windows, he noticed residential curtains.

Reaching into his truck's interior, he pushed a long blast on the horn. "Answer your freaking phone!"

The voicemail message started again. Growling, he slapped the top of his pickup's roof and immediately shook his hand in pain.

His wife was going to snap at him like a furious alligator. Their daughter's wedding was tomorrow, and he'd promised that morning to pick up the anniversary clock she'd ordered as their gift. It wasn't like he'd intentionally forgotten. Work preoccupied his mind until he was halfway home. He'd driven straight here once he remembered. It wasn't his fault they were closed. Well, to hell with her. He was in no mood for her scorn.

Starting the pickup, he stomped on the accelerator and brake. Squealing tires drowned out the saxophone. Continuously smashing both pedals, he tortured the asphalt until smoke rose from it. At the same time, he roared his frustration in an outburst of insane howling. Finally, wearing the devil's own sneer, he released the brake and raced through the Quarter's streets, determined to get to Al's Tap as fast as he could. There he'd get a well-earned bottle of Heineken among friends and let the viper stew in her own venom.

Tapu was aware of the enraged customer in front of his clock store. He didn't need security cameras to tell him. The excessive noise from the man was enough. But even better than that, as a shaman, he could examine a person's heart. The man's emotional pain filled Tapu with sympathy.

Had he not been in the middle of a ritual in the backroom, he'd have answered the phone and given the husband his clock. The husband's heart was a good one, but anyone can become overwhelmed by life. The poor fellow was in the mood to take rash action. Now Tapu'd have to rush the ceremony and try to deliver the wedding gift before the husband made his situation even worse.

Quickly he reached for a powerful dried root. No, such an impulse was wrong. Guilt stopped his hasty action. He was dealing with a dead soldier's regret. One who had been courageous, and also a good man. Respect was called for as he performed the ceremony. He must honor the man with a reverent ritual.

But what about the father-to-be? The fellow needed his intervention, too. He'd have to think of some way to fix the wedding gift crisis and keep their daughter's wedding day from becoming a parental divorce trigger.

The workshop behind the clock store was as dim as a room with a night-light. Behind Tapu rose floor-to-ceiling shelves. They contained an assortment of clocks and watches of all ages and in various conditions of working order. All of them needed repair and attention. To the right and left of Tapu, there were two walls with benches and cupboards. The right one held tools and clock parts, and the left wall held ingredients for shaman magic rituals. The fourth wall exhibited a simple bedroom-sized window decorated with a dingy flowered curtain.

On the right and left benches, a fat candle burned on each. Upon a six by four foot rectangular table in the center of the room sat a soccer ball sized cast-iron cauldron glowing with the light of a small fire.

Tapu stood before the cauldron with a wristwatch in his left hand and a pinch of dried plant roots in his right. While gently blowing on the fire, he sprinkled the roots onto it. When a wispy white smoke curled upward, he passed the wristwatch back and forth, cutting through it.

"Do you feel thicker? More dense?" he asked the ghostly soldier before him. Tapu could still see through the man in an Army E2 dress blue uniform.

The ghost nodded.

"Good. You talk to me. I tell you when I hear you. Okay?"

He waved the watch through the smoke repeatedly, each time assessing the solidness of the dead man. After a few more passes, he heard, "… see my baby." It was so faint Tapu missed hearing the first part of the soldier's words.

But what little he'd heard was enough to know the phantom's need. Why it had stayed after death. He yearned to see an infant before moving on into eternity.

Experience had taught Tapu it was rarely the elderly who became ghosts. Actually, he didn't know that for sure, but he'd never met one. In his experience, it was always the young. They often had unfinished business or were passionate about making amends. Sometimes there was a fiancée to say goodbye to and sometimes a family relationship they wanted to mend. The dead had painful yet simple, common desires. Which meant he could usually help them.

Reading the name badge and insignia on the uniform, Tapu said, "Private Taylor, you die in Afghanistan or in US?"

Taylor's voice was faint, but Tapu could tell from lip movement that he said Afghanistan.

"I sorry, Private Taylor. I can give you last twenty-four hours of your life. Yes. But it be in Afghanistan., not in America. Do you know? Will US Army fly you home to see baby? If no, you no see baby before death."

The phantom's expression reflected both disappointment and anger.

"If you no want to continue ritual, I stop now. You go. Fly away now to future place."

Taylor pointed to the wristwatch in Tapu's hand. His volume was that of a whisper. "Does it work?"

"Yes. If no continue ritual, I give to sad lady who brought it for repair. Your widow, yes? But if we finish ritual, it be on you wrist for living of last day."

Taylor words sounded as if he were underwater. "If I end up back in Afghanistan, I'll deal with it." The specter looked at the ceiling and struggled to keep his composure and lost. Tears ran down his face. "I must see my baby son." After another moment of sorrow, his posture came to attention. His face instantly controlled and absent of tears. "I'll go to my commander and request an emergency video conference. I'll make up some excuse. Offer to run an errand. Whatever it takes. I must see my baby before going on patrol. My final patrol."

"Okay," Tapu said. "You know Earth rotates, yes?"

The ghost looked annoyed.

Tapu continued, "No one die alone. Spirits of universe life energy, notice when anything die. Even if bugs die, they sad. Understand?"

"They remember Mother Earth's position in solar system and universe. My prayer to life spirits will be for you to relive you last full rotation of Earth." Tapu pointed to the side of his own head. "Your ghost mind will start last day. Your ghost mind will remember all. Remember life as ghost, too. Understand?"

The soldier looked puzzled, but he nodded.

Even if Taylor didn't understand now, it would become clear to him when he began his do-over day.

Tapu blew on the fire and dropped more dried roots into the little cauldron. The coals were nearly out, and the roots failed to catch. Scooping up more twigs and dried moss, he puffed and fed the coals until the white fragrant smoke reappeared. Once again, he waved the wristwatch back and forth through the magical smoke. Looking up from time to time, he could see Taylor's uniform morphing from his burial attire to his combat uniform.

Deciding the magic was strong enough, he said, "Please, touch watch now. Then last day starts. You will have free will. Understand free will? You do what you can do. What US Army let you do. Understand? I not guarantee you see baby."

With a quick nod, Private Taylor saluted him, touched the watch, and both winked out.

Tapu's part of the do-over day was complete. From now on, the actual results were up to Private Taylor.

Walking to the wall switch, Tapu flipped the ceiling light on. He quickly blew out the candles and put the cauldron into its fireproof box. Lack of air would snuff the unburnt embers out. Such coals were too precious to waste.

The ingredients for his ceremonies came from his childhood home in the Amazon basin. For generations, his family had produced healers. His maternal grandfather and elderly mother were the current shamans of his tribe. Each had their own physically challenging routes through the jungle to the various villages. On their journeys to heal and perform ceremonies, they each led about an apprentice who learned to gather the rare ingredients that went into the magic potions and medicines. Because they were rare, Tapu tried to use as few of the ritual ingredients as possible.

A clamor of bells, chimes, chirps and music box tunes shattered the silence. From the store's salesroom, every grandfather clock, cuckoo clock, musical and dancing timepiece produced pandemonium. What time was it? Oh, no! Could he still get the wedding gift to Al's Tap before an inebriated father-of-the-bride left in his pickup?

Hurrying to the salesroom, Tapu retrieved the anniversary clock from under the checkout counter, gift-wrapped it, and smiled. To him the result was a work of art. Returning to his workshop, he sat cross-legged on the floor, and took a tiny sip of one of his potions. Astral projection was fairly easy for those with a shaman's aptitude. Since he was five years old, he'd enjoyed exploring the Amazon with out-of-body experiences.

Breathing deeply and slowly, his mind expanded outside into the night. Seeking the father-of-the-bride's heart, he jumped his spectral attention to the souls in Al's Tap. Gently, he touched each one until he found the father. His spirit was fully engaged with a cluster of friends. Tapu could feel that the man was happy now and going to be settled there for a while.

Despite sneaking the wedding gift into the fellow's Ford truck, the man was probably still going to be flailed by his wife for being out so late. Ah, well. Tapu could only help the foolish so much. Unwise behavior, such as staying at the bar too long, usually leads to painful results.

Since there was no need for haste, he stayed within the speed limit as he drove over to Al's Tap, broke into the father's pickup truck, and placed the wedding gift on the floor of the passenger side.

Breaking into vehicles wasn't a shaman tradition. He'd learned that skill in boarding school. His tribe's teenagers attended middle and high school in a large town hundreds of miles downriver from their tribal lands. Fortunately, his top grades in school led him to a college opportunity in America and not a life of petty crime in Brazil.

After delivering the wedding gift, he settled into his living room recliner to watch an episode of 'Grande Sertao: Veredas'. The mini-series was as close to his beloved Amazon River as he'd get for a long while. Maybe forever. True, he loved New Orleans. It was his home, and his life was good because of his mildly profitable store. Still, Brazilian entertainment filled an empty place in his heart. Who knew that Brazilian TV and movies were available in America on Amazon Prime?

***

Four weeks later, a muscular ghost wearing a dark blue suit walked in with a thirty-something-aged woman leading along three children, ages between six and ten. Except for the ghost, everyone was wearing T-shirts and shorts. Tapu noticed the kids were empty-handed. No texting or playing games on their phones.

"Do you buy pocket watches?" the woman asked. Her demeanor suggested she expected Tapu to say no.

"Yes, please may I see it?"

While she dug in her purse, Tapu noticed the ghost drifting around the store examining the clocks. He ignored his children and wife.

"Here," the woman said, then noticed Tapu's attention was distracted. "You kids, don't be touching stuff."

Tapu took the pocket watch and said, "Children okay." Looking back at them, he added, "I see they no have cell phones."

Her face reddened. "It isn't against the law, is it?"

"Sorry," said Tapu. "Just curious. Most children on phones all the time."

With a sarcastic laugh, the mother said, "Ha. Yeah, they used to. Can't afford them no more since their father died. How much will you give me for the watch? We don't need charity, but I need you to be fair with me."

"I can buy you watch. I give good price."

The woman's mood became calm. "How much?"

"One hundred dollars. Okay?"

She opened her mouth to say something, then stopped and looked down at him. Most Americans were taller, and towering over him often led them to behavior that dismissed him as a child. In this case, her expression became sly. Moving her eyes up and down his body, he felt her assess his intelligence.

"That's outrageous. It's worth two hundred dollars."

Since leaving Brazil, he had been used to being dismissed as subhuman. His thin, brown, indigenous stature considered unworthy of respect. Despite wanting to help her financially, he would need to do it in such a way as to prevent her from offending the life spirits. That could lead her toward some type of punishment by them. Better to risk offending her pride with charity.

"I think it valued $50 new, yes?" This let her know he knew its approximate value.

The woman looked at her children, Tapu felt her attitude change to one of concern. Turning her attention back to him, her expression hardened.

She needed money, and she was going to lie to get it. Why did she think charity was bad? But cheating him was okay. Americans were crazy people.

Before she could speak, Tapu said, "You no want charity, yes? Pawn shop two blocks away. Later, when things are better, you can buy watch back. Okay? Watch can be collateral, yes? Like loan, like business, understand?"

Her appearance didn't change, but he could feel her hostility flare. "I'm not going to any thieving pawnshop. It's an antique worth well over two hundred dollars."

Her antique assertion saddened him, but he understood why she was lying. She was angry that she had to accept charity from a little brown man. Swindling him was her way of maintaining her self-respect.

Fine. It didn't matter. Actually, it did. It hurt. But he was going to be merciful. She was never coming back for her husband's piece of junk pocket watch. Because he knew the true value of the timepiece, a pawnbroker deal should satisfy the life spirits that his transaction was charity. She was not cheating him, even if she thought she was.

"Okay, I be like pawnshop for you. Come to counter. We write two-hundred-dollar deal, yes?"

Pen in hand, he asked, "What you husband name?"

"He went by Butch, but his real name was Terrance Robineau." She shook her head. "He thought Terry was a sissy name, then the fool named our oldest, Terrance Robineau, Junior. Go figure."

"Easy to figure. Husband love son. His name claims son. You understand, yes?"

Olivia looked at Tapu in amazement. Like he'd said something profound. "Huh. I think you may be right."

Leaning over the bill-of-sale, he said, "I need you spell Terrance

Robineau. That a tough one."

She huffed and spelled it so slowly he knew she was ridiculing him.

"What you name?"

"Olivia Robineau. Do I have to spell that, too?"

"Yes, if you want to continue form. We quit if you don't want."

"Whatever. Keep going."

Under the glare of her displeasure, he pressed on through the rest of the bill-of-sale. Finished, he held the pen out to her. She scribbled a mess that was supposed to be her signature.

After that, he held out $250 in small denominations.

Olivia took the cash without counting it. "You kids stop messing with the music box. It's time to head to the bus stop."

Tapu waved his hand. "Good luck." Then in a whisper he said, "Butch, you stay."

Almost at the shop door, Olivia turned around. "What?"

"Have good lunch today."

"Sure," she said, and left.

After the front door closed, he said, "Come, Butch. I make you offer you not refuse." Looking at the ghost's empty expression, he knew his "Godfather" humor was lost on the man.

"Butch, you want to help family, yes?"

With a scowl, the ghost nodded.

"Family need money. Olivia know where you life insurance policy is, yes?"

Butch frowned.

"You have life insurance, yes?"

Butch shook his head.

Tapu sighed. "Never mind. The deal is I can make you live last day of life again. When you live again, you can help family, get money. Yes? Understand?

The dead man pursed his lips. Then he glided towards Tapu, speaking angry, silent words. The specter's manner was menacing. Tapu could tell Butch thought Tapu was being stubborn. Did he mistakenly think the shaman had the power to restore life for more than 24 hours?

"No get knickers in bunch," said Tapu. Then he added, "Do not hope for self. You die. Try help family. Understand?"

Butch swung at Tapu and punched at the nearby clocks. Every time his fists passed through. Despair crazed the man.

To calm the ghost and gain his cooperation, Tapu said, "I not sure. Maybe you not have to die. I never saw such a thing though." Tapu shrugged his shoulders. "Maybe you different? You go now. Follow family. Return this place tonight after store closes. We perform do-over ritual. Okay?"

The ghost winked out without a polite salutation.

Tapu sighed. That whole family very rude.

***

That evening, the shaman busied himself with gluing a chocolate-colored German cuckoo clock back together. It was owned by a woman who looked like Olive in the Popeye cartoons. The poor woman had been dusting all of her wall decorations when her favorite had fallen and broken into several pieces. Distraught at the damage, she'd come in that afternoon with redden eyes from crying. He assured her, he could make it like new.

When Butch arrived at sunset, Tapu was still working on it. He didn't bother looking up at the ghost towering over him from the center of the table. Why did this dead man have to be such a jerk?

"Please, Mr. Robineau, you get off my table now, okay? You disrespecting me."

Butch sank through the table and walked out of it.

Replacing the cuckoo clock with the cauldron, the shaman started the do-over ritual by lighting the cauldron and large fat candles with a camping lighter gun.

Butch cocked his head and one eyebrow while looking at the device.

"No need to do anything special to light ceremony fire." Spinning the igniter by its trigger guard, Tapu pretended to blow smoke from the end of his old west six shooter.

The ghost stared with a blank expression.

"Okay, I not funny. We get down to business."

Tapu turned off the ceiling light and began chanting to the life spirits. The cauldron fire grew stronger each time he added a magical ingredient. Passing Butch's pocket watch back and forth through the smoke, Butch thickened.

"You talk and I tell you when I hear you, okay? Tell me why you ghost? Why you stay and not go to eternal peace place? For children?"

Butch hesitated, then nodded and continued to talk with his volume on mute.

The ghost's hesitation told Tapu that Butch was not concerned about his family at all. His focus was only on himself. As a result, he'd had to think for a second about how he should answer the question. Tapu had seen the man's selfish heart earlier and hoped that by sending him off to follow his family around that day, his ambition would have changed to providing for them. It failed.

"I have idea for you help family financially. Do you want to hear?"

Butch shrugged.

"On do-over day, you go right away and buy term life insurance. Buy all you can. Policy voids if you do suicide? You no can do crime either? Understand?" After a pause, Tapu asked," How you die?"

Butch whispered, "A drunk driver hit my motorcycle."

"Ha! I hear you now. Good. I think you can buy lot of term insurance. You no wait. Go when agent office open, yes? Take much money, yes?"

Butch shook his head. "Don't have none. Bought a motorcycle off a guy that morning."

"You death day is do-over. Can do anything over. No buy motorcycle on do-over day. Okay? Buy term life insurance. Understand? Protect family, yes?"

Butch made the 'wrap it up' finger gesture while asking, "Are we about done here? When does my do-over start?"

"Please touch pocket watch."

The ghost snatched the watch, and both winked out.

***

Olivia's voice yelled down the hallway, "Get up! Now! Breakfast. If you're not ready in thirty minutes, I'm leaving without you. Got it? You'll be walking to Carols's again. I mean it. Get up!"

His wife's shouted words woke Butch with a jerk. His hand slapped a solid chest. A strong pull of air filled his lungs. "I'm alive!" Barking a laugh, he tossed off the bedsheet and ran down the hall to hug each of his kids, who were still in bed of course, and finally embraced and twirled Olivia around in the kitchen.

His wife tried to be angry and push him away, but he kissed her cheeks, her nose, her eyes and a long kiss on her mouth.

She laughed. "This isn't getting you out of the doghouse if you blow our savings on a motorcycle. We need new tires."

"Yes, yes," Butch said. "I'll buy you tires. I'll buy you that air conditioner. What else do you want?"

Suspicion reflected in her voice, she asked, "Were you gambling last night?"

"No. I've got a new gig. Down on Bourbon Street."

"You're lying. No one on Bourbon Street will ever hire you again."

"They have and I start tonight."

Olivia looked at the kitchen wall clock. "I've got to go. We're going to be short a waitress this morning, what with Heather out of town for a wedding."

Butch froze like a statue. The drunk who killed him. He was involved in a wedding.

"Butch. What's the matter? You don't look so good," Olivia said.

"I'm okay. You've got to go. I'll see you later."

Olivia kissed him and said, "Kids, grab your Pop-Tarts and get in the car."

Watching their Toyota SUV back out of the driveway, he decided he needed to get ready for the day ASAP. If he had only twenty-four hours from the time of his death, he'd wasted four hours of it in bed sleeping. It wasn't fair. It should have started with him awake, dressed, and ready to jump into action. Nope. Apparently, a do-over meant his day would start exactly as it had: in bed, sleeping.

Pressurized hot water spraying from the showerhead was glorious. Since becoming a ghost, he hadn't felt such amazing sensations of water beating on his head, his hair, his face, his torso. He didn't want it to stop. Yet he must, because now he was experiencing another fresh sensation: hunger.

After ten minutes before a sizzling skillet, he sat down to fried Spam, scrambled eggs, and two slices of cinnamon raisin toast. Feeling alive was something he'd never savored, and he was grateful for the chance to focus on it now.

Speaking of focus, he opened the notepad app on his cellphone to create a list. 'Pawn trumpet'. He'd lied to Olivia. He didn't have a gig on Bourbon Street, but he needed an excuse for leaving that night. Next item "buy gun." Maybe he could get that at the pawnshop, too. It would save time. Third item 'buy tires.' Maybe he'd do this first. Rather than ride the bus all over town today, if he had their car, his chores would be easier to do. "Buy air conditioner'." He'd put that in one of the living room windows.

And now, for the grand finale, item five, "Kill Jared Schmidt", the drunk driver who'd killed him. He could wait outside Al's Tap until closing. Jump out of the shadows and force him into the alley. Make him cry, beg for his life. He'd make him kneel. He'd tell the guy to open his mouth and suck the gun. Then he'd tell him who he was and pull the trigger. Yeah, that would be great.

Wait. Even better. Since he wanted the guy to know everything about the man he'd killed, first he'd spend the night buying the guy beers. He'd tell him stories about his childhood, love of music, and his children. He wanted the drunk to know exactly who he'd killed on the motorcycle.

What about buying life insurance like the little brown shaman wanted him to? Fine. If he had time. On his list, before killing Schmidt, he inserted 'buy life insurance.' There, now everyone should be happy.

What should he do after he shot his killer? Better drive their Toyota home so Olivia can get to work tomorrow. What then? He didn't know. There wouldn't be much time left until he died again.

A terrible thought occurred to him. The police would figure out who had bought the murder weapon if he had bought it from a pawnshop. They'd come straight to his home, and Olivia would know what he had done. It would horrify her. And his kids would experience shame and bullying. He'd have to think of something to keep that from happening.

Looking at the kitchen clock, he noted it was time to head to the bus stop.

An hour later, he had the car keys, and Olivia and he were standing outside the Village Inn front door. Butch held her in his arms and kissed her until an old couple pushed open the interior door to exit. Olivia pulled him out of the way of the exterior doors.

"Thank you," Olivia said.

She'd said it to Butch, but the old lady said, "You have a good day, too, Honey."

After the couple walked on, Butch held up the SUV's keys. "The next time you see this beater; it'll have four new tires."

"I've got to get back," she smiled and kissed his cheek.

Over her shoulder, a grotesque face peeked around the building corner. He jerked in shock. She turned to look. "What is it?"

"Nothing," he said and pecked her on the cheek. "I'll see you later."

As she went inside, the nightmare face peeked around the building again. Butch dashed after it, but there was no one there when he got to the corner. Feeling unsettled, he decided it was someone pulling a prank. Weird. It wasn't even close to Halloween.

Time to get hopping. After the tires were on the car, Butch paid for the most expensive air conditioner the big box store had. His family deserved the best. The checkout clerk directed him to pull around to the loading dock, and said a couple of guys would load it into his car for him.

While backing up, he could see two men in the warehouse's shadowed interior doorway. After popping open the car's back door, he got out and headed toward them. They were both wearing hoodies over their heads. The hands holding the air conditioner had scarlet skin with black hooked predator claws. Both turned with devilish faces to look at him. "There you go, sir."

Butch staggered back with a scream, tripped and fell onto his back.

"Are you okay?" They were normal-looking young men in their big box store uniforms. No hoodies or devil faces in sight.

"You were…" Butch stopped speaking. "Yes, I'm fine." They reached to help him off the ground. "Don't touch me!" he said, scrambling in a crab walk away from them. "I'm fine I said."

Alarmed and creeped out, he sped away. Two blocks later, he pulled into a fast-food parking lot until his shaking stopped. What the hell was going on? He'd never had hallucinations before. Even as a ghost. What was happening to him? Who would know? Maybe that shaman guy. Putting the Toyota in gear, he drove to the French Quarter.

Butch was surprised to see the shaman in the open doorway of the shop as he pulled to the curb in front of the clock store. "How did you know I was coming?"

Tapu answered, "Life spirits tell me. You come in, please. I make you café au lait. Okay? Then we talk."

Behind the workshop was Tapu's office in what had once been a break room. Butch watched the little gnome busy about getting down mugs, microwaving the milk, and brewing the coffee. On a dish, he set out powdered sugar covered beignets. Pointing to the mugs now containing café au lait, Tapu said, "Please, bring coffee."

Seated across the table from each other in the workshop, Tapu took a large swallow from his mug and nodded to Butch. "You drink. Is good."

Butch didn't feel like drinking anything. His stomach was churning. But he took a small sip and set the mug down. "I'm seeing things. Demons"

Tapu dipped his beignet in his coffee and took a big bite. Powdered sugar ended up on the tip of his wide nose. "Is good. You eat, please. I tell you what life spirits say to me."

Tapu waited. Butch sighed, then performed the same dunk and bite that Tapu had.

Tapu said, "Life spirits say you have murder in your heart. They sent demons to warn you. Do not kill Jared Schmidt."

Butch felt his jaw tighten. His fists clenched. "That drunk took my life from me! I have a right to justice!"

It was Tapu's jaw that tightened this time. The little shaman shook his head. "You not have right. Life spirits show me your death. You die in accident. Mistake. Schmidt, full of guilt pain."

"I'm going to kill him, and you can't stop me."

"You correct. I cannot. Now you will go to peace place. You murder Schmidt, life spirits will punish you. Please think of family being with you in peace place. You good man. Enjoy do-over day now. Help family. Do not do this evil thing."

Without a word, Butch shoved the table and shot to his feet, his chair tumbling backwards. "You call the police; I'll beat you into a coma. Understand?"

Butch expected to see Tapu cringing with fear. Instead, the shaman remained calm and looked sad.

Back in his car, Butch drove to a large pawn shop. After he pawned his trumpet, he examined the pistols. The clerk explained the process of buying one. It was infuriating. It wasn't possible for him to hide his identity. Butch told the clerk he'd think about it and left.

Back in the Toyota, he searched the internet for sporting goods stores. Maybe he could buy a big hunting knife or a bow and arrows. A fresh idea made him laugh. A crossbow. Yeah, Schmidt would pee his pants.

On his way to the store, while stopped at a light, he noticed an insurance sales office in a strip mall. What the heck. It wouldn't hurt to check it out. In about an hour, he had a $100,000 term policy. Who knew there were companies that sold term insurance without a medical workup or history? He should have done this years ago.

The last stop had been the sporting goods store. He set his new purchase in the back of the Toyota. Before closing the car's hatch,

Butch stared down at the crossbow lying next to the air conditioner. A chill flashed through him. The weapon was a horror. Far more menacing than a gun.

Feeling someone behind him. Looking over his shoulder, he whirled around. Six zombies stood in a semicircle, blocking escape. Their eyes looked hungry. The one on his right grabbed his throat with both icy hands and bit off his cheek. Butch screamed, and they disappeared. Shaking with adrenaline, he slammed the car hatch and headed home.

Despite the grisly warnings, Butch would see to it that Jared Schmidt was getting the punishment he deserved. Where was the justice if his killer lived? And why did the life forces resist righteous justice? What was not right about it?

When he died the first time, he chose to remain a ghost rather than move on into eternity. What if he chose to remain a ghost again? It hadn't been so bad, had it? They had never punished him as a ghost, and he had hated Schmidt since learning at his funeral who had killed him. Would he be safe from eternal punishment? He hoped so, because that drunk SOB was going to die.

***

That evening, Butch picked Olivia up from work on new tires as he'd promised. While she heated a can of baked beans and fixed a lettuce salad, he grilled hamburgers. Then the family dined in an air-conditioned house he'd also promised. Butch hadn't seen Olivia this happy in years.

He'd worried that she didn't love him anymore. He knew their marriage had not turned out to be as wonderful as she'd expected, and it was his fault. He was a good enough trumpet player, all right. But he argued with any bandleader trying to tell him how to play it. It had gotten him fired repeatedly. Each new gig was at increasingly low-life bars. In time, the money and tips were less than they could live on and she had to take a job waitressing.

He helped her wash the dishes and then showed her the term life insurance policy. The thing scared her.

"Butch, what are you planning? You're not going to kill yourself, are you?"

He took her hand in both of his. "No. Never. I just realized there was a way to protect you I'd never thought of before. I'm going to be with you forever."

It was a lie, of course. They only had a few hours left in his do-over day. If he became a ghost again, maybe he could convince Olivia to become a ghost, too. Then they'd never separate for all eternity. They could watch their grandchildren, great-grandchildren and so on for centuries.

Butch kissed her. "I've got to go."

She kissed him. "I want to come watch you tonight."

"No!" The word came out too quickly. He forced a smile. "The first night of a new gig is pretty bad." He touched the side of her face with his palm. "Come next week. It'll be better."

"Okay. I'm still on the early shift, anyway. Heather is driving back tomorrow." She stood. "I've got to get the kids to bed. See you in the morning."

His heart felt like it was being squeezed by a gorilla. It was urgent that he touch each of them again. "Wait. Let me help you, and then I'll go."

"If you say so," she said, looking at him in disbelief. He'd never been one for parental chores. A new interest in them was spooking her again, that he might be contemplating suicide. He was sorry about that, but he had to hold them physically one last time.

***

At Al's Tap, Butch left the crossbow in the back of the Toyota, and walked into the neighborhood bar. The smell of beer filled him with comfort, like cinnamon rolls hot from the oven. He slid onto a bar stool and ordered a Bud.

Behind him, a man said, "Hey, Jared, I hear your daughter roped you into painting her living room this weekend."

"Who told you that?"

Butch swiveled his stool sideways so he could see the man speaking.

"My daughter told me. They talk, you know."

Jared said, "Well, no one told me."

"We might have if you'd bothered to stop by. We piss you off or something?"

The discussion in that part of the bar went silent. Patrons looked anywhere but at Jared. Everyone knew about him killing the motorcyclist guy because he'd been driving while intoxicated.

Jared took a deep breath and let it out slowly. "I've had things to do."

"Well, you're here now. Let me get you a refill."

When the man left the table, Butch walked over. "Mind if I join you? Jared, isn't it? My name is Butch."

"Sure."

Once Butch sat down, Jared stared at him. "Do I know you?"

"Maybe. I was in the news a few weeks back." Butch gave him a big smile. "You might have seen my picture. I was sitting on my motorcycle."

Jared went white. "Who are you?"

"Wow, man, you look like you've seen a ghost. I told you. My name is Butch. I'm a trumpet player. You've probably seen me playing in a band or a parade around the city somewhere."

Jared stood up. "I've got to go." Then he hurried to the door.

Jared's friend called out. "Hey Jared. What about your beer?"

Without a glance or word back, Jared exited the bar. Butch hurried out the door after him.

He ran to his Toyota and fetched the crossbow from it. When Jared turned on his headlights, Butch knew exactly where to aim. He pulled the trigger. The bolt shot into the engine and killed it. He reset the bowstring and loaded another bolt. It was time he and Jared had a little talk.

At Jared's Ford pickup truck, Butch aimed the crossbow again. This time at Jared's frightened face.

"Roll down your window."

Jared held his hands up and said, "No."

"You think that glass is going to stop this bolt? Roll down your window. I just want to talk."

Jared lowered his left hand and rolled the window down a quarter of the way.

Still aiming the crossbow, Butch said, "I want justice from you, Schmidt. How are you going to give it to me?"

Jared wept. "I never saw you until I stood over your body in the street. I've suffered depression and regret every damned day since. You want justice? Kill me. I want freedom from this excruciating guilt."

Butch watched the tears roll down his killer's cheeks. Looking at Jared over the tip of the bolt, he said, "I know you didn't mean it. I know it was an accident, and I forgive you." He dropped the crossbow to his side. "Forgive yourself." Butch turned to walk away. Jared's question stopped him.

"How are you alive?" Jared asked.

"I'm not. Magic is strong here in New Orleans. You won't see me again. "

With that, Butch drove to the Mississippi levee and cast the crossbow into the river.

Back in his Toyota, he flipped open his pocket watch. Less than two hours of his life remained. What did he want to do with them? Return home? Olivia and the kids were sleeping. He turned the ignition on. Zydeco music came from the radio. Music. Yeah, listening to live music sounded perfect. He wanted to die with Bourbon Street jazz in his ears.

***

At breakfast the next morning, Tapu scrolled through the local news sites on his phone. Jared Schmidt was not in any of them as a murder victim. That was a relief. However, there was a man who'd fallen into an open manhole near Bourbon Street. This morning, construction workers found his body. Authorities were withholding the man's name until they could notify his next of kin. Tapu hoped this fellow wasn't Jared Schmidt either.

The life spirits never told him what happened to the ghosts he performed the do-over ceremonies for. Occasionally, he learned something from the local newspaper or TV stations. But usually not. The results remained a mystery. Yesterday's do-over would probably remain one, too.

Time to get to work. The sad lady's German cuckoo clock would not fix itself.

Deadfall

Michael Van Natta

It is said that if a human can think a thing, no matter how outrageous it is, then it's simply a matter of time until they or some other human makes it happen in the real world. That's where I come in.

Call me Gunderson. I'm a cop in Detroit, city of my birth.

My chief texted me that Friday morning, tasked me out northwest to the bedroom Community of Novi, Michigan, to see about a missing woman. I was still just a rookie then, a new cop on the streets, still learning.

Since the case in Connecticut, missing persons had become kind of like my default specialty. But this case was routine. A ho-hum search mission for a confused woman with Alzheimer's who just wandered out her door into the unkown. Husband can't find her, is a bit muddled himself, he calls the hospital who's CEO calls—not the Novi police—but my chief who's an acquaintance of his, who then put me on it.

You got to start somewhere and you gotta always go with what you got. There was the husband, Smithson "Smiity" Dewillier, who made the call to the Henry Ford hospital branch in Novi ER to see if his forty-eight year old much younger wife had suffered some unfortunate accident or otherwise somehow shown up there. Wife: Early onset dementia.

I started with the husband. It's always the spouse.

* * *

After the forty-five minute drive northwest from the city cutting against the grain of rush hour traffic, I Googled my way to the residence. The Dewillier's mansion sat on a forty-acre forested spread abutting Walled Lake, its shores the habitat of Wayne County's rich and famous. Unlike the others, the Dewillier home was built ages before the others–gilded-age money.

The ornate heavy wooden door opened to a tall woman dressed in a blue and white uniform, her dark hair so severely pulled and tied back I wondered if it was the reason her eyebrows seemed perpetually raised. Instead of a greeting, she offered only a stare down her nose.

Most people look down at me. I'm a small woman.

I hadn't bothered going to the station to change into my uniform. I'd driven from my home in street clothes, my Glock 19 in my front right pocket.

"Good morning, I said, plastering a practiced smile on my face, trying for my best musical voice.

"Yes." She had a low voice and it wasn't a question. "You are detective?"

So, not from around here.

"Good morning," I said again. "Yes. I mean no. Not a detective. But I'm an investigator. My boss in Detroit sent me here to help."

"Oh." She paused. "Yes, Yes."

She looked to be younger than me. "Is Mr. Dewillier here?"

"Yes. Please wait," she said, and with effort, pushed the door closed.

Huh.

It was early April and still cool under the perpetual overcast skies that cover Michigan from Labor Day to May Day, clotting up the better judgement of its more damaged citizenry. After a few long minutes, waiting while a chill but light breeze fluttered though my curls, the door came crunching open again and Sophia led me back through a dark hall to a tiny cube of a greenhouse-like room in back, overlooking a wide lawn that led to the lake. Thin lacy ice hugged against its shore.

A compact elderly man sat in a withered uncomfortable-looking wingback. Sophia wordlessly pointed to an upright chair on the other side of the claustrophobic room and left.

The man, dressed in new jeans and a gray plaid chambray under an old-fashioned still shiny black smoking jacket didn't seem to notice me as I sat.

"Hello," I said, flashing my best smile. I have really white teeth. "Are you Mr. Dewillier?"

He didn't react in the least. Immediately, he reminded me of Billy Bob Thorton twenty years older. Had to be in his mid-seventies. A triangular face, longish bed-head of sticking-up gray hair. Age-spotted hands with gold rings. An ornate tarnished silver amulet thingy hung from a chain across his chicken-skin neck. His eyes were red. From crying? In his left hand he gripped a black enameled walking cane.

"I'm ..."

"You are here about the cat." It was a statement. His eyes remained cast out, unfocused, toward the lake, The single parlor wall was decorated with photos of buildings that looked like fancy college dormitories. A fat Siamese lay sleeping on one of the window ledges. The dark foreign accent lady—Sofia, she'd told me—entered with a tray of cups and a carafe. "Unless you like tea?"

"Coffee's fine," I said. She withdrew.

"I'm Officer Gunderson from the Detroit Poliice."

The man looked at me as if trying to remember the name of a long-ago friend. "Police. Yes."

"Is Sophia a relative?" I was thinking Dewillier might be her sugar daddy.

"No, he said, his words drawn out. "Sophia is our maid. Our cook."

"I understand you can't find your wife? Darla, is it?"

He turned in his chair, lifted bleary heavily-lidded eyes. "Darla is ... was ... not in the house when I woke up. The front door was ...was wide open. We—Sophia and me—we called for her, looked in all the rooms but we did not find her. She must have gone out.

You see, she gets con … conf … she can't think straight. It's worse at times." He screwed up his face, as if looking into a stiff wind. "Nights can be bad."

His voice sounded as if it came from deep in his chest. "Have you gone looking for her outside?" Have you called neighbors? Friends?" I was hoping this would be quick and easy. Get in, get done, get out. She might be on the property somewhere. Even so, I remembered how expansive the property was.

"No," he said. "I do not know where to start." His face started to come apart, pieces flying away in an unseen derecho. The arm holding the cane trembled about.

"When did you last see her?"

"When Sophia put her to bed. Last night. I kissed her bye, night, night … like I do all the nights."

"And she was okay? Then?"

"Good. Not worse."

"Is Sophia a nurse? Besides being the maid and the cook?"

"She's my daughter …" He shook his head back and forth calling to mind a horse beleaguered by a swarm of flies. "Not my daughter …. my friend's daughter." He bent over his knees, lay the remains of his face in his hands and shook.

I waited, leaned over and put a hand on Dewillier's shoulder once and then removed it. "Who's your friend?"

"Jeffrey," he said, words muffled, from far away. "Jeffrey…Jeffery … Oh, God …" he lifted his head. "I can't think now… can't think of his last name. I will. Later. I will …." He looked away, seemed to fall into himself.

Something was off. Not just his speech pattern. But odd. Like maybe planned? Or over-dramatic? But then again, I'd not had much contact with people with dementia—outside of my own little private dementias—and despite my gut feeling, I waved the notion away.

"Is your cat ill?" I asked. The grey Siamese lay breathing but otherwise hadn't moved.

He looked again my direction. "Cat? What cat? I don't have

a cat."

I let that go. "Is there anything else?" I asked. "Anything unusual about her in the last day or days that would help find her? Has she been talking about going out anywhere?"

He shook his head, sniffed once, and rose in his chair. "No. She … her talk is not real good now. She keeps repeating stuff. She … Oh, God. She shouts the one word, *Fuck*, all the time. She never ever cussed before. Also, shouts *Contessa*. He frowned and crouched in his worn red leather chair, as if to avoid the onslaught of something I couldn't see.

"Contessa, Contessa. I haven't thought about her for years. I don't think Darla has either."

"Who is she? Contessa?"

He looked away into the near distance. I watched as his eyes grew wide and then he looked down. "Just a friend we both knew. Years ago now."

"You haven't seen her lately? This Contessa? Either of you? She hasn't contacted you, or Darla?"

He shook his head. "Years ago."

"Do you know of anyone who might be looking to hurt or do harm to your wife? Or to you? Anyone who would want to see her disappear?"

He ratcheted his gaze toward me and his eyes focused. His pupils dilated. His mouth puckered. A look of pure hate painted across his continence. I recoiled, involuntarily, pulled back in my chair, started to raise my hands as if an object had been hurled at me but his expression melted and he turned back toward the window, shook his head again.

Sophia brought in a silent coffee urn and two cups. He drank and I, too, took a sip. When Sophia left the room, I asked again. "Is Sophia a nurse?"

That long confused pause. "She may be. She's been here a lot of years. She may be a nurse. She does real good with Darla."

"Listen, I'd like to call the Novi police, if that's okay with you? They can have a team of pol … people out here and do a good thorough search of the property and look for clues in the house." I looked at him, nodding. "Is that okay?"

He pivoted in the chair. His face tightened and he clenched his jaw, raised his voice. "You're part of them, aren't you? You just like all of them!"

Like the time before, as if he didn't remember what he'd just said, he turned away. Seemed then to change, soften.

He began to tell me things, as if I was just a neighbor, dropped by for a Sunday visit. He said he couldn't trust the local cops. He told me in his simple and truncated way how they had been in the house many times—too many times, he said—and things had come up missing at times after their "little sick calls." He wouldn't abide by it, he said. He grew adamant. Despite the childish way he spoke, his eyes were now sharp, focused.

After more questions, I'd learned a few more details about their life together but not really anything to help find Mrs. Dewillier. She owned a passel of nursing homes across the Midwest. He was the Chief Operating Officer. Hence, the cash.

"Have you two been married a long time?"

"Well, if twenty years is a long time, then I guess." He smiled for the first time, benevolent and dour, in the way a funeral director might.

I hazarded a guess. "You both started the company after you were married? Or did one of you own it before?"

He nodded, then shook his head, and his faint smile vanished, replaced by that far-away look. "She would not go into one of her own homes. Didn't want that. Ever. I had to watch her get sick, suffrage ... suffer." I hate that. When she got worse, real bad, I called the ambulance and they took her. She had to stay there in that strange hospital room for three days while they stuck her all the time, scanned her, wired her, probed her. Then, her time was up and it was time to go to ... Rosalie Center. But she refused to go there."

Dewillier's wrinkled cheeks grew red. He tapped his cane twice on the tiled floor. The cat startled, raised its head, opened its coppery eyes. Then laid its head back down, shut its eyes again.

"So she came back here. Cost a ton and she didn't go to the rest home in the end." He looked at me. "Doctor said they couldn't keep her any longer. Even in our own goddamn wing, they said she had to go to the rest home. She just wanted out." He got that distant look again but then came back from wherever he went.

I could see an undercurrent of fury heating up his cheeks. He reached up to his heart and grabbed the silver pendant there and squeezed it, as if it gave him strength. When he let go, I noticed the embossed swirl of snakes around a single human-like eye.

I pointed and asked, "That's beautiful, Mr. Dewillier. Where did you get that?"

"This?" He lifted it again. "I … years ago …" He let it fall back to his chest. "I can't think. In … across the sea …" He shrugged and winced.

Dewillier told me how sameness and routine was helpful for Darla's condition, how they had a special moment every morning when weather permitted. They'd take a walk through the woods to their "special place" where they'd have a light picnic brunch and he'd give Darla her medications.

At my suggestion, he put on a heavy coat and, holding my arm, he led me outside, over the greening-up lawn and along the path through the dense woods.

After five minutes, we came to a sheltered area, a clearing where a wood picnic table was set up. A metal trash can leaned against a tree nearby and while Dewillier eased himself down on one of the benches, I grabbed a quick-see. It was empty. No other identifiable items to indicate human goings-on. And no wife.

"Darla gets so much fun … so much … ease here." A faint almost-smile traveled across his face. "It is the best part of her day …. Mine, too."

I nodded. All around, a million other places the wife could have stumbled into. Several paths led off in different directions from the clearing.

"Do you—the two of you—ever take a hike from here? Go some-where else? Like down one of these paths? Or out to the lake?"

"No. Like I said. We need consis … she needs things to be like they were."

"Mind if I take a quick walk down one of these paths?" He'd started to shiver, despite the pillowy white down parka I'd helped him into at the house. "I'll just take a minute," I said.

He nodded, I think. It might have been a shiver but I think he nodded. So I ambled down the most worn path. I couldn't really see more than fifteen feet or so before the dense trees and thicket obscured my view. Still, this was the most logical place to find her. Alive. Injured. Dead.

I walked far enough away and called Novi to get them out to the property, with explicit instructions to park on the highway and walk in. I needed their help and didn't want Dewillier or Sophia see them searching. By the time I caught a glimpse of police activity through the parlor window—they're not real crafty, these guys—Dewillier and I were warming by a small fire in the parlor, hot coffee again in our hands. He'd turned tearful and I had to wait it out, asked if he'd like a pastor or a social worker to come by. He briefly got that look again—scared me again—but he shook it away. "Leave them out of this. I have Sophia."

On the walk out to my vehicle, I felt as if I was being watched. I turned back once but all the curtains were closed.

A black Escalade roared up the drive and out popped an animated tall man in a brown overcoat and movie-star hair. A gold glint of ear rings, both sides.

"Who are you?" he asked as we closed.

"Who are you?" I said. I ask the questions here.

"Ken Grandquist. I'm Mrs. Dewillier's lawyer. Have you found her yet? Is Smitty okay?"

I'd still not told him my name. "And you're here why?"

"News travels fast."

"Uh huh." I looked at the flashes of uniforms among the trees.

"Is he under suspicion?" He must have guessed my role.

"Suspicion of what?"

The tall lawyer grit his teeth. "You know. Anything." He shot me a million-dollar smile.

"We're doing all we can to find Mrs. Dewillier. Why do you ask?"

"He's … Smitty doesn't always make sense. I assume you've talked with him so you know. I kind of feel I need to be around when anything official happens."

"Official? Like what does that mean?"

My client and her husband have some … some pending matters before the court right now."

"Like what?" This man had given me more information than any other source.

"Ah … sorry. Attorney-client privilege. You get that. What's your name, by the way?"

I handed him my card and my make-nice smile. He stepped around me but stopped. "Why is Detroit here, by the way?"

"Long story," I said and walked away.

After I got in my Mustang, headed off toward town, heater blasting full, two vehicles appeared behind me. A blue SUV and a two-toned pickup. One turned off at the first corner, the other went straight as I got on the four-lane. Neighbors.

* * *

Back at the precinct, at my tiny desk, I called Novi for any updates but there was nothing. No bodies, living or dead. No signs. Then, I called the hospital, got a Dr. Brentwood in the Novi ER on the line and he agreed to talk to me despite the usual HIPPA crap.

"She was here as a patient a month ago. Husband brought her in, wanted her committed to a nursing home. Darla is well-known here and this time she was pretty sick. We had to admit her, work her up, treat her, to which she responded and got better. On the third day, we were ready to transfer her to Rosalie Palliative Care but she wouldn't have anything to do with that. Made quite a scene. Ultimately signed out AMA."

"AMA?"

"Yeah. Against medical advice, We had to send her home."

"What was Mr. Dewillier's response to all this?"

"Mad as a cat in a sack of dog turds. I think he filed a lawsuit."

"A lawsuit? For what?"

"Not sure, exactly. We did everything right. I mean, the man likes us … or used to anyway. He's a big donor, or has been in the past. There's even a hospital wing named after him. Dewillier Dialysis Unit. I'm maybe talking out of school here. There are a lot of people smarter than me you could talk to. Believe me, Dewillier has the Board's full attention right now. Word has come down. 'Treat with kid gloves.'"

Next, I called the CEO, a man by the name of Kilroy Kranovich. He was busy, according to his secretary, but after I identified myself, he was on the line in less than a minute.

"Mr. Kranovich, my name is Geri Gunderson. I'm an investigative officer from the Detroit Police Department."

"Oh, yes. Captain Stickler was gracious enough to help us through this."

"I was wondering about that. I've been up to the house and met Mr. Dewillier. He's beside himself but he has support people by his side. We're actively looking for his wife as we speak. I'm sure we'll find her soon. Why did you call Chief Stickler? Why not the local cops?"

"It's a long story, detective."

"Officer. I'm not a detective. I've got time to hear it if you do."

The phone went dead. I thought I'd lost him. "Mr. Kranovich?"

"I'm here." He cleared his throat. "Let's just say Smitty … Mr. Dewillier … has had his share of health problems lately. He's not acting himself." Another pause on the line, then, "He's been a real friend of the hospital over the years. A big supporter of what we do for the community. Financially and otherwise. He has a large extended family and we take care of all of them. As patients. Let's just say we'd like to keep relations smooth with Mr. Dewillier? To be honest, since the latest Medicaid cuts, we're lucky to still be afloat. We'll be okay, I think, if we keep bailing."

* * *

I didn't learn much more from Kranovich. After I hung up, I jumped in my car and headed over to Brueggers Bagels for breakfast. I find the huge bagels way too chewy but their donuts rival Krispy Kremes. On the way, I got a text from the chief. They'd found Mrs. Dewillier. In the woods, as I suspected. I plugged the Dewillier address into my device for the second time that day and flipped around on the freeway.

She'd been found about three quarters of a mile from the home, on the edge of where the forest leaves off and the beach starts. When I arrived at the scene, the Novi County Medical Examiner was there. Most of the line cops had left but a couple were still trampling through the nearby forest for clues.

"Blunt force head trauma, I'm afraid. Didn't know what hit her. I'm Dr. Davos, by way," the ME said, rising from the side of a heavy-set woman in a maroon robe and black-striped pajamas lying face down and dead. The back of the woman's—Darla's—head was a blob of dark purplish congealing blood and squished between white bone fragments, greyish gelatin pudding that I thought resembled my idea of cerebellum.

"Geri Gunderson, Detroit Police Officer."

Davos stood, brought herself to her full height, smiled, peeled off a blue latex glove and shook my hand. "Of course. We heard you were coming up. So nice to meet you finally."

She spoke with a faint accent. Australian?

"Finally?"

"We've all heard about you of course."

I didn't allow her to go on. By then, it was practically all I ever heard. My reputation proceeds me. "What's the story?"

Her smile faded. "Pretty straightforward. Woman has advanced dementia, goes for a walkabout. Has the unfortunate luck of wandering under a tree with a large compromised branch ready to break away. Must have hit her square on."

"Man," I said. "What are the chances of that?"

"It happens. Although you're more likely to die from a meteor hit, in a plane crash, from a lightning strike, or a hundred other freak accidents. A widowmaker is extremely rare."

I looked around. The dead woman was about my height, but much heavier. Probably went two fifty. She had blonde hair, chin length, most likely dyed. The depression in her skull was large enough to pour a cup of water into. Blood-smeared gray brain matter was clearly visible. Some tree bark fragments.

The ME knelt beside her and began dictating into a dedicated device, I took out my phone and began grabbing pictures. Beside her left shoulder laid a tree limb maybe five inched across and six of seven feet long, counting the twigs at the outer end. I paused then. Something not right here. Same feeling I got before when talking with Dewillier.

I scouted around the perimeter, which meant slipping through the dense growth of shrubbery and saplings that had obscured the body from discovery. Rustling came from my west and south. The pair of uniforms rummaging for clues. The air had that particular odor of summer camps and early spring gardening.

Then it hit me, or rather didn't hit me. A slight breeze but essentially no wind. No gales or gusts that penetrated the canopy. My hair barely moved. I looked up. The tops of the trees were not swaying, not being buffeted by a wind that might shake loose a six-inch diameter limb. Through a visual cut in the forest, I could see the lake. Certainly not a whitecap day.

The ME and the other cops thought I was crazy when I declared a crime scene. They made some noise about jurisdictions but I ignored that. I went back to my car and got a roll of yellow tape from the trunk and spooled it around trees. The two other Novi cops came up and watched, shaking their heads. I'd just made a whole lot more work for everyone. But there were just too many circumstances all aligning at once. I didn't like it. So it would be a crime scene until I declared it wasn't. Act accordingly.

I called Stickler and reported in. She had my back. I went to inform Dewillier, give him the bad news. After he'd finished a short bout of wailing and cursing, he insisted on seeing his wife. I didn't object–I felt sorry for him. Also, I needed a positive ID. When he and

I got there, a full forensic analysis had gotten underway, a team of three techs blowing out clouds of frozen breath who shot me evil eyes while they photographed and took swabs.

I watched the bereaved husband as he was allowed to bend a knee to his dead wife. The ME had turned the body over and Mrs. Dewillier's face in her death mask grimaced without judgement at the overhead clouds. That didn't seem to bother Dewillier. Perhaps she always grimaced in life? He was told not to touch her but did so anyway. Kissed her, he did. He kept asking, "Why? Why?" He cried but hardly a tear fell or froze on his cheeks. Then, "It's all your fault, all your fault." I don't think he meant it for his wife or me personally but I made a note to ask him.

Back at the house, Sophia told me Mrs. Dewillier occasionally went to church at a small Lutheran chapel a mile away and I called. Reverend Aldos Borsch agreed to come immediately.

Next, I paid a visit to the lawyer Grandquist in Novi. His office was an up-scale remodeled dance studio—the sign was still above the door—next to a fast-food Coney Island drive-up. After ten minutes of being ordered to sit in a drafty and dusty outer room by a bimbo with a nail file, he opened the one inner door and called me in. It's wasn't like he had other clients.

"I wondered if I'd see you again. And here you are. Heard you're suspicious. Declared a crime." He lifted a giant convenience store orange plastic mug and drank something from it. "Get you a coffee?"

It did not look appetizing. "No thanks. I just have a few questions." He didn't offer me a seat but I sat anyway in one of the upholstered chairs facing him over a large polished birds-eye maple desk.

He smiled his toothy lawyer smile. "Fire away."

"Mrs. Dewillier is dead, if you didn't know. Looks like an accident. Widowmaker, they call it."

"Yes, I've heard. Smitty called, distraught." He set the mug down. "Terrible. So why are you here again?"

"I understand Mr. Dewillier has a lawsuit pending against the local hospital. Related to an illness and an admission of your client there.

"Is that a question?"

"Of course it's a question."

The lawyer looked around his office as if seeing it the first time. "I'm afraid I …"

"I've already downloaded the court documents. Can't we just cut to the chase?"

Grandquist cleared his throat. "He–he's not my client. Darla is. He's suing the hospital for a million dollars plus another two million for pain and suffering."

"For fraudulent billing?" A statement posing as question. Two can play at this game.

"For that, yes. Of course it's all true. The doctor—Dr. Brentwood, I think his name was—racked up a charge for everything he could think of and then some. Smitty's got a case but unfortunately, for both he and I, no real chance of winning. Every single test can be construed by the defense as medically necessary."

"Doesn't sound fair," I said.

"It's why health care costs so much these days. It's a business, like any other."

"Huh."

The lawyer Grandquist opened a drawer and pulled a file, slipped on readers and paged through it. "Darla's bill totaled one hundred nineteen thousand and some change. That includes the ambulance ride, itself almost forty grand."

Astounded, I tried not to show it. I recalled the time I'd gotten extensively sewn up in a Connecticut ER after a car wreck a few years back. The bill had been eight-something. Thousand.

"Smitty's real problem is he'd been trying to get his wife admitted to a nursing home for a year or more. She won't have it. In her will, she confers upon me—not Smitty—the power of medical attorney." He chuckled. "Ironic, isn't it? She's got the fifth largest nursing home corporation in the country and she will not partake of what are the best care options available anywhere. She could benefit greatly. Not to mention it's completely free for her. She owns the damn things."

"I heard that. So, do you think she should have gone into a nursing home?"

"Oh, absolutely. But what I think is irrelevant. So is what Smitty thinks."

"She has a will?"

"Well, it's a revokable trust, actually. And he's been—Smitty that is—he's been coming at me to change the document. I've drawn it up with the alterations at his insistence but he could never get her to sign."

"Change it how?"

"Removed the clause about an endowment to the hospital for one."

"He must be really pissed at the hospital. And for another?"

"Huh? I'm not following."

"You said for one. Is there another change he's wanting?"

"Well. Yes. The trust names her cousins and nieces and nephews as beneficiaries of the entire business. Smitty and Darla never had children of their own. Smitty gets the house and property which as you know, is not insubstantial. But he's served as general manager since they married two decades ago. I do see his point but again, what I think doesn't count."

"His point? What point?"

"He wants a fifth of the business and then also a sum for Sophia."

"Sophia? The maid?"

"Caregiver in chief, more like. He wants her paid for back wages and then ongoing for as long as Smitty lives. Longer, actually."

"Just who is this Sophia?"

"Sophia came with the marriage. She was—and is—Smitty's personal assistant. And then, when Darla could no longer take care of herself, she stepped up and took on the role of her personal caregiver, a help necessary to keep her in the house. He thinks she ought to be compensated. I tend to agree, but Darla strongly objected."

"What's Sophia's story? Why does it feel like there's a whole lot more you're not telling me?"

The lawyer stared at me, as if sizing me up. stood, walked to the door and pushed it shut. "This is not to go into any official record? On background?"

"For now, okay. Background. If I need to bring it out … if a crime has been committed … I may be forced to use it."

He waved a dismissive hand. "I guess it'll have to be okay. My client is and always will be Darla, not Smitty." He went back to sit behind his desk.

"I happen to know that Sophia is Smitty's daughter. He's naturally protective."

I nodded. It surprised me and it didn't. Something wasn't right.

"He finally confided in me—or confessed maybe—some years back. See, Mr. and Mrs. Dewillier honeymooned in Italy and eastern Europe after their …" He scrunched up his eyes. "… 2007 wedding. Apparently, Smitty found a diversion, a dalliance, during the second week of the trip. I didn't know them then, of course, but I've come to believe neither he nor Darla were ever suited for each other. So he met a woman that should have been a dalliance but instead became the love of Smitty's life. On their honeymoon, if you can believe that. But he left that woman in Europe. I mean, think about it. All that money? A secure lifelong occupation? He left her. I might have done the same. But … maybe not."

The lawyer looked off in the distance. "He showed me pictures once. A real classic Romanian beauty. A gypsy. She apparently called herself that." He pulled his chair forward. "Stunning woman. But he left her, this Contessa, hard as that must have been, he left her and sailed back across the pond, and Contessa? Never to be heard from again. He told me the last words she had for him were an indecipherable and vituperative tirade in screaming Romanian. And eight English words that he heard quite distinctly and remembers to this day. *I curse you until the day you die!*"

He let that sit in the air. "Smitty didn't know she was pregnant, of course."

"Oh shit," I said. "He discovered that?" Then I thought again. "He must have."

"Sophia found Smitty somehow. Credit the internet. She grew

up in a foster home in Romania. Cut free at eighteen. Worked as a housecleaner. After she contacted him, he arranged for her travel, for her relocation, the adoption. She's a full U.S. citizen, at least as the constitution stands now. Give credit to Smitty."

A knock on the door and the bimbo poked her head through, let her eyelids droop. "Hank's on line one," she said, looking not at Grandquist but at her freshly polished nails. Glitter Red.

"Jesus, not today, Bindy. Tell him I'm busy. I'll call him tomorrow."

Bindy? Really?

"Bindy said nothing, rolled her eyes, closed the door, disappeared.

"Belinda's good at what she does," Grandquist said. "If I could ever get her to do what she's good at."

"Good help is hard to find," I said.

"Tell me about it. Anyway, Smitty. He was a sly one. Darla never knew any of this. Or at least she never let on if she did. But give him credit again. He hired Sophia as his personal assistant. Got her some real American education. Accounting. Darla hated being slowly replaced as head of household but what could she do? I think now Darla probably always suspected Sophia was who she was. Smitty never admitted it to Darla. But then again, he refused to fire Sophia. And as he started to lose it, he started wearing that amulet on his neck, the one Contessa had bought him from a Romanian street vendor' By then, Darla was getting out of sorts.

***

Heading back to Detroit, on an especially winding and tree-lined section of Magellan Drive, I spotted the same two-toned pickup coming up fast in the rear-view. Something absolutely aggressive. Why? What the …? Related to the Dewilliers? It made no sense. I was about to take evasive action—pull over and pull my pistol — when the back window shattered, followed in rapid succession by plunking as bullets pierced metal. I ducked as low as I could and hit the accelerator. Automatic weapon? Then the windshield spiderwebbed and my rear-view mirror ricocheted off the dash, bounced and flew away. I felt a hard hit to the top of my head from something and then I woke up in Novi Henry Ford Emergency Room staring at the smiling face of Dr. Brentwood. My chief sat at the bedside, squeezing my hand.

She gave me the run-down.

Eight shots through the vehicle. Count my blessings, only one had hit me. A bullet meant for my brain had struck a glancing blow, knocked me forward which bashed in my nose on the steering wheel. I don't have memory of any of this. The chief ran led the investigation personally. These were the facts so far. The chief vowed to find the people responsible.

It'll never be the same. My nose, I mean. Also, air bags deployed right in my face. First degree burns over my destroyed nose, a few blisters but mostly like a bad sunburn. Brentwood released me after I refused to be admitted for overnight observation. I'd had concussions before.

***

Investigations so far have failed to find the perpetrators. They're real, though, and they're out there. Someday, I'll bring them to justice. And whoever put them up to it.

***

Handwriting analysis of the signed trust documents by experts in the field testified there weren't sufficient differences in the signatures to say it wasn't Mrs. Darla Dewillier's signature at the bottom of the trust document. Smitty had bought and paid for the best specialists. The lawyer Grandquist, who represented Darla's estate, also had brought in his best. Told me once again that his client was Darla. It did come out that Smitty's wanted to change the document. Had to. Through it all, Dewillier had that hateful look.

That always haunted me. That Smitty Dewillier would get away with it like that.

A week after it all started and two days after Darla went into the ground, I had to close the case. The ME would not change the cause of death to "uncertain" and I had no specific evidence a crime had been committed. And no evidence my shooting had any connection at all. All I had was strong suspicion. We'd managed to locate the two-toned pickup. It had been reported stolen the afternoon after my shooting. It checked out but the perps were in the wind.

***

Five months went by. I'd forgotten all about the Dewilliers. I was in the middle of another missing person's case and my partner, Ochoa, and I were closing in on a murder suspect in a botched liquor store robbery. I got a call from the lawyer Grandquist.

"You hear the news?" he asked when I finally got him back on the line. I hate playing phone tag with lawyers but it seems to be part of the deal.

"What news? The trust has been thrown out?"

"No, no. I dropped the appeal. I don't believe for a minute that was Darla's signature on the document but you have to admit, it was nearly perfect."

I'd seen the document as we were closing down the case. I couldn't tell, couldn't swear it was Smitty's doing. Nobody could, it seemed.

"He got the best lawyer he could buy. Beat me fair and square."

"That's pretty sad news. Justice for sale like that."

"Well, that's not all the news." While I waited for him to go on, I heard him swallow, painfully visualized the Big Gulp mug at his lips.

"Like Darla, Smitty was getting the *Old Timer's* disease. After she died, he went downhill pretty fast."

"So maybe some justice does exist in this world?" I thought about how much money this lawyer had made over the years representing Darla Dewillier and, rumor has it, now Mr. Smithson Dewillier. So maybe just some justice. For the lawyer Grandquist, anyway.

"The doctors recommended he go into a nursing home and he resisted for awhile. Sophia, of course, didn't want that either. But in the end, he could see the handwriting on the wall. He told me he wanted Sophia to have a real life, so he signed the paperwork.

For the new home they'd just built and for which he'd provided the legal name–Contessa Memory Center."

"Jesus," I said. "Has he no decency? Where the justice in that?"

The lawyer chuckled then excused himself. "I shouldn't laugh but you know the saying? 'What goes around comes around?'"

"Like 'What you sow, so shall you reap?'"

"Do not enumerate your fowl feathered progeny before the process of incubation has fully matured."

"What?"

"Don't count your chickens before they're hatched."

"Oh." Despite it all, it was hard to not like the man.

"So here's the sad story of the end of Mr. Dewillier. And it is sad, really. I can't help but think of that curse Sophia's mother Contessa laid on Smitty all those years ago."

"You don't believe stuff like that do you?"

"Doesn't matter what I believe. Smitty believed it, At the end especially. Told me for weeks, Contessa had been appearing in doorways at the mansion. Scared hell out of him. That Contessa had been helping him with his urinal. That Contessa made the best scrambled eggs. He stopped sleeping, stopped eating. went downhill like a snowball, little things at first that grew into an avalanche. Mostly, I think he was hoping to escape his ghosts when he checked into the home."

"He was mistaking Sophia and Contessa?"

"You're one smart cop, Gunderson, I'll give you that. I don't know for sure. Anyway, when they were wheeling him into the brand spanking new Contessa Memory Center, it was a very light-wind day. Nobody could fault the wind."

I bolted up in my chair. "What? What happened?"

"The sign above the door was a make-shift wooden thing, temporary, until they could get the real sign finished and installed."

I could see where this was going. "No. Don't tell me."

"Hit him square on top of the head. He apparently died immediately."

"Jesus," I said. "He died? Just like that?"

"I'm afraid so."

I took a big breath and watched the events of the last months travel by in fast-motion.

Grandquist went on. "The only good thing I can see that came out of it was that Mrs. D never wanted to go in a nursing home and Mr. D actually did want that. She got what she wanted and he didn't. He never set foot—or wheel as the case may be—inside."

"I guess that's something at least." I thought about it. "And Sophia?"

"Yeah. After Smitty signed the Memory Center contract, Sophia moved back to Europe. Greece actually. Lives on some island now."

I chewed my bottom lip.

"I know, I know. You might have suspicions about that. You've met Sofia once but I've known her for years. She's the sweetest thing. Not a hint of a bad bone in her body. And …" he lowered his chin, looked at me as if confiding a secret. "Not really smart enough to pull off something like that."

I thought about that. Maybe. Maybe not.

"I see what you're thinking. Don't waste your time or energy, Gunderson. Leave dead dogs lie, as they say. Sophia is the doer of many kind deeds, has done a ton of good in the world. She deserves what she's got. It is a kind of justice, too, don't you think?"

"Maybe," I said, scratching my head where the wound had never fully healed.

"Maybe not."

Fallen Flowers

J.L. Wheaton

We kept her room just as it was the day she left for school two years ago. The day our daughter, Rose, never came back. News of the school shooter rocketed me into a stupor of disbelief, anger, and grief so deep it shredded my soul.

The doll she loved still slouched in the toy stroller. The baby cam, unplugged, allowed to reside on top of the bookshelf, dust-laden and forgotten. Glitter stickers decorated a sheet of paper taped on the wall–a reminder of her eighth birthday three years ago. The last birthday she would ever have. Her bedcovers remained tousled, with the neatness sensibility of a child in haste to catch the school bus.

My husband, Mark, and I kept her bedroom door closed most of the time, because the torture of her absence was too much to bear. But sometimes I've crept into her room in the middle of the night. The darkness seemed to soothe some part of me with her presence even though I'm unable to see her, or comb her blonde curls, or kiss her soft cheek goodnight. Her room was the place I would go to cry until my tears were spent, where I'd wipe my soggy face with a multitude of tissues that gathered around me like fallen lily petals.

***

One night, just after the second anniversary of her death, I slept with Mark in our bed when I was awakened at 2:00 am to a crackling sound. Faint and unusual, the disturbance set my heart pounding. I held my breath to listen, thinking it might have been a dream, but the noise repeated. Something from inside our closet.

I slipped out of bed to investigate. Moonlight filtered through the parted curtains, creating patterns of shadow and light. The crackles grew from a faint scratching to a discernible white noise when I opened the closet door. The source seemed to originate from a dusty cardboard box tucked away on a shelf. I hadn't thought about the obscured and forgotten collection of odds and ends in years. Crackles became static, like an old radio with faulty reception. I removed the box, trying to be as quiet as possible. I didn't want to wake Mark. He had just arrived home from his evening maintenance job and fallen asleep.

I peeled back the creased flaps and searched inside. Bits and pieces I had decluttered years ago jumbled around in a disorganized collection of unneeded possessions. I had intended to give the contents to charity but, like so many tasks, ignored after our tragedy.

My hand met a plastic-encased object. I pulled it out and held it. The old baby monitor we used in Rose's room to watch her crib emanated a faint illumination. But the crackling had stopped. A strange dot of light flittered across the screen inside Rose's bedroom. My hands trembled. I looked at Mark, still asleep. How could a dot of light appear on an unplugged screen?

Curiosity overshadowed my fear when I tiptoed barefoot down the hall to Rose's room. I paused outside the closed door to listen. Nothing stirred on the other side. I turned the knob, and the door creaked open. Standing at the threshold, I peered inside. Nothing was amiss. No crackling sounds or dots of light. Nothing disturbed. A long-held breath escaped between my lips. Easing the door shut, I returned to our bedroom. The monitor displayed only a dark, blank screen. I shoved it back into the box.

***

The next day I told Mark about what happened. He hugged me in a sympathetic embrace.

"I miss her too. There's been times I wanted to see her so badly." His chin dropped. "It was probably a dream," he said, "or maybe some kind of battery glitch. I'll take the box of stuff to the second-hand store today."

I nodded. "You're probably right. It just seemed so real." But I couldn't stop thinking about it.

The next night I went into Rose's room after Mark went to sleep. I lay in her bed, clutching her little cotton nightgown against me over my heart. Her scent still lingered there, mingling with my own. Each passing year stole more of her fragrance away.

I fell asleep there on her twin bed, my tears still refusing to hold back, even though my screaming sobs had diminished with the passage of time.

My eyes fluttered open when I heard her whispers in my ear. Her voice, soft and sweet, just like I remembered. "Mama."

I sat up straight and blinked, rubbing my eyes. She stood before me, perfect and beautiful, like on her last birthday. Her rosebud lips formed a smile.

"I miss you, Mama. And Daddy." Her entire body glowed with an incandescent shimmer.

My heart pounded so hard I thought it would burst through my chest. An intense joyfulness filled me with warmth. I stretched my arms toward her.

My eyes squeezed tight when I embraced her, relishing a happiness not experienced in such a very long time. But I couldn't feel her flesh or the weight of her body against me. I opened my eyes, and she stood at the end of the bed, her ethereal presence mesmerizing.

"There will come a time when you will be happy again, Mama." Her voice sounded so small, so childlike. "You'll have to leave here."

"I'll never leave here," I said. "I can't. Your room is all I have left of you."

Her glistening blue eyes deepened to the color of an October sky. "Someday you will have to. There is a flood coming. I don't know how to explain it, but when you celebrate my next birthday, you'll understand."

Little by little, parts of her image faded, curling around the edges like a flower's spent bloom.

"No, don't go, Rose. Please! I want you to stay."

"I want to stay too, Mama, but I can't." She looked over her shoulder. "See my school friends? They're waiting for me."

I saw only my darling Rose. No one else. Her face shone last, before disappearing. Desperate to hold on to her, I clutched at thin air. Tears blurred my vision. I couldn't stop any of it.

Her voice trailed off. "Don't be afraid, Mama. I love you and Daddy so much. There is joy where I am." Her sweet giggle dissolved into silence. Devastation filled me. Losing her all over again.

The remainder of my sleepless night tore at my thoughts, trying to process what I had experienced. What did Rose's message mean about a flood? About leaving here? Was it just my imagination?

After Mark and I finished breakfast the next morning, he cleared the table while I stared out the open dining-room window like a zombie. The curtain fluttered in a passing breeze. Billowing outward until it retreated, held captive against the window screen. My hands clenched my coffee cup as if it too would vanish if I let go.

"What's wrong, Babe? You feeling okay?" He sat next to me.

I wanted to spare him the crazy account of the previous night. But I couldn't. With all we've been through together, he deserved to know, no matter how unbelievable it sounded.

He listened to my tale pouring out of me with patience. His shoulders slumped and his lips turned down when he gathered my hand in his. For a long moment, he said nothing.

"Babe, we both miss her so much." His voice cracked, and he took a long breath. "I know you felt this was real."

I interrupted him. "You think I'm crazy." I hung my head. "Maybe I am." I pulled my hand from his and covered my face. I wanted to hide my anguish.

He put his arm around me. "Listen, we can go back to the counsellor again. Maybe change your antidepressant."

I nodded, agreeing with his logic. But deep inside, I knew what I saw was real.

***

Weeks, then months passed without incident. Every occasional rainstorm or flash flood warning kept me on edge. On those days, I wouldn't leave the house. My depression lessened with the help of our survivor support group. I never brought up in our sessions what I had witnessed that night in Rose's room.

The day of Rose's birthday arrived under sunny skies. No forecast of rain. Mark and I held a quiet celebration at home with just the two of us before he had to go to work that early evening. I went to bed early.

The ringing of my cell phone woke me. I picked it up, squinting at the glowing red numbers. 11:00pm. Mark's voice on the other end sounded apologetic.

"Sorry, Babe, for waking you up. But can you pick me up? My car is out of gas."

I groaned. "Can't you call a cab? I'm a little groggy."

"Sure, I could. But I'm only about ten minutes away. It's okay, I'll try to get a ride."

"No." I sat up. I didn't want him stranded in the dark looking for help. "Where are you?"

He told me his location.

"Okay. I'll be there in a few minutes."

I couldn't shake the uneasy feeling when I got into the car and drove the sparsely traveled road under the partial moonlight. I had reached our rendezvous point when I saw Mark's stalled car parked on the opposite side of the road.

In the blink of an eye, my attention shot to a rustle on the road ahead. The next second my headlights beamed onto something I couldn't quite identify until a shudder raced through me. A flash of a disembodied hand. Fingers wrapped around an automatic weapon. I yanked hard on the steering wheel and swerved. Plummeting downhill, tearing through long grass. The windshield splintered. I pitched up and forward. My body twisted and hurled against the seat belt. The car rolled, crashing with an abrupt slam and jolt. And settled with a boom and a splash.

Dazed, I gathered my bearings, struggling to clear the fogginess that surrounded me. The world didn't look right. Grasses and tree trunks reached downward, framed against the sky. Only the sky was upside down. I was upside down. The swishing sound of turbulent water preceded the pungent odor of a rancid river. Frigid, slimy mud crawled around my scalp. Intense cold stunned my skin. My wild thrashing did little to stop the pull of the sinking car and rising water that reached my nose. I beat my fists against the window, holding my breath.

***

My eyelids blink halfway open, protesting the brightness of the white room. Muffled sounds of children playing at recess, only far away, echoed. Diminutive, foggy shapes surrounded me, with child-like voices murmuring in indistinct conversations. I squeezed my eyes shut. An annoying beeping repeated in a timed rhythm. My eyes opened and focused on my surroundings. Recessed lights in the ceiling tiles glowed. The pinching irritation on the top of my hand was from an IV drip. The hospital gown felt soft but overly large. I reclined on a hard bed, covered by a sheet.

"Oh, thank God," Mark said, releasing a sigh. "You're awake."

My eyes turned toward Mark. He stood next to me, wearing his worried expression. "We're in the hospital." He stroked my forehead, brushing my hair from my face. "Doctor Wellborne says you'll be fine, maybe a little sore, only minor cuts and scrapes."

I groaned, muscles screamed with each slight movement.

"What do you remember?" he asked.

My voice sounded raspy. "I remember you pulled me from the car. I must have passed out then."

Mark looked confused. "I found you by the riverbank and called 9-1-1. The paramedics assumed you were thrown out when the car impacted the water. You almost drowned."

"No, I remember the feel of hands pulling me out of the car." I looked at his large hand that held mine. "Small hands under my shoulders. Small but strong." I swallowed, and tears stung my eyes. "It was Rose."

He smiled and kissed my forehead.

A man in a long white coat walked into the room. "I'm Dr. Wellborne. Glad to see you awake. How are you feeling?"

"Sore, but other than that okay."

A pleasant smile crossed his lips. "You're lucky to be alive. If your husband hadn't been there within minutes after your car crashed into the water … well, that would have been another story. The good news is you're going to recover."

Mark looked at me with glistening eyes. "That's not the only good news."

Dr. Wellborne drew closer and nodded. "The baby will be fine, too."

"What?" My eyes widened. Mark grinned through his tears.

"It's still early. I didn't know until we got to the hospital," Mark said.

My mouth dropped open, and happy tears mimicked those of my husband. The realization hit me, and I touched my abdomen. "I'm pregnant."

***

Months passed. I healed from the accident and concentrated on the arrival of our unborn child. We decided the baby would spend the first few months in a bassinet in our room. Mark and I hadn't discussed where the permanent room would be, but we both knew we had to make a choice. Our small house had only two bedrooms.

New hope came when we attended our survivor's support group one day. A move to help victims of gun violence was underway. Especially focused on the parents. A large organization had volunteered to collect the deceased children's belongings and move them to a museum. The permanent display would provide facts about school shootings to raise awareness of remedies.

We tearfully agreed to donate many of Rose's possessions, leaving her room to her sibling she would never meet. Rose would have wanted it that way.

About the Authors

Stephen L. Brayton

Stephen L. Brayton is a Sixth Degree Black Belt in the American Taekwondo Association and a Marketing Associate for a software company.

He began writing as a child; his first short story concerned a true incident about his reactions to discipline. During high school, he wrote for the school newspaper and was a photographer for the yearbook. For a Mass Media class, he wrote and edited a video project.

Current publications include Alpha, the first of his Mallory Petersen action mystery series, and *Night Shadows*, the first in a supernatural series featuring a homicide detective and an FBI agent.

He is the editor and contributing author of *The Peace Tree Mystery*, a story set in the Knoxville, Iowa/Lake Red Rock area.

He has also been published in numerous anthologies of fiction, poems in Lyrical Iowa 2018-2025, and articles in issues of *Plant Engineering*.

Deb Miller

Deb Miller enjoys writing unique short stories that showcase unusual professions, settings, or historical periods. Her contributions to print anthologies include mysteries and ghost stories. Her interests include traveling the world by cruise ship, binge-watching ancient archeology videos, and a previous career in IT. Deb is working on her debut novel titled *Fox Hunt on the Prairie*.

Joann Schissel

Joann Schissel is author of *Before It's Too Late*, a women's fiction novel released in 2024. She has several short stories published and earned an Honorable Mention in the University of Iowa's Write Now Micro Story Contest in 2024. Her fiction writing interest began after retiring from decades of employment in marketing and graphic design in Des Moines, IA. She currently lives on a vineyard with her husband and together they own and operate a winery and write novels.

Note: not all authors are included here.

Michael Van Natta

Michael Van Natta has been hard at writing fiction for the last thirty years and has published a novel, *Leo's Birds*, and many short stories. He is the founder and long-time facilitator of the Marion County Writer's Workshop (est. 2003), and co-owner of *Back Roads Literary Review* (est. 2022). He and his wife, Joann, also own and operate Nearwood Winery and Vineyards in Knoxville, Iowa. He is a retired family physician who loves to play golf, guitar and fish for trout.

Geraldine Birch

Geraldine Birch has been a newspaper reporter most of her life, having worked for various community newspapers in Southern California and Arizona. Her work included a ten-year stint as a free-lance writer for the *Los Angeles Times*.

In 1991, she moved to Sedona, Arizona, where she worked as a reporter, editor, and political columnist for the *Sedona Red Rock News*. Birch's political column "Gerrymandering," was awarded a first place national award by the National Newspaper Association.

Her writing has also appeared in the *Arizona Republic*, the *Christian Science Monitor*, *Opium*, *Six Hens*, The *Santa Fe Writers Project*, *Reed* Magazine, and she was a finalist in the 2022 Bellingham Review's Annie Dillard Award for Creative Nonfiction. She is the author of three books, *The Swastika Tattoo*, a historical fiction; *Vision of a Happy Life: A Memoir*; and *Sedona: City of Refugees*, a fictional romance set in Sedona, Arizona.

Larry Brown

Larry Brown is a retired military officer who writes short stories and is working on three novels. As a member of Marion County Writers Workshop since 2005, he has written hundreds of short stories, co-wrote three radio scripts and authored one script. Many of his tales of mayhem have been published in anthologies. Larry resides in Knoxville, IA.

C.B. Butler

C.B. Butler writes (mostly) speculative fiction from the Saint Louis suburbs, where he lives with his wife and three children. He has previously published in *Coffin Bell Journal*, *Fifty-Word Stories*, and *Page & Spine Fiction Showcase*. He is currently self-publishing a science fiction series on his own website and is shopping another novel around.

Rose Wilson

I'm R. (Rose) Blackerby Wilson and while I would like to have someone else write my bio, I don't like writing my own as if I were someone else; so here goes: I like reading different genres and therefore like writing the same way. I have written novels (two) and short stories (a gazillion) and love dabbling in children's books. The latter is borne from my besottedness (?) with my two grandchildren. You can find my online presence by searching the internet using my full pen name.

I love, love, love cats and dogs but am looking for a person to be my agent.

Pamela K. Kinney

Pamela K. Kinney gave up long ago ignoring the voices in her head and has written horror, fantasy. science fiction, a children's fantasy picture book, poetry, nonfiction ghost books, and a nonfiction shapeshifters/indigenous mythology book ever since. Her horror short story, *Bottled Spirits*, was runner-up for the 2013 WSFA Small Press Award and considered one of the seven best genre short fiction for that year. Several of her books have been the Book Fest Award winners. Her newest release is *Nowhere Land*, a horror novel, plus, her urban fantasy novel, *How the Vortex Changed My Life*, both published by Dreampunk Press. Her upcoming nonfiction ghost books are *Haunted Surry to Suffolk: Spooky Tales Along Routes 10 & 460 East* from Dreampunk Press coming winter 2026, and *Paranormal Appalachian Trail* coming 2027 from Schiffer Publishing. She is a member of the Horror Writers Association, Virginia Writers Club, and James River Writers.

Michael Chatham

Michael Chatham is a writer living in Massachusetts. He has been writing for nearly 20 years, however, this is his first publication. Most of his work, whether serious or satirical, involves some level of societal or political criticism.

Bailey Primus

Bailey Primus is a graphic designer by day, writer by night. Located in rural central Iowa, she enjoys writing creepy short stories and children's books.

Joy Wright

J.L. Wright is an internationally published author and poet of Cross-country Boy, Unsettled Joy, Homeless Joy, and Unadoptable Joy. Their work has also appeared in Taj Mahal Review, Solstice Magazine, GNU Journal, Creekside Review, and a myriad of anthologies, including Peace Poets, Whatcom Writes, The Writer's Corner, Texas Bards, and All the Lives We Ever Lived. They lived near Chico, CA during the Campfire in 2018.

R.H. Riffenburgh

R. H. Riffenburgh, winner of the Odin Writers Award, has published a five-star novel, poetry, several short stories, four editions of a leading medical research textbook, and 165 scientific articles. He writes fiction in retirement at home in San Diego. A PhD and professor emeritus, he has previously been a company CEO, government scientist, Navy undersea diver, NATO officer in Europe, and medical researcher.

L.A. Curry

Lisa A. Curry is a full-time graphic artist and is a member of a local writers group, where they write and share short stories every week. A lover of sci-fi and horror, she is currently working on her first novel and lives in Texas with her husband and two very snuggly cats.

Ember Purrian

Ember resides in South Africa, has a great affinity for cats, fantasy, and horror. Currently she is being held captive by five cats, but over time they might multiply. She has always been a little eccentric, has a unique creative style, and loved drawing and writing since she was a child. Writing has been a hobby but feels like she can climb the heights and reveal her brain to the world ... even if some day.

Teresa Tallman

Teresa lives in the desert Southwest with her husband and trusty foster failure, Suki. Writing is her second career, and she enjoys every moment of learning about this great passion. Her favorite genre is cozy mysteries and paranormal cozies.

ACKNOWLEDGMENTS

This is the sixth edition of Back Roads Literary Review Anthology series of which I have been proud to be a part of. It's been an interesting journey, not without its twists and turns, but as always, after all the hard work, quite satisfying and rewarding. I'm pleased that so much enthusiasm for writing remains in an industry seemingly ever-evolving to meet the challenges of the modern world. We have had more attention and have attracted more writers for this edition than ever before.

A special gratitude is owed to the members of the Marion County Writers Workshop here in central Iowa for early foundational support and ongoing efforts to provide this platform for emerging and aspiring writers. With nearly universal federal defunding of all things human, and the consequent disappearance of the University of Iowa's Summer's Writing Festival–the premiere institution that for thirty eight years has supported writers of all stripes and from many countries, and on which the Marion County version is modeled–it's time for us writerly folks to step up and, where we can, fill the void.

Special gratitude goes to Joann Schissel for the hard work and imagination for her original cover art, layouts and formatting.

Our Thoughts on the Current State of Writing and Artificial Intelligence

Many long discussions have been had here regarding the best way to handle the rise of artificial intelligence and large language models in our publications. Surveys and data appears to show that more writers are using this tool than not, that more writers are not acknowledging its use to readers than are, and that it—and it's use—continues to evolve, becoming more accepted as a standard tool of writing, much like low level platforms that arose years ago to assist with menial tasks of spelling, punctuation and are now completely mainstream.

Opinions are, like its use, all over the map. The hope here at *Back Roads Literary Review* is that its use will serve creativity and not the reverse, will provide an easier path toward the learning of writing skills, become a trusted "partner" at the keyboard, and creative "muse," much like writing workshops function. And that its use enhances the quality of works and not just gives us a flood of dumbed-down generic stories by writers who have become dependent on AI, forgetting that writing can be had from machines but stories come from living people, from lived experiences, asking on the page the difficult questions.

About the cover

The cover art is intended to express the idea of commonplace objects in nature, like an ant, scaled and patterned to create a sense of fear. Even the smallest presence, removed from its everyday environment, can instill a sense of dread–the "what-if" in both art and literature.

The cover art started with a royalty-free image of an ant and manipulated in Adobe Illustrator. Generative AI played no part in the creation of the artwork.

Visit www.BackroadsLiteraryReview.com
for more information about us or to purchase this
issue our other publications.

For more information about Marion County Writers
Workshop, visit our Facebook page. Workshop
sessions are held weekly in person or via Zoom.

www.ingramcontent.com/pod-product-compliance
Lightning Source LLC
Chambersburg PA
CBHW032259310726
48973CB00008B/2460